GALAXY'S EDGE

EDITED BY MIKE RESNICK

ISSUE 39: July 2019

Mike Resnick, Editor
Taylor Morris, Copyeditor
Shahid Mahmud, Publisher

Published by Arc Manor/Phoenix Pick
P.O. Box 10339
Rockville, MD 20849-0339

Galaxy's Edge is published in January, March, May, July, September, and November.

ISBN: 978-1-61242-464-4

SUBSCRIPTION INFORMATION:
Paper and digital subscriptions are available (including via Amazon.com) . Please visit our home page: www.GalaxysEdge.com

ADVERTISING:
Advertising is available in all editions of the magazine. Please contact advert@GalaxysEdge.com.

FOREIGN LANGUAGE RIGHTS:
Please refer all inquiries pertaining to foreign language rights to Shahid Mahmud, Arc Manor, P.O. Box 10339, Rockville, MD 20849-0339. Tel: 1-240-645-2214. Fax 1-310-388-8440. Email admin@ArcManor.com.

CONTENTS

THE PURSUIT OF THE PANKERA

A PARALLEL NOVEL ABOUT PARALLEL UNIVERSES

A NEW WORK BY

ROBERT A. HEINLEIN

The original working title for this novel was *Six-Six-Six*

COMING SOON

For more information please go to

www.ArcmanoBooks.com/heinlein

THE EDITOR'S WORD

by Mike Resnick

Welcome to the thirty-ninth issue of *Galaxy's Edge*. We're pleased and proud to present new and newer writers such as Lou J Berger, Shawn Proctor, Floris M. Kleijne, Christopher L. Bennett, Eleanor R. Wood, R.D. Harris, Rick Norwood, Auston Habershaw, and Robert Jeschonek, as well as old friends Joe Haldeman, Kristine Kathryn Rusch, Nancy Kress, and Kevin J. Anderson. We've also got our regular features: Recommended Books by Richard Chwedyk, science by Gregory Benford, literary matters by Robert J. Sawyer, and part two of the Joy Ward interview with Gordon van Gelder. And we've also got the sixth segment of our serialized novel, *Tomorrow and Tomorrow* by Hugo winner Charles Sheffield.

So what will your great-grandchildren do to amuse themselves?

The answer is: pretty much what your parents did—and that includes the heroes they dream about. (No, not basketball players and the like. HEROES.)

Let me explain.

You see, there was a time when heroes were springing up all over the landscape—and the good ones never leave. The 1930s were an exceptionally fertile time for the creation of heroes who struck a responsive chord in the public's hearts (which, after all, is where one responds to heroes). Everyone knows about the comic book heroes, Superman and Batman, who are well into their 60s now with no signs of slowing down.

But I have in mind another batch of heroes, who began a little earlier, and who give every indication of lasting just as long: the pulp heroes. We'll come to their present and their future in a moment, but first let's examine their past.

It all began with a radio announcer known as The Shadow. That's right; a radio announcer.

Street & Smith Publications owned a title called *Detective Story*, which also became a radio show. And to introduce the show, an announcer would come on in a creepy voice, ask the audience if they knew what

they were about to experience, laugh maniacally, and tell them that "The Shadow knows…"

Then someone decided that this shadowy announcer was such an interesting property that they ought to copyright him, so they planned to do a one-shot magazine called, not surprisingly, *The Shadow*. The head honchos at Street & Smith decided that if they were lucky, they might even get a second issue out.

They miscalculated by 323 issues. That's right; before the Shadow bit the dirt, he'd appeared in 325 issues of his own magazine—and had been portrayed by Orson Welles on his own radio show. (The radio show didn't have a lot to do with the *real* Shadow. The Shadow of the pulps didn't have the power to cloud men's minds, he had no romantic interest in Margo Lane, and although it got quite complicated, he wasn't even Lamont Cranston.)

Well, with sales taking off to the point where the magazine was soon selling a million copies per issue and was so popular it had to go semi-monthly, it didn't take long for Street & Smith to figure out that the public liked continuing heroes. So they created another—Doc Savage, the Man of Bronze. While the Shadow was cast in the traditional mold of the detective (though there was nothing traditional about his slouch hat, his fiendish laughter, and his blazing guns), Doc was a worldwide adventurer who righted wrongs all over the globe, usually against super-villains who seemed, at first glance, to have supernatural powers (but who never really did—until the very last adventure, "Up From Earth's Center", where Doc goes mano a mano against Satan himself). Doc and his band of followers appeared in 188 "novels" (many were really novellas) before his magazine vanished from the stands.

Most of the Shadow novels were written by Walter Gibson under the house name of Maxwell Grant. (Why? Simple. One day Walter notices that the Shadow is making Street & Smith rich, and he's still getting five hundred dollars a novel, so he goes in and demands a raise. They say no. He threatens to leave. They say, "Fine, and next week there will be another Maxwell Grant, and who will know the difference?" He stayed.)

By the same token, Lester Dent wrote most of the Doc Savage novels, though the only byline ever to appear was Kenneth Robeson.

Pretty soon other publishers were jumping onto the hero bandwagon. There was the Spider, a paranoid version of the Shadow, who killed people if he thought they were even contemplating crimes, and who had body counts that dwarf the average Arnold Schwarzenegger movie. (New publisher, same principle: none of the Spider's readers knew that Grant Stockbridge, the official author, was usually Norvell Page.)

There was Ki-Gor, a Tarzan clone who appeared in far more novels than the original ever did. There was Captain Future, who traveled the solar system righting wrongs that were out of Doc Savage's domain. There were flying heroes such as G-8 and His Battle Aces, and Dusty Ayres; group heroes like the Secret Six; undercover heroes like Operator #5 (who spent thirteen full issues—a wordage total approaching *War and Peace*—fighting back The Purple Invasion); there were the Phantom Detective, and the Ghost, and the Whisperer, and the Black Bat, and Captain Satan, and Taboo Dick, and Doc Harker, and tons of others.

And then one day the pulps were gone, and so were the heroes. If you wanted to find heroes in the 1950s and 1960s, you had to look at the comic books, where the plots were watered down, the characters simplified, and everyone wore colorful long underwear.

But there is something in the hero pulps that refuses to die. By the 1970s, George Pal had made a Doc Savage movie, and had purchased the rights to make a lot more. (He never did, but he planned to. I know; I have the screenplay to the unmade sequel.)

Then the comic books, seeking something that *didn't* have the proportional strength of a spider (whatever *that* means) and *wasn't* a visitor from Krypton, discovered the hero pulps, and soon Doc Savage and the Shadow had their own magazines again—only this time they were comic book magazines.

Bantam began publishing the Doc Savage books, and while it took them a quarter of a century, they eventually brought out every last one of them—and a couple of brand-new sequels. James Bama made as much of an impression on a new generation of readers with his interpretation of Doc as Walter Baumhofer pulp covers had made on their parents' generation.

Other publishers followed suit, though none had quite the same phenomenal success. Three or four different ones picked up the Shadow over the years (and Belmont actually commissioned some new—and truly dreadful—Shadow novels). The Spider found a number of paperback publishers, including one who tried unsuccessfully to update all the references in each story.

But, anachronistic as they were, the heroes refused to die. In the 1990s the Spider came back in book form again, this time with the original pulp cover illustrations. The Shadow became a big-budget movie starring Alec Baldwin, Tim Curry, Sir Ian McKellen, and Jonathan Winters. Tarzan, a pulp hero before there *were* pulp heroes, was a huge success as an animated film.

And what's on tap? Dwayne Johnson has signed to take his shot at playing Doc Savage. There are Shadow and Doc and Spider fan clubs all over the world.

My guess is that all of the major pulp heroes will soon have their own interactive computer games. Most of them are already featured in role-playing games.

The one thing you can be certain of is that as entertainments continue to evolve—as they have evolved in the past seventy years from pulps to comics to books and movies—the heroes who refuse to die will evolve with them. I don't know exactly what your grandchild's relationship to the Master of Men (the Spider) or the Man of Bronze will be, but I know that he's going to have one.

You want a guess? The computer jockey of the future will not follow the path of William Gibson's case in *Neuromancer*. Far from being an embryonic criminal, he—and all his friends—will tie in to a story that is interactive to the nth degree and *become* Doc Savage, giving orders to Monk and Ham, and duking it out with John Sunlight. A maniacal laugh will escape his youthful lips as he explains to his enemies that the Shadow knows. He'll fight Kerchak for the kingship of the apes, flit around the solar system with Captain Future or the galaxy with the Gray Lensman—and if he's just a little bit on the odd side, he'll don his Spider disguise and kill thirty or forty people because he suspected they were contemplating doing evil deeds.

He'll emerge unscathed for lunchtime, stare at the row of books his parents inherited from their grandparents, wonder why anyone would bother *reading* about heroes when they could *become* them, and then, his lunch over, he'll go back to the computer just in time to save America from the Purple Invasion.

Lou J Berger is an active member of the Science Fiction and Fantasy Writers of America (SFWA), and has published short stories in Daily Science Fiction, and a handful of anthologies. He can be found on Facebook and on Twitter (@LouJBerger) or at LouJBerger. com. *This story, a recent finalist in the Writers of the Future contest, marks his eighth appearance in* Galaxy's Edge *after an absence of two years.*

THE WALKING MAN

by Lou J Berger

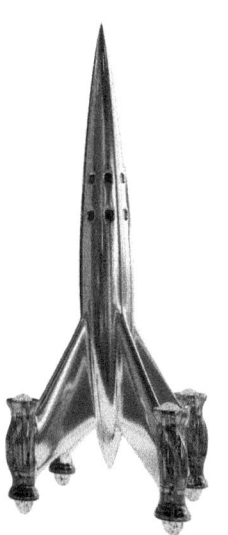

Old Joe stopped wiping the bar with his rag and cocked his head, listening hard to something I couldn't quite hear. A wagon clattered by outside, sending a fresh wave of glittering dust motes through the swinging doors.

"It's coming," he announced, flipping the filthy rag over his shoulder and lifting the hinged section of the bar out of his way.

I got up slowly, because I dreaded its arrival.

We followed him outside: me, Sweet Sue and the marshal who had just arrived from Denver on the morning dirigible.

Fanning herself, Sweet Sue looked down the dusty lane that passed for a road in Dry Gulch, Utah. Across the way, people gathered on the boardwalks and stared into the desert, where sunlight hammered the landscape into stark contrasts of green sage and reddened sand.

The marshal stood beside me and looked around. "Say, Quincy, what's coming? What did he mean?"

I shifted the wad of tobacco from my right cheek to my left. I wasn't about to explain a goddamned thing.

He waited for a long moment, shrugged, and gazed down the road.

Through the shimmery heat, a golden head rose into view, followed by shoulders and arms. Finally, legs.

As the automaton drew near, we heard its gears grinding, followed by the plod of one metal foot after another, striking the bone-dry earth.

In its arms it cradled a grisly burden, the worst mistake I ever made.

The marshal gasped. Davey Heep's skeletal remains lay dust-choked and filthy in the crook of the automaton's arms, the skull resting hard against its sternum. All his flesh had rotted away, with iron-hard bands of sinew and gristle, calcified in the Utah sun and dark as worn leather, holding him together.

Sunlight glinted off the automaton's head, which faced forward until the machine drew near. It then turned and fixed me with a baleful gaze, yellow gas-light flickering behind clear, quartz eyes. Pain, manifesting from guilt, twisted my gut.

I met the automaton's stare until it looked away. Then it clanked its way out of town, tenderly carrying Davey's corpse, disappearing into the badlands for another three months. It would return, though, regular as clockwork. It always did.

Every clank of its metal feet drove a stake deeper into my heart.

A sigh bled from the crowd, and they drifted off to do their business, whispering to each other, some darting furtive glances in my direction.

I followed Sweet Sue, her petticoats whispering against meaty calves, back into the cool air of the darkened bar, where Old Joe set up three shot glasses of rye on the scarred, wooden bar-top.

I went to my regular table, with my back against the wall, facing the door.

The marshal counted the drinks. "Who doesn't get one?"

"Quincy don't drink no more," Old Joe rumbled, lifting a glass in salute. "Here's to ol' Davey out there, rest his blackened soul." He gulped the brown liquor.

I watched Sweet Sue sip hers. The marshal glanced at me, lifting his eyebrow with an unasked question before emptying his own glass.

Not a drop of liquor had trickled down my throat since the night Davey died, and I wasn't about to pick the habit up again with a lawman in the room. I needed my wits about me.

After fidgeting, the marshal leaned forward, scraping his chair legs through sawdust.

"What in tarnation *was* that thing?"

Old Joe glanced my way, sighed, and said, "Buy a bottle, and I'll tell you what I know."

The marshal stepped up to the bar and dropped a gold coin on the beaten wooden top. The coin clanked and rolled for what seemed like an eternity before settling flat, and Old Joe made it disappear into his apron before plunking down a full bottle

of whiskey. The marshal took the whiskey back to his chair.

Sweet Sue fanned herself while Old Joe talked, his voice rich and smoky, unlike the cheap, watered-down whiskey he served.

"Davey Heep was the meanest cur that ever came into Dry Gulch," he said. "From the moment we first saw his pinched rat-face three years ago, when he stepped off the Chicago dirigible and decided to make our fair town his home."

The marshal nodded. "And somebody here killed him. Shot him in the back."

He turned and gave me a long, hard look.

I picked at a callus on my thumb.

Old Joe kept his eyes on the marshal. "Davey came in, asking about where he might register a mining claim. I told him that the general store was a good place to start, and he disappeared like lightning was chasing him. He was back in an hour, with an overloaded mule tethered out front carrying a pickaxe, a bedroll, and enough pemmican to last the whole winter.

"Davey drank a whole bottle of rotgut that night and swayed his way out to that poor mule. Somehow, he managed to climb aboard. That animal carried him and his gear out of town and up into the canyons where he wandered around and finally staked a twelve-acre claim."

The bartender pointed his rag in my direction. "Quincy, here, had been running that claim with his partner Nick, right up until Davey said it was abandoned."

Old Joe had the grace not to mention that I had spent most of my time in his bar while Nick did the hard work in the harsh sun, picking tiny golden grains out of black sand. I kept myself busy spending my share, drowning myself in liquor and the soft caresses of plump-thighed women.

I'd left Nick in those canyons, sweating alone under a hot sun while cool, clear creek-water flowed like molten glass across those gold-veined granite rocks.

Old Joe frowned. "Quincy, you okay with me telling this?"

I shrugged.

"Anyway," he continued, "Davey came back a couple of days after he left and registered that twelve-acre parcel, called it his own. He told the claims office that it was abandoned, and the sheriff went up to look at it. Said it did look deserted, with no sign of Nick. Quincy wasn't, ah, in a condition to contest the claim."

I had been blind drunk at the time. The claim office's week-long waiting period came and went while I was shacked up with one of Sweet Sue's night ladies.

Old Joe kept talking. "Davey ordered state-of-the-art equipment from Saint Louis, and it arrived two weeks later. During that time, he fumbled around and managed to pull half an ounce of gold from the creek bed, using what Nick had left behind."

I scratched my stubbly jaw.

When I'd finally heard the news, I'd gotten sober and gone back to the claim. While Davey snored under a lean-to, I found, in the blue moonlight, the rock he'd used to murder Nick. Nick's heel marks still scored the sand right to the cliff where Davey had hurled my partner's body into the canyon.

I knew, standing in that ghastly moonlight, that Nick was dead and I'd killed him as surely as if I'd swung that rock myself. I also knew, as sure as Nick's body rotted somewhere below, that if I killed Davey that night, I'd be dead in a week, strung up under the big maple in the town square.

And that wasn't acceptable. So I quit the booze and lived as frugally as a man can, waiting for the right moment.

Old Joe spat brown juice into a spittoon. "Davey's equipment arrived, and he started pulling an ounce of gold, maybe two, every month after that. He spent most of his time working the claim, sleeping up there, but would come down on Fridays with a sack of gold dust and sometimes a nugget or two.

"He was the kind of man who flaunted wealth, and he hired our best carpenter to build him a monstrosity of a house on the edge of town."

I stared at my calloused hands. Wagonloads of lumber went into that house, along with gilt chandeliers, and the fancy glass that Davey had ordered all the way from New York City. The house, once finished, had glowed like a Christmas ornament.

"When that walking automaton first stepped off the train," Old Joe said, "Davey was right there to fasten a jeweled leash around its neck. The instructions that came with it told how to make it loyal, and Davey lost no time making that poor contraption his walking, clockwork slave."

The marshal chuckled, his big grin wide. "How can a machine be a slave? That's like calling a wind-up clock a slave. It's nothing but gears and brass casings, designed to do a job."

Old Joe put gnarled fists on the bar top, his mustache bristling in anger. "Now listen here, Marshal. Maybe you're used to machines being mere tools, but that machine has got heart, and it loved Davey, despite him being the most scurrilous sumbitch that ever trod these streets!"

The marshal swallowed, his smile withering like a corn plant under a noonday sun.

Old Joe wiped his mouth, nodded a time or two, and then recommenced.

"We took to calling that thing the Walking Man. It followed Davey for the first month or so, its brass legs trying to keep up with Davey's dartin' stride, wearin' that leash and collar like a badge of honor instead of the insult it truly was."

The bartender's eyes developed a faraway cast, and he glanced toward the doorway. Western sunlight slanted in. Outside, a horse walked by, pulling a wagon, chains clanking and dragging in the dirt.

Old Joe poured another shot of rye and threw it down his wrinkled throat. "Sweet Sue knows the rest of it."

Sweet Sue beamed, still flapping that fan, trying to keep ahead of the rivulets that trickled down her neck and into the impossible chasm of her deep décolletage. "Well, you were telling it so pretty, I couldn't possibly match your oratorical charms."

The marshal shivered when he heard her sultry voice, and his mouth fell open. I reckon I couldn't blame him.

The first time I heard Sweet Sue speak, I'd been surprised that such a massive woman might have such a beautiful voice. She sang jest fine in the church choir, but her speaking voice hinted at forbidden pleasures doled out in a darkened room redolent with chamomile.

I guess the marshal heard it, too.

Sweet Sue switched her fan to her other hand.

"Well, I owned the Pleasure Palace at that time," she said, "and Davey wasn't quite as bad as Joseph says. He was a regular customer, and the ladies couldn't wait until he walked into our parlor."

I snorted. She glanced my way and arched a painted-on eyebrow, her mouth quirked, and I cast my eyes back down to the tabletop.

It had long been my suspicion that Davey's sudden wealth had allowed Sweet Sue to sell the Pleasure Palace and retire in luxury.

These days, she spent her days in the bar, drinking small glasses of thick, sweet plum wine and somehow never seemed to get drunk.

"Davey would leave the Walking Man in our parlor while he dallied upstairs with one of my girls," she continued. "And I would try to engage it in conversation, you know? It would sit in one of my overstuffed Victorian chairs, brass hands folded in its lap. I would serve tea and cookies, but it never partook.

"Once, I snapped at it. I felt terrible afterward, but I demanded to know why it never tried my cookies. When I knew Davey was coming, I would spend all morning baking those cookies, just to be civil to that machine. And it never ate a single one."

Her face grew pink, and she fanned all the faster.

"It turned to me with those terrible, flickering eyes, and it apologized, in the most cultured voice you ever heard. Said, 'Thank you, ma'am, but I'm not equipped to eat.'

"You could have bowled me over with a turkey feather to hear that thing whip such a phrase like that. It turned away, fixin' on the upstairs landing, which was where Davey had gone with one of my girls. After a bit, it turned to me and said, in a small voice, 'I don't know why he visits this place. Is my company not sufficient?'

"I felt bad for that poor contraption. It had no earthly understandin' of a man's needs, how a man can spend his days toiling in the heat, pulling gold from a river, but eventually needs to feel something other than cold stones and mud between his fingers.

"A man needs to touch a woman's softness, to smell her scent, to lay his lips agin' the long curve of her graceful neck, to remember why God made him the way he is."

Sweet Sue jerked, her eyes flying wide open, as she realized what she'd been saying. Her eyes darted over to the marshal, and she giggled. "Sorry, Marshal. I didn't mean to go on like that."

I glanced at the marshal, whose face had gone crimson. I chuckled, but covered it by clearing my throat.

"Later that fall," she said to the marshal, "during the Thursday night poker game, Davey sat right where you are, dealing out a hand. I was by the piano, dozin' in the heat. One of the half-breeds that lazes around town came busting through those swingin' doors and shouted that Davey's house was on fire."

The marshal rose halfway out of his seat. "On fire?"

Sue glanced at me again. "Quincy, here, was in that poker game, too, but had stepped out back for a few minutes. He wasn't here when the half-breed broke the news."

I felt a stirring in my gut and opened my mouth. "I was…indisposed…that night."

The marshal spun around, gave me a hard look. "You saying you had the trots?"

I thought about shooting him right then and there, but took a deep breath instead, stood, and walked to the bar. Old Joe handed me a tall glass of sarsaparilla, and I took it back to my seat. "I reckon you're right," I said. "Something must not have agreed with me that night."

Sweet Sue continued. "Everybody rushed outside, seeing Davey's architectural masterpiece burn, black smoke boiling into the evening sky and yellow flames dancing like Injun braves. The whole town grabbed buckets and set up a line between the horse troughs and Davey's house.

"When the first bucket hit the burning planks, a single shot rang out. A few moments later, that brass machine walked out of the darkness and into the firelight, holding Davey in its arms."

"I saw it myself," Old Joe said. "Davey was back-shot and the exit wound was ragged and bleeding, just under his ribcage. Blood bubbled out of Davey's mouth and he struggled to breathe, cradled in that machine's shiny arms like a babe held by his momma. He kept pointing at the burning house, saying 'Take me home,' but the Walking Man didn't seem to understand. It just held him there, looking first at Davey and then at the fire, which had engulfed the house. Davey spluttered and squawked, his mouth full of blood. 'Take me home,' he said, and then he died.

"That machine stood there for God knows how long, staring at the fire. When the roof caved in, the Walking Man headed straight out of town into the canyons, carrying Davey in his arms."

Joe closed his mouth with the finality of a shovelful of dirt hitting a coffin's lid. The marshal's mouth had fallen open again, and he looked from Old Joe to Sweet Sue and then back to me.

"Are you serious?" the marshal shouted. "Did nobody think to ask Davey who shot him? Was Quincy on the water line?" He pointed right at me. "Why won't anybody come out and tell me that the man who killed Davey is sitting right there?"

Stunned silence filled the bar, and neither Old Joe nor Sweet Sue looked at me.

I sipped my drink, collecting my thoughts. Seeing those twin boot heel marks up on the bluff had changed me. I'd made a vow beneath that dead moonlight: I'd bring justice to Nick's killer, no matter how long it took.

The marshal stared at me for a long time, then cleared his throat. "Say, Quincy. Where exactly *were* you when Davey got hisself backshot?" The question hung in the air like a hemp noose.

Sweet Sue switched hands and fanned herself even more vigorously. Old Joe took the rag off his shoulder and rubbed it in wide circles across his spotless bar.

The fans whirred gently above us.

I looked into my glass, threw back the last of the sarsaparilla, and set it carefully into the little ring of water it had made on the table.

There wasn't a soul in town who didn't suspect me of backshooting Davey. Hell, they knew it, certain as the sun rises and sets, but not a single person had ever said it outright.

That night, when everybody had bolted down to the fire, I had just returned from splattering kerosene along the walls of Davey's house and setting it alight. I'd hurried to the bar, entered through the back door, then followed the crowd to admire the show. Not another man, woman, or child was paying us the slightest attention, their every thought on the conflagration.

For the first time since that blue, moonlit night on the bluff, Davey and I were together, alone.

Only Davey's golden man-servant followed us outside, focusing its attention on Davey.

Yet, I took my chance.

Drawing my six-gun, I fired into Davey's back, two feet in front of me. His hat tumbled off and then he pitched forward, sprawled into the street, a hole in his denim shirt turning redder and redder. I stared at the still-smoking gun in my hand, horrified at what I'd just done. Only cowards shoot men in the back.

Davey hauled himself up on his hands and knees. He whimpered, and the machine knelt beside him.

"How may I help you, sir?" it asked in a voice as clear as a bell.

"Take me home," Davey gasped and then looked at me, his face contorted in pain. "How did you know?"

I watched him bleed.

The automaton gathered Davey up as if he weighed nothing. It glanced at me, its eyes burning with gaslight or maybe even something hotter, then it had walked toward the fire.

"I was busy putting out a dangerous fire," I finally replied to the marshal. "Before it burned down the entire town."

After some consideration, the marshal shrugged and looked at his empty shot glass in his hand.

"I can't prove who shot Davey Heep, and I suspect nobody around here would tell me, even if they knew, even if I asked them directly. What I *do* know is that a man is dead and somebody needs to pay for that crime."

He lifted his eyes and looked at me, hard.

"My problem," he continued, "is I can't imagine any earthly punishment being harsher than whatever Davey's murderer is experiencing right now, knowing he backshot a man instead of letting justice take its course."

He emptied the last of the whiskey bottle into his glass and held it aloft.

"I'm going to go back to Denver and mark this case closed. But first, if you don't mind, I'd like to make a toast."

We all raised our glasses, despite mine being empty. "To the Walking Man."

Copyright © 2019 by Lou J Berger

Shawn Proctor's work has appeared in Crab Orchard Review, Daily Science Fiction, Amazing Stories, Flash Fiction Online, Podcastle, *and elsewhere. This is his second appearance in* Galaxy's Edge.

UNICORNS ON ALL STREET, FAIRIES IN THE COFFEE SHOP

by Shawn Proctor

I may have been the only person to have seen her the night she did it. But everyone saw what came after.

The small woman climbed a rickety ladder, crowned by streetlight. In one hand, a bucket of ebony paint. In the other, a fat brush. Her curly hair rustled as she twisted the brush tip in her mouth, lips bringing the bristles to a point, then dipped it in the black paint and reached up to the sign. She sang to herself in a deep alto melody a song that I couldn't place. A sparkle fell from her sweater as she worked.

It was the sparkle that made me stop. Made me put down my briefcase and stare at the woman beneath the Wall Street sign. "What are you doing?" I asked.

"Just stealing a letter," she said without looking away. She kept painting until the "W" was gone from the sign. I looked again. I swore it was not erased, but had actually vanished.

✿

The next morning I walked from the subway up to the street and glanced up at the street sign. It was still changed, still reading "All Street." I laughed to myself and walked to where the statue of the charging bull faced the new statue of a brave girl. A half-man, half-bull circled both statues, leaning over each to get a better view. The creature covered his mouth with a hoof and whispered, "Breathtaking."

A sextet of winged horses flew in a "V" overhead, and business men and women stopped in front of the New York Stock Exchange to stare. Traffic jammed. Swarms of fairies dashed in and out of coffee shops. A gray finger poked up through the sewer grate to tease a stray cat.

I walked into the lobby of my office building, and the security guard stopped me. "We're closing for today, miss," he said, sneaking glances at the gremlins loosening screws inside the revolving door. "Stop that!" he shouted at them, and rolled a magazine into swatter. The gremlins squealed and scampered away.

I walked back out to All Street and narrowly missed being run down by a galloping unicorn carrying a tower of donuts on its horn. "Watch it with that," I said, mostly out of habit, ones baked in from living in the city for a decade. "I mean, excuse me."

The unicorn swept its tail past my face, and I smelled cream and strawberries. A hot dog vendor next to me stopped slinging sauerkraut for a moment. "Wack-a-doo horse smells like cookie dough," he said. "Warm cookie dough."

The rest of the morning, I joined the rest of the people—tourists and New Yorkers of every kind, from office bigwigs to construction workers—who shot video and photos of nymphs and satyrs and cats made of shadow until their phones and cameras ran out of charge and memory. *If I see that little woman again, I'll be sure to thank her*, I thought.

✿

By the end of the second day, All Street had adapted to the fantasy creatures. They made signs advertising magical coffee and "Get your picture with the Jubjub bird! $5!" and my office and the stock market opened on time, just like any other day, despite the mess left by the roving Bonnacon. Tourists still came, but I had accounts to manage, stocks to move from some two-letter company to some three-letter company. Still, I couldn't help but stare out the window at the spaghetti-long dragon that seemed to pass by every half hour, its leathery mustaches fluttering. *Tomorrow, I'm going to talk to a dragon*, I thought. *Or a unicorn. But most definitely not a Bonnacon.*

At the end of the night, I shuffled from the elevator and saw a familiar shape underneath the streetlight. It was small—bigger than the creatures we were calling kobolds and smaller than the Minotaur. I ran out to meet her. "There you are."

"And there you are," she said, her face dim under a straw hat.

"Everyone is talking about the creatures you sent here."

"Oh, I didn't send them. I only stole a letter," she said. The woman nudged a bucket with a paint-splattered knee. "And I just gave it back."

Sure enough, I looked around and saw no dragons or unicorns or any magical thing anywhere. Not even the gremlins. The street was empty then, and it seemed to me sadder, without wonders around every corner flitting and flying and scampering. But it was just the same old Wall Street. "If I had known it was temporary—"

"You would have savored it more."

I nodded.

"They all say that," she said, and tapped the paint can shut with a small rubber mallet. "Then they go back to rush-rush-rushing."

I looked at the revolving door of my company, still marked with a large "Out of Order" sign. "I don't want to," I answered.

The woman tipped her head back, gray and brown hair bunching in her scarf.

"I mean it, not like those other people," I said.

The woman set everything down, even her straw hat, and walked very close. She put a hand up to my ear and whispered, "So steal some letters of your own."

I watched her continue walking, all the while singing that same tune I knew but didn't quite know. I set the wide hat on my head, and picked up the bucket and brush. A sparkle fell from its tip to the dark street. I started down the escalator to the subway, every word, every sign an open invitation.

Copyright © 2019 by Shawn Proctor

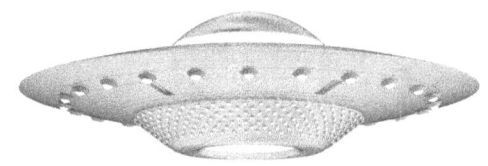

Joe Haldeman is a multiple Hugo and Nebula Award winner, the author of an acknowledged classic (The Forever War), *and a former Worldcon Guest of Honor.*

CIVIL DISOBEDIENCE

by Joe Haldeman

I'm old enough to remember when the Beltway was a highway, not a dike. Even then, there were miles that had to be elevated over low places that periodically flooded.

We lived in suburban Maryland when I was a child. I remember seeing on television the pictures of downtown Washington after Hurricane Hilda, with the Washington Monument and the Capitol and the Lincoln Memorial all isolated islands. My brother and I helped our parents stack sandbags around our Bethesda house, but the water rose over them. Good thing the house had two stories.

That was when they built the George W. Bush Dam to regulate the flow of the Potomac, after Hilda. (My grandfather kept mumbling "Bush Dam... Damn Bush.") That really was the beginning of the end for the UniParty, a symbol for all that went wrong afterward.

The politicos claimed they didn't cause the water to rise—it was supposed to be a slow process, hundreds or even thousands of years before a greenhouse crisis. I guess they built the dam just in case they were wrong.

Then there were three hurricanes in four weeks, and they all made it this far north, so the dam closed up tight—and people in flooded Maryland and Virginia could look over the Beltway dike and see low-and-dry Washington, and sort of resent what their tax dollars had bought. Maybe what happened was inevitable.

Over the next decade, the dikes also went up around New York, Boston, Philadelphia, and Miami. The Hamptons, Cape Cod. Temporary at first, but soon enough, as the water rose, bricked into permanence. While suburbs and less wealthy coastal towns from Maine to Florida simply drowned.

By the time the water got to rooftop level, of course all those towns were deserted, their inhabitants relocated inland, into Rehab camps if they couldn't afford anything else. We spent a couple of years in the Rockville one, until Dad had saved enough to get into an apartment in Frederick. It was about as big as a matchbox, but by then we two boys had gone off to college and trade school.

I was an autodidact without too much respect for authority, so I said the hell with college and became a SCUBA instructor, a job with a future. That was after I'd been in the navy for one year, and the navy brig for one week. Long enough in the service to learn some underwater demolition, and that's on my website, which brought me to the attention of Homeland Security, about a day and a half after the Bush Dam blew.

Actually, I'm surprised it took them that long. Most of my income for several years had been from Soggy Suburbs, diving tours of the drowned suburbs of Washington. People mostly come back to see what's become of the family manse, now that fish have moved in, and it does not generate goodwill toward the government. They've tried to shut me down a couple of times, but I have lawyers from both the ACLU and the Better Business Bureau on my side.

I returned to my dock with a boatload of tourists—only four, in the bitter January cold—and found a couple of suits and a couple of cops waiting, along with a Homeland Security helicopter. They had a federal warrant to bring me in for questioning.

It was an interesting ride. I'm used to seeing the 'burbs underwater, of course, but it was strange to fly over what had become an inland sea, inside the Beltway dike. The dam demolition had been a pretty thorough job, and in less than a day, it became as deep inside the Beltway as outside. They can fill up the collapsed part and pump the water out, but it will take a long time.

(The guy who did it called it "civil disobedience" rather than terrorism, which I thought was a stretch. But he did time the charges so that the flooding was gradual, and no one but looters drowned.)

Since I was a suspected terrorist, I lost the protection of the courts, not to mention the ACLU and the Better Business Bureau. They didn't haul out the cattle prods, but they did lock me in a small room for twenty-four hours, saying, "We'll get to you."

It could have been worse. It was a hotel room, not a jail, but there was nothing to read or eat, no TV or phone. They took my shoulder bag with the book I was reading and my computer and cell.

I guess they thought that would scare me. It just made me angry, and then resigned. I hadn't really done anything, but since when did that matter, with the UniParty. And not doing anything was not the same as not knowing anything.

The smell of mildew was pervasive, and the carpet was squishy. When we landed on the roof, it looked like about four stories were above the waterline. I couldn't see anything from the room; the window was painted over with white paint from the outside.

Exactly twenty-four hours after they had brought me in, one of the suits entered through the hotel-room door, leaving a guard outside.

"What do you need a cop for?"

He gave me a look. "Full employment." He sat down on the couch. "First of all, where were you—"

"I get food, you get answers."

"You have that backward." He looked at the back of his hand. "Answers, then food. Can you prove where you were when the dam was sabotaged?"

"No, and neither can you."

"What do you mean by that?"

"Food."

Yet another look. He stood up without a word and knocked twice on the door. The guard opened it, and he left.

A few minutes later I tried knocking, myself. No result. But the man did come back eventually, bearing a ham sandwich on a Best Western plate.

I peeled back the white bread and looked at it. "What if I don't eat ham?"

"You left a package of sliced ham in your refrigerator on K Street. You ordered a ham sandwich at Denny's for lunch on the twenty-eighth of November. I checked while they were making the sandwich."

Now *that* was scary, considering where my refrigerator was now. I tore into the sandwich even though it was probably full of truth serum. "If you know so much about me," I said between bites, "then you must know where I was at any given time."

"You said that neither you nor I could say where we were when the dam blew."

"No…you asked where I was when it was *sabotaged*. That could have been a week or a year before the actual explosions. The saboteurs were probably back in Albania or Alabama or wherever by then."

"So where were you when it blew?"

"At my girlfriend's place. It rattled the dishes and a picture fell off the wall."

"That's the tree house she's squatting in, out in Wheaton?"

"Home sweet home, yeah. Her original apartment is kind of damp. She paid a premium for ground floor. Wrong side of the Beltway."

"So we only have her word for where you were."

"And mine, yes. What, you don't have surveillance cameras out in Treetown yet?"

"None that show her place."

I guess it was my turn to respond, or react. I finished the sandwich instead, slowly, while he watched. He took the plate, I suppose so I couldn't Frisbee it at his head, take his keys and gun, subdue the guard, steal the helicopter, and go blow up the New York dike. Instead I posited: "If the saboteurs could have been anyplace in the world when it blew, what difference does it make where I was?"

"You weren't in town. It looks like you knew something was going to happen."

"Really."

"Yes, *really*. We got a warrant, and a Navy SEAL forensic team searched your apartment."

"Are my goldfish all right? Water's kind of cold."

"It's interesting what's missing. Not just toiletries and clothes, but boxes of books and pictures from the walls. Your computer system, not portable. All the paper having to do with your business. Your pistol and its registration. You moved them with four cab rides between your apartment and the Sligo dock, all two days before the Flood."

"So I moved in with my girlfriend. It happens."

"Not so conveniently."

I tried to look confused. "That's why you're on my case. I'm one of the dozens, hundreds, of people who moved out of D.C. that day or the next?"

"You're the only one with underwater demolition training. On that alone, we could haul you down to Cuba and throw away the key."

"Come on—"

"And you were already on a watch list for your attitude. The things you've said to customers."

"The apartment was too expensive, so I got back my deposit and moved out. My girlfriend—"

"A week before the first of the month."

"Sure. It was—"

"In a blizzard."

"Yeah, it was snowing. No problem. Or the cabbie's problem, not mine. We wanted to have Christmas together."

"For Christmas, you just sort of boated through twelve miles of blizzard. By compass, for the fun of it."

"Oh, bullshit. I just kept the Beltway to my left for ten-some miles and turned right at the half-submerged Chevron sign. Then about a hundred yards to a flagpole, bear left, and so forth. I've done it a hundred times. You try it with a compass. I want to watch."

He nodded without changing expression. "One of the things we lost when the dam blew was a really delicate sniffing machine. It can tell whether you've been anywhere near high explosives recently. The closest one's in our New York office."

"Let's go. I haven't touched anything like that since the navy. Four or five years ago." I'd been in the same house with some, but I hadn't touched it.

He stood up very smoothly, one flex, not touching the arm of the couch. I wouldn't want to get into anything physical with him. "Get your coat."

I got it from the musty closet and shook it out, shedding molecules of mold and plastic explosive. How sensitive was that machine, really?

He knocked twice, and the cop took us to an open elevator. The buttons for the bottom four floors were covered with duct tape. The cop used a cylindrical fire department key to start it. "Roof?"

"Right."

"Where's my stuff?" I said. "I don't want to leave it here."

"We're not going anywhere." He buttoned up his coat and I zipped mine up. We got out of the elevator into a glassed-in waiting area and went out onto the roof. There was no helicopter on the pad. Not too cold, high twenties with no wind, and the air smelled really good, almost like the ocean.

I followed him over to the edge. There was water all the way to where the horizon was lost in bright afternoon haze, the tops of a few buildings rising like artificial islands in a science-fiction world. Behind us, the Beltway, with almost no traffic.

"It's quiet," I said. Faint rustle of ice slurry below us. I peered over the rusty guardrail and saw it rolling along the building wall.

"They said 'Power to the People.' This isn't power to anybody. It's like the country's been beheaded."

I didn't say that if you're ugly enough, extreme cosmetic surgery could help. I might be in enough trouble already.

"Whoever did this didn't think it through. It's not just the government, the bureaucracy. It's the country's history. Our connection to the past; our identity as America."

That was something Hugh was always on about. The way they wrap themselves in the flag and pretend to be the inheritors of a grand democratic tradition. While they're really alchemists, turning the public trust into gold.

"Hugh Oliver," he said, startling me.

"What about Hugh?"

"He disappeared the same time you did."

"What, like I disappeared? I left a forwarding address."

"Your parents' address."

"They knew where I was."

"So did we. But we've lost Mr. Oliver. Perhaps you know where to find him?"

"Huh-uh. We're not that close."

"Funny." He took a pair of small binoculars out of his coat pocket and switched them on. The stabilizers hummed as he scanned along the horizon. Still looking at nothing, he said, "A surveillance camera saw you go into a coffeehouse in Georgetown with him last Wednesday. The Lean Bean."

Oh shit. "Yeah, I remember that. So?"

"The camera didn't show either of you coming out. You're not still there, so you must have left through the service entrance."

"He was parked in the alley out back."

"Not in his own car. It had a tracer."

"So I'm not my brother's car's keeper. It must have been somebody else's. What did he—"

"Or a rental?"

That much, I could give up. "Not a rental. It was clapped-out and full of junk."

"You didn't recognize it?"

I shook my head. Actually, I'd assumed it was Hugh's. "Why did you have a tracer on his car?"

"What did you talk about?"

"Business. How bad it is." Hugh's a diver; not much winter work. Idle hands do the devil's work, I guess. "We just had a cup of coffee, and he drove me home."

"And what did you do when you got home?"

"What? I don't know. Made dinner."

He put the binoculars down on the railing and pulled out a little sound recorder. "This is what you did."

It was a recording of me phoning my landlord, saying I'd found a cheaper place and would be moving out before Christmas.

"That was at six twenty-five," he said. "When you got home from the coffeehouse, you must have gone straight to the phone."

I had, of course. "No. But I guess it was the same day. That Wednesday."

He picked up the binoculars again and scanned the middle distance. "It's OK, Johnson."

The big man slammed me against the guardrail, hard, then tipped me over and grabbed my ankles. I was gasping, coughing, trying not to vomit, dangling fifty feet over the icy water.

"Johnson is strong, but he can't hold on to you forever. I think it's time for you to talk."

"You can't…you can't do this!"

"I guess you have about a minute," he said, looking at his watch. "Can you hold on a minute?" I could see Johnson nod, his upside-down smile.

"Let me put it to you this way. If you can tell us where Hugh Oliver went, you live. If you can't, you have this little accident. It doesn't matter whether it's because you don't know, or because you refuse to tell. You'll just fall."

My throat had snapped shut, paralyzed. "I—"

"You'll either drown or freeze. Neither one is particularly painful. That bothers me a little. But I can't tell you how little guilt I will feel."

Not the truth! "Mexico. Drove to Mexico."

"No, we have cameras at every crossing, with face recognition."

"He knew that!"

"Can you let go of one ankle?" He nodded and did, and I dropped a sickening foot. "Mexico returns terrorists to us. He must have known that too."

"He was going to Europe from there. Speaks French." *Quebec.*

He shrugged and made a motion with his head. The big man grabbed the other ankle and hauled me back. My chin snapped against the railing, and my shoulder and forehead hit hard on the gravel.

"Yeah, Europe. You're lying, but I think you do know where he is. I can send you to a place where they get answers." He rubbed his hands together and blew on them. "Maybe I'll go along with you. It's warm down there."

Cuba. Point of no return.

My stomach fell. Even if I knew nothing about Hugh, I knew too much about them.

They couldn't let me live now. They'll pull out their answers and bury me in Guantanamo.

Johnson picked me up roughly. I kicked him in the shin, tore loose, ran three steps, and tried to vault over the edge. My hurt shoulder collapsed, and I cartwheeled clumsily into space.

Civil disobedience. What would the water feel like? Scalding. Then nothing.

Copyright © 2005 by Joe Haldeman. First appeared in Future Washington, *ed. by Ernest Lilley.*

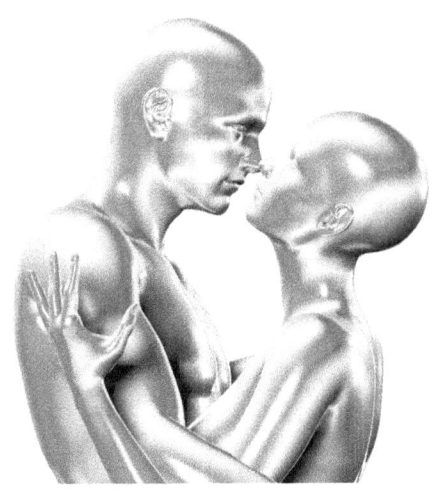

Floris M. Kleijne is a Writers of the Future winner and has had short stories published on Daily Science Fiction, *in* Factor Four Magazine, *and in* Reckoning, *among others. This is his third appearance in* Galaxy's Edge. *www.floriskleijne.com*

THIS IS KILLING ME

by Floris M. Kleijne

"Don't do it," Mansour's death pill implored. "Shut up." Turning on the hot and cold bath faucets, he felt the suicide tablet judging him as he filled a glass at the sink. Apparently, someone had had the immensely stupid and patronizing idea of imbuing the pill with a basic counseling AI. It had started chatting as soon as he had unwrapped it.

Steam from the bath blurred the mirror, and that suited him just fine. He was in no mood to look at his pale, drawn face. He wanted to lower himself gently into the scented water and sink into oblivion. Never having to face another empty, dreary day. Never again having to suffer the alternating bouts of soul-destroying boredom, despondency, and mind-numbing grief that had colored the past months in shades of black and gray.

Now this.

"I won't shut up," the pill said. Mansour wanted to hear smug self-righteousness in its voice, but in truth, it sounded kind more than anything. He couldn't even feel pissed at the thing. "You're throwing away your life, and for what?"

"You tell me." Mansour placed the water glass on the edge of the tub and tested the water with his elbow. Not quite scalding. Perfect.

"What do I know? I'm just a pill. *You* tell *me.*"

"What would be the point? You think you can change my mind? You don't know nothing about me. You don't know nothing, period! You gonna bring the love of my life back to me? You gonna fix my debts? Find me a job? No, really, tell me: You? Gonna? Fix? My? Problems?"

"I can't fix your problems, of course." The pill lay motionless, but from its tone, Mansour imagined an apologetic shrug. "But what I can do is listen. I'm a good listener."

With rough, crumpling motions, Mansour began to take off his clothes. He was damned if he was going to spill his beans to half a gram of poison.

"Listen," it continued, "if you called 911 right now, EMT would be here inside ten minutes, and you would get the help you need. But if you're not doing that, the least you can do is talk to me. No harm, no foul, right?"

Naked, he stared at the heap of clothes on the tiles. With a sigh, he picked them up and folded everything into a neat stack on the toilet lid.

The thing had a point. If he was doing this anyway, he might as well talk it out first. It couldn't make him feel any worse, and even if it did, that would only make the deed easier in the end, wouldn't it? And at least the damn pill, with its canned responses, wouldn't try to make him feel better, or worse: fix him.

Dropping the pill into a plastic cup, he placed it beside the glass, and lowered himself into the water.

With a deep sigh, Mansour began to talk.

☼

"And you know the worst part? Telling you all that took all of five minutes. The whole crappy disaster of my life fits inside three hundred seconds. And if you thought it would make me feel better to talk about it, think again." Mansour sank his head between his knees. "This is stupid. I'm talking to my suicide pill."

"It's not stupid."

"You know what?" Mansour sat up in the bath, causing a wave to splash over the edge and soak the rug. "You're right, it's not. You know what's stupid? You're a frigging kill pill, and you're trying to talk me out of it. What's that about? You afraid of being swallowed?"

He paused, but the pill kept its silence.

"Good. Cos I'll tell you what I think. I think it's disgraceful that they would do this. Put a frigging AI shrink into a pill. You have no idea. No. Idea. Not a damn clue how hard it was to go and get my scrip filled. I even had to sign a bloody NDA first, God knows why! The only thing that kept me going was the idea of this moment, this bath, an end to it all. And you want to interfere with my right to die? Why?"

"Statistically speaking, the fact that you even engaged in conversation with me means you probably don't actually want to die."

"And that makes it OK, you interfering? You're right: I don't want to die. You thought that would be my huge therapeutic breakthrough? Well, you're wrong! It's not about wanting to die, it's about not wanting to live."

Mansour threw his head back to scream, but a tremendous sob came out instead, and in moments, his crying shook his body and blinded his sight.

"It's going to be okay," the pill whispered, "it's going to be okay."

With deep, sighing breaths, Mansour slowly got his crying under control.

"Yeah? How's that?" He had tried to reach for cynicism, but heard eagerness in his voice instead.

"You're suffering from traumatic depression. A lot of bad things have happened in your life, and you've lost the ability to cope. Temporarily. With the right help, you can get past this."

"And this is the right help? Talking to my suicide pill?"

"Of course not. But you qualified for professional help the moment you opened my wrapper."

"That's…" Mansour ran a hand over his face. Yeah, what was that? For the first time in months, a lightness settled in his stomach that he could only call hope. "Are you even lethal?"

"Oh yes," it said. "If you swallow me, you die. But as long as you're talking to me, you're not killing yourself."

"So should I shove you in my ear instead, huh? Are you going to keep talking to me for the rest of my life?"

"No. Not the rest of your life."

"How long, then?"

"Just long enough," it said, and this time, the smugness in its voice was unmistakable, as outside the bathroom window an ambulance siren screamed ever closer. Mansour closed his eyes and felt his lips twitch in what might have been a grimace, or a smile.

"Hey, pill?"

"Yes?"

Mansour opened his mouth to say 'Fuck you'. But what came out instead was, "Thanks."

Copyright © 2019 by Floris M. Kleijne

Christopher L. Bennett has written fifteen Star Trek *novels to date. His short stories have appeared in* Analog, Daybreak Magazine, Alternative Coordinates, *and now* Galaxy's Edge.

THE MELODY LINGERS

by Christopher L. Bennett

He sang to resurrect her. He sang and she was there beside him on the stage. The songs made her real to his fans, and in return the fans made her real for him again.

Jeran had spent a year crafting the songs, perfecting their lyrics to capture Tikeji's essence—her quirky turns of phrase, her thoughtful convictions, the giving kindness in her heart. He had honed the melodies and rhythms to evoke the lilt of her voice, the arpeggio of her laughter, the silken heat of her body as she writhed atop him. But it had not been enough to bring her back. So he had gone to sea and studied with the dolphins, trading song for song. For them, singing embodied the world, created it, shaped it. They sang to the world and it sang back to reveal itself: the shapes and movements of life, the urges and emotions within their podmates and foes and prey, all limned through sound. Their language was dimensional, tangible, a vocabulary of form, motion, and attitude. Through their example, Jeran had learned to shape his harmonies to embody a physical form, to pulse with the very beat of life.

But he could not do it alone. Beside him, Ganalyn danced, acting out the role he had trained her to fill. She had Tikeji's midnight skin, her ravenous grin, her lissome, long-legged frame. But she was merely the receptacle. The energy came from his fans: teenage girls and young women who fantasized of being Tikeji so they would know Jeran's love. Wyrd crystals throughout the amphitheater, enchanted to resonate with the one in his hand, carried his voice to their ears as if he stood intimately close to each one, his song imprinting a detailed image of Tikeji in every mind. Ganalyn's attire and movements evoked Tikeji, making her the focal point for their cathexis, anchoring the Wyrd spirit their collective devotion made manifest. Her face and body and mind transformed until it was his wife who danced beside him,

her divine beauty restored to the world for one more night. By willing themselves to be Tikeji, letting themselves become part of her, his fans had made her real again…at least for a little while.

His joy fired the concert's final triumphant chords, the music thanking the audience for their gift. As he released them from their ecstatic trance, they staggered and many swooned. As always, his road crew hurried out to tend to any who were overwhelmed.

But Jeran's attention was solely on Tikeji, living again and ready to be with him. He took her hand, and the music of her laughter accompanied their run back to his dressing room. They had to hurry, to seize every precious moment before she faded.

As always, there were fans who intercepted them backstage. Still bound to Tikeji's essence, still loving Jeran as she did, they cried out to him, offered themselves to him. "You *will* be with me tonight," he assured them as always, "for it was your passion, your vitality, that brought my Tikeji back to me. Now, please, my love and I need to be together." They sighed at the romance of it all and let the couple pass, satisfied by their vicarious role in achieving the reunion.

Jeran and Tikeji were already tearing at each other's clothes as they fell through his dressing-room door. It was a few moments before he noticed that someone else was inside, clearing her throat: a stern, fortyish woman with unusually pale bronze skin. A prominent scar intersected her left eye socket, in which an amber crystal glinted.

Jeran groaned as he and Tikeji pulled apart. "We're a long way from Tazanbi, Inspector Khar. You have no jurisdiction here."

"Unless I can convince the Bekarya City Guard of the danger you pose," Temen Khar replied.

He scoffed. "Not this again. I assure you, Inspector—everyone in that audience was a willing participant in the Wyrdworking. Including the Guardmaster and her daughter, who are both here tonight."

"I don't doubt you have them in your thrall." The inspector believed her tone-deafness made her uniquely immune to his "hypnotic" music, no doubt a mask for her jealousy of those who could appreciate it. "But what of your own conscience, Mr. Sadarin? Surely by now you've verified the reality of the suicides."

Jeran sighed. "I concede that the rate of *reported* suicides among the girls and young women who attend my concerts is four times the national average. But that doesn't mean I'm *causing* them. Maybe girls who are already suicidal come to my concerts seeking hope. Maybe I'm unable to bring enough of them out of it."

"According to their families, most were not depressed prior to your concerts."

"And what parents know everything about their children at that age? Inspector, my songs are about love, about joy. They inspire people with the message that love is eternal." Tikeji snuggled against him reassuringly. "That's why my fans *voluntarily* concentrate on the vision of Tikeji that I create for them. In turn, their shared energy and will give substance to that vision through the Wyrd. Yes, it takes a lot out of them, but no more than dancing or sports. It doesn't hurt anyone."

"No, I'm sure it doesn't hurt impressionable adolescent girls to be exploited for your sexual gratification."

"I told you back in Tazanbi—I never take advantage of any of them. Tikeji's the only one I want to be with."

"The woman you are with is not Tikeji Sadarin. She's merely possessed by a Wyrdwraith manifested through your audience's collective focus. You *are* taking advantage of at least one person."

Tikeji had had enough. "Ganalyn is a Sibal temple concubine, Inspector," she said. "It is her sacred calling to submit her body to the workings of Wyrd."

"Hers is an honored role among her people," he told the skeptical inspector. "And right now, thanks to my fans' love, she *is* Tikeji. My new style lets me create something far more than just a glamour or an echo of memory. Music has a soul, Inspector Khar. It has life. This woman is no mere eidolon of my wife. I've recreated her."

"Your wife is dead, Mr. Sadarin. I shouldn't need to tell you that. It's the fixation that's driven everything you've done for the past three years."

"But at least you have your Wyrdwraith and your temple whore to distract you from your grief. Those girls out there, the ones whose emotions you exploit to feed this wraith, don't have that comfort. All they have is what your 'special' music infects them with—obsessive love, grief without resolution,

dependence on something they've lost. Once you go away, once the object of their obsession is torn from them, many fall into deep depression. Many of those kill themselves."

"Or rather, you murder them."

Tikeji stepped forward, protecting him. "Get out."

Khar's eye stayed fixed on Jeran. "What will you have your wraith do to me if I don't, sir?"

He clasped his love's shoulders, persuading her to move aside. "Don't be absurd. Tikeji would never hurt anyone, and neither would I."

"Wouldn't you? I wired inquiries to my Tynilaean counterparts. They informed me that you've booked the largest sound-equipped arena in Xendiraj. That you've funded a project to tie its amplification system into their new telegraph grid, and to distribute crystal repeaters all over the human lands."

"I'm one of many backers who see the potential of Tynilaean innovation. Imagine what it will mean for all Thayara to transmit sound across great distances at the speed of lightning."

"So you can drain energy from more enthralled victims than any single Wyrdworking since the Siege of Numeshai."

"Just a little from each person. Freely given, but enough in total to power the greatest working the world has ever seen."

She shook her head. "Hundreds of thousands of minds caught up in your web of despair and obsession. All of them feeding this wraith, this reflection of your devouring grief, making it more powerful than any Wyrd-god in history. The toll could be incalculable."

"My music embodies a woman who had more love and goodness in her than anyone I've ever known!"

She moved closer. "You think I don't understand what your music embodies? I lost my husband in the Erinthean Blockade. I'd have thrown myself into the sea if I hadn't had a daughter who needed me. You, though—you're so used to success and entitlement that you can't accept a loss and move on. And you'll sacrifice countless others before accepting what you can't have."

"You're just afraid of progress." He reached out to his wife. "Look at her. Tikeji holds on longer after every concert. The repeated Wyrdworkings are reshaping flesh, bone, even brain. If this works, imagine what it could mean. We could conquer death itself!"

Khar sighed in dismay. "It's as I feared. You think you can make her transformation permanent. Does Ganalyn know what will happen to her consciousness if you succeed?"

"Her legal consent is on record." He clasped Tikeji's shoulder. "I recognize the magnitude of Ganalyn's sacrifice, Inspector. But she has chosen this path to restore another's life."

"There is no restoration here! However elaborately conjured your wraith is, it's still nothing but a resonance. It goes both ways, did you know that? The Wyrd field resonates with our thoughts, and our thoughts resonate with its patterns. It's a loop that feeds and strengthens the wraith by intensifying the very urges that create it."

"I know the theory!"

"Then you should know that however perfect the illusion, ultimately that creature you call Tikeji Sadarin is driven by nothing more than mindless hunger for feedback. It will do whatever is necessary to preserve and promote its own existence. No matter how many people have to suffer."

"You're wrong, Inspector. She is my wife! She's *exactly* as I remember her."

Her real eye, stonier than the crystal one, held his gaze. "That proves she's only an illusion. A real person would never stop surprising you."

"I've had enough!" Tikeji swung a fist at Khar's face. The inspector dodged it easily and flung her onto the couch.

"You see, Mr. Sadarin?" Khar asked. "Nothing but base self-preservation."

He ran to Tikeji's side. "Get out!" he cried. "My wife has a right to live again! She wasn't done yet!"

This time he was certain he saw both of Khar's eyes flash. "Don't talk to me about losing people before they're done. Not after all the lives you've ended prematurely." She opened the door to leave, then turned back. "My girl is thirteen. If I try to forbid her from listening to your telegraph performance, I'll just guarantee she will. I'll do whatever it takes to put you in prison before that happens."

"Get out, get out, *get out*!" Tikeji screamed, shoving the inspector out into the hallway. "You have no right to stop the concerts! No right to kill me again!"

Outside, his fans' voices rose in anger at what they'd overheard. By the time Jeran reached the door, they were mobbing Khar, screaming, "No, you can't!" "Don't stop the music!" "Don't you hurt Tikeji!" "Jeran, we love you!" Security needed to pull them away so the inspector could pass, but the roar of fury followed her out, for there were still thousands of girls in and around the arena. Jeran was gratified to hear his loving fans standing up for him and Tikeji.

But Tikeji was already dragging him back to the dressing room, clawing at his clothes, devouring him with her dancing lips. She was in rare form tonight, intense, aggressive, overwhelming. For an immeasurable time, he was aware of nothing but her.

Until he realized that his road manager had been calling his name for several minutes. Until she informed him that Temen Khar had been torn apart by the audience.

He thought it a joke or a metaphor until he saw the blood on the manager's clothes, the haunted look in her eyes. He ran out toward the arena, but his crew held him back. Tikeji wrapped her arms around him from behind, holding him firmly. "It's all right, love. She won't bother us anymore. But we need to get out of here."

"No, it can't…I have to talk to them…my fans… such sweet girls, how could they do this?"

"She brought it on herself, my love. They couldn't bear to see you hurt any more than I could."

"But how did they even know?"

She pulled on his arm. "There will be questions. People wondering if her crazy theories were right. We have to get out of town before the city guard arrives. Come on!"

Jeran stared at her. "Tikeji…did you know this would happen?" The fans would still be linked to the spirit they had conjured. *A Wyrdwraith induces its own pattern in the minds around it…* "Did you… *make* them kill her?"

"Darling, how could you think that?" She put her arms around him. "Her own hate must have inflamed the crowd, brought her fate on herself. Remember, Jeran: she wanted me to die again. Is that something you could've permitted?"

She kissed him long and deeply. After a moment, his hesitation ended and he kissed her back. "Of course not, my love. We'll always be together."

As for Ganalyn…well, it was her calling. And he had certainly paid extravagantly enough for her service.

☼

Jeran had enough friends in high places to suppress the truth of Khar's death and allow his band to leave Bekarya before too many questions could be raised. He extracted their promise that provisions would be made for Khar's daughter. It wasn't the same as bringing her mother back, but it was what there was, for now.

Feeling Tikeji's urgings pricking at his mind even after her embodiment faded, he accelerated the concert schedule, booking the fastest passenger locomotive north into Tynilae. He reduced the concerts en route to the barest minimum necessary to sustain the imprint.

But he soon learned from his contacts in Bekarya that a startling number of concertgoers had taken their lives since his departure—more in four days than there usually were in two weeks, with more expressions of guilt in their notes and journals. The questions about Khar's death were becoming harder to suppress. Jeran had to pay handsomely to keep the news from spreading north.

Yet he found that Khar's words lingered in his ears. "Does it trouble you?" he asked Ganalyn as they rode in his private train car. "That Khar might have been right?"

"The loss of life is always sad," the temple concubine told him as she prepared their tea. "But life is impermanent. Wyrd endures. It is Wyrd that I exist to serve." Her accent, the liveliness in her voice, the grace in her movements—they were so much like his wife's now. Yet she retained the humility and Sibal philosophy that were Ganalyn's. It was an enticing combination, and he knew she would give herself to him readily. But he was faithful, never taking pleasure from this body unless his wife inhabited it—although he allowed the band and roadies to partake freely of Ganalyn's concubinal services so long as they treated her with the respect due her calling. At least that let her contribute something of her own.

"And what of your own sacrifice? Do you miss the woman you were?"

Her lips compressed. "It is not a temple servant's place to take pride in herself—only her service. And the life I had before the temple…there are many memories I would prefer to lose."

In the past, Ganalyn would have betrayed nothing of her own feelings. Now, she was a sounding board for his doubts as his wife had been. He studied her face. "But you are uncertain."

"I obey the will of Wyrd."

"Do you really believe the Wyrd has a will? That I'm not just imposing my own will, my own desires, on a mindless field of force?"

"The Wyrd is within our minds, our hearts. By serving the Wyrd, I serve all life." She held his gaze. "And the will of the Wyrd cannot be defied once one has committed to its service."

"Even…if it did get people killed?"

"The Wyrd in them would endure." Her eyes glistened with bated tears. "Just as the Wyrd in me will endure once I no longer exist."

He studied her face, unable to look away. There was so much of Tikeji in her now, but it blended with Ganalyn's own features and character to create a new beauty he'd never quite noticed before. Would it be so wrong to stop here? To let her live as Tikeji and Ganalyn, a merger of the best of both? Did the last of Ganalyn really have to die to satisfy him? Did more teenage girls have to die?

He sighed, knowing it for the fantasy it was. "I couldn't stop even if I wanted to, could I?" Jeran asked. "She wouldn't let me."

"I don't see how you could, Jer—Supplicant," she replied. "The spirit is bound to us. Her will is our will."

"And we must serve it," he intoned with heavy irony. Even now, he could feel Tikeji's presence looming. She hovered constantly, anchored to Ganalyn. He couldn't fight her will to live if he tried.

Ganalyn paused in thought. "And I assume you could not craft a song that would…unmake her as you have made her?"

He stared at her, even as he felt Tikeji's attention fall sharply on him. "No," he said after a moment. "No, the very idea is a contradiction. The song-working requires defining the subject in great detail, focusing total concentration upon it. How could I fixate on her and let her go at the same time?" The pressure on his mind eased as the wraith was reassured.

"As I thought, Supplicant."

Her question lingered in his mind. He knew he had to cast aside all doubts and finish what he'd started…but the moisture glinting on Ganalyn's cheek made it harder. He reached out and tenderly brushed the tear away. "Ganalyn…I'm sorry. But Tikeji is all I live for. I have no choice but to see this through."

She took his hand in hers. "I also live only to serve. You owe no apology…to *me*."

✧

As they drew nearer to the great Tynilaean city of Xendiraj, Jeran sequestered himself to refine the songs for the far-reaching performance that would originate there. "This will be the one," he said to his band. "Every detail must be more perfect than ever before." To that end, he told them apologetically, he would need to take direct control of the entire performance, Wyrdspeaking the music into their minds, guiding their muscles as they played. They grumbled, but they were compensated well enough to be loyal. He practiced the technique with them, but with the old songs rather than the new, secret versions he was crafting. "This is the music that will restore my wife to me for good," he explained. "It must come solely from me—and from her. It must be an embodiment of our special bond. I need your energy, your passion, but the guiding will must be pure for this working to achieve the necessary precision. We're breaking new ground here, my friends."

The band conceded, accepting that Tikeji's wraith was Jeran's true collaborator now. Whatever it took, she would ensure her resurrection.

And he would see this concert through at any cost.

The great arena in Xendiraj held forty thousand eager fans. It was the greatest concentration of energy and devotion Jeran had ever felt, even before he began to perform and bond to the audience through the Wyrd crystals. And the telegraph lines transmitting the sound throughout two continents would bring him the energy of hundreds of thousands more, an army of young women committing themselves to Tikeji's final embodiment. With that kind of power, a man could accomplish miracles.

As Jeran sang, he felt the wraith's power grow almost instantly. Ganalyn's features, already so close to Tikeji's, took on her aspect before the first song

reached its coda. The embodied wraith joined him in the familiar song, reinforcing the acoustic patterning that solidified her essence. She writhed with passion, reveling in the body she now claimed as her own forever, beaming with ecstasy as Ganalyn began to die within her.

Jeran wept as he watched her, as he felt her embodied in the song. She was so beautiful, so full of life and passion. So much like the Tikeji he remembered.

But the real Tikeji would die before harming a mouse.

And so he began the secret song he had been crafting in solitude for weeks. At first, the wraith sang along with the melody and lyrics she expected. But then he introduced his new refrain. The melody meshed with hers, the lyrics echoed, but they were inverted. Into a song of devotion and celebration of Tikeji, he injected a new theme of resolution and release. He sang of his wholehearted love for her, and then he sang of letting it go. He sang of his overarching despair at her loss, and then he sang of finding peace and moving on. He paid tribute to her life, and then he bade it farewell.

He had known since Khar's death that he was in the thrall of a predator that would kill thousands to sustain itself, with him as its instrument. But he couldn't just stop, or it would have compelled him. Ganalyn's suggestion, to unmake her the same way he had made her, had offered his only ray of hope. But how could he use his music to dissipate the wraith when the essence of the enchantment required a song that defined and embodied it?

Through counterpoint. Through inversion. That was the brilliance of music. A single work could contain two opposing themes and bring them into harmony, each resolving the other. Jeran had realized he could fixate the audience's love and passion and energy upon the essence of Tikeji, yet at the same time direct that energy toward accepting her death, detaching from dependence upon her. They were two opposite states of mind and heart, but the new song would show the audience how they could harmonize and become one. As it had helped him to understand how he could love her completely, yet still let her go.

The hard part had been hiding this new work from the wraith when it could sense his very will and desire. The harder part still had been knowing that more girls would suffer despair and death because he would not have the power to stop it until today, on this stage. But now, with half a world's worth of energy flowing into his Wyrdworking, he could finally atone for what he had inflicted upon them.

Jeran saw the protest in the wraith's eyes as he exorcised it, a fury that contained nothing of Tikeji. But she was bound by the song, dependent on the ritual. The song was what made her, and until she was whole, she had to follow where it led.

But there was one more thing he had to do. The counterpoint pattern was merging with the wraith's pattern, cancelling it, bringing the tension of its existence to a resolution. Soon the wraith would dissipate forever. But only the pattern would be gone. The immense energy being fed into that pattern could not be destroyed, only released. Already, he could feel the heat beginning to radiate from Ganalyn's body.

So Jeran Sadarin began his final song. A song of confession, of acceptance that Tikeji lived only in his memory, that the wraith he had created was only an extension of his own desire and denial. That he had used and exploited others to feed his selfish obsessions, deluding himself that he was sharing something beautiful with them. He sang to free them all, and he took it all upon himself.

And with that, the trapped, silently screaming wraith was pulled from Ganalyn. The temple concubine choked out a single hoarse cry and fell to the stage, scorched but breathing, free from his thrall at last. With his lyrics, Jeran bound the dissolving wraith to his flesh. He felt the heat filling him from within, but he clung to his concentration, pouring his whole being into finishing the song, finishing the wraith.

Tikeji would have wanted him to live—to move on and find new love, new peace. But his actions had made that impossible. The only way he could honor her now was by setting himself aside on behalf of others. It was not suicide; she would never have tolerated that. But someone had to bear the brunt of the wraith's fiery demise, and he would not allow anyone else to suffer for his selfishness—least of all Ganalyn, whom he had exploited so shamelessly.

She would never be truly herself again, in body or in mind. But Jeran hoped that enough of Tikeji's independent spirit had been imprinted on Ganalyn that she could make full use of the freedom she would gain from his death.

In a way, Tikeji would live on after all. But she would live for herself, not for him. That was how she deserved to be honored.

The energy tore through him now, burning him from the inside. It was not mere physics; the dying wraith was lashing out, taking him down with it. But he had the passion and will of half a million fans to give power to his song. The flesh of Jeran Sadarin was immolating, but his song lived on, self-embodied, carrying itself to its own inevitable resolution. For a few shining moments, Jeran truly was the music. It was how any musician would want to go out.

He held the last note for as long as he could, sensing the band retreating, the roadies pulling Ganalyn to safety, the audience running for the exits.

And then he finished with a bang.

Copyright © 2019 by Christopher L. Bennett

Kristine Kathryn Rusch is the only person in the field's history to win a Hugo for her fiction and another one as best editor.

LITTLE (GREEN) WOMEN

by Kristine Kathryn Rusch

First, let me say, I hated *Little Women*. Oh my God. Awful. And—spoiler alert!—by the time Beth died, seriously? I was ready to kill her myself. I have no idea why you teachers still assign this book, except maybe to introduce us to Louisa May Alcott the woman, who is a hell of a lot more interesting than any book she ever wrote. (Sorry about the "hell," Mrs. McGill, but really, I mean, sometimes you gotta say what you gotta say. And oops, yeah, I know, this aside should be its own paragraph. It looks weird that way, so I'm not going to do it.)

Second, here's the stuff you asked for, even though we both know you know it:

My name is JoAnne May Michaels, and yes, it's a coincidence that my first name is similar to the first name of the "heroine" in *Little Women*. The similarity stops there. First, no one calls me Jo and lives. I'm J-May, thank you very much, except when I'm in trouble, and then my mom calls me JoAnne (if it's not that bad), JoAnne May (if it's bad) and JoAnne May Michaels Get Your Butt Over Here (if it's life-and-death bad).

My parents, sisters, and I live in Alamaloosa, Oregon, and, since we're pretending that the person who's reading this doesn't know me, I'll tell you where Alamaloosa is. It's in the foothills of Siskiyou Mountain Range, not too far from where they butt up against the Cascade Mountain Range. If you can say The End of Nowhere, you're seriously understating where I live.

But the schools are good, because Alamaloosa is what my mom calls "a bedroom community" of Ashland, Oregon. I looked it up: Mom's wrong, because Alamaloosa existed before Ashland and has an industry (mining) and besides, Ashland, with a population of 20,000, isn't big enough for a bedroom community, but it's snobby enough for a bedroom community, so I guess that counts.

The reason I'm telling you about the schools (even though the real you knows the schools) is pretty simple: My parents, who love the backwoods and The End of Nowhere, moved *here* to get me a good education. Not Portland (2.5 million in the metro area) or even Eugene (350,000 in their metro area). Nooo. My parents moved *here*, because it was the only place in Oregon with good schools and nothing surrounding them except mountains, trees, and the occasional lost Shakespearean enthusiast. (Because Ashland is the home of the largest regional repertory theater in the United States, and that dang theater [which we students have to go to every year whether we want to or not] specializes in Shakespeare.)

So why am I doing this, like, totally nineteenth century introduction to this totally twenty-first century essay? Because (1) I can and because (2) I don't expect you to believe me and because (3) it's a freakin' assignment. (Thought I forgot, didn't you, Mrs. McGill?)

Here're the details:

From: Mrs. McGill's Honors English, home of this year's stupid *Little Women* assignment (with asides by J-May, addressing the audience, whoever they may be, including Mrs. McGill, who already knows I hate *Little Women* with a burning passion. [And yeah, I know what an aside is. I've seen too much Shakespeare]).

Assignment: Here it is, verbatim, underlines, italics and all:

Write about the most unusual day of the past year.
Establish what your real life is like.
Show why the unusual day was *unusual*.
Convince me that this unusual day is worth remembering.
Use one of the essay formats we've seen in our reading.

Okay, so what I've got here is an *informal* essay, almost like a letter, addressed to a real audience. Got that, Mrs. McGill?

Except I know what you're going to say. You're going to say that I'm not really using one of the essay formats from class, and you'd be right. I'm a heavy reader and I love essays and I know this is a real essay format, but it's not one of the ones you assigned, and screw it anyway.

I'm really not using one of your essay formats, because I already know I'm going to fail this damn thing. (Pardon my French, or should I say my Old French, since the word comes from that language [not German, like I originally thought].)

I know I'm going to fail, even though I'm following the rest of the assignment *to the letter*. Got that, Mrs. McGill? I'm doing what you ask.

It's not my fault you're not going to believe me.

✧

A Day in The Life of J-May Michaels:

I get up. I go to school. I go to the Watering Hole, which is the tavern my parents own, where I sit at the bar and do my homework. I do not drink. I do not let my friends into the tavern to drink. We all know that I'm not supposed to be there, but I am there, because my parents need cheap help, and the county sheriff spends his off hours in the booth behind the antique jukebox that came with the tavern, and he doesn't care, so no one else cares either, so, as my dad would say, Mrs. McG, don't get your undies in a bundle.

I clean the stockroom, sweep everything before the evening "rush" (the locals, who arrive after work for burgers, and the occasional lost Shakespearean, looking for atmosphere), bus tables, and report any creep who grabs my butt. Everyone's usually gone by ten, and my dad locks up, not that it means much, since we're in—hello!—Alamaloosa and—double hello!—we live upstairs.

Weekends, not much different, except no school, but usually extracurriculars or something "special" down in Ashland at the university or at the Shakespeare Festival. Then more cleaning, sometimes homework, and a date. (I wish. Just kidding on the date thing.)

There it is, the exciting life of J-May Michaels.

Now, enter Little Green Men.

Too soon?

Okay, let's back up some.

It's February. I'm sitting at the bar, crouched over pre-calc, which isn't that bad, even though everybody says it's bad, but Mr. Cohen, he says I have a gift for mathematics and I should take pity on

everyone, and by pity, he means I should tutor the less fortunate, but I'd rather poke my eyes out with a stick or sweep the bar every afternoon, whichever keeps me out of the Learning Lab with the Lame-os.

There's a Diet Coke fizzing to my left and a plate of nachos cooling at my right, and my tablet already has some sticky fingerprints on it, which Mom will yell at me about, because she says I shouldn't eat and do homework on the iPad at the same time.

So I'm trying to figure out the always-true, never-changing trig identities because, gifted or not, sometimes I don't remember everything right away, when something plops into my soda and I jump.

Because at the Watering Hole, we get spiders. Big huge garden spiders that look like they're straight out of the Forbidden Forest in Harry Potter, but they're harmless and annoying, and I hate it when they just fall randomly off the ceiling.

So I pick up my glass, hoping that maybe ice cracked loudly or something instead of falling spiders, and I stir the soda a little with my straw.

And that's when I see a little green hand, waving the universal sign for "help-I'm-drowning" around an ice cube.

I'm thinking that the wavy-thing is an effect, caused by me stirring the soda, so I pull the straw out of the liquid, and the hand reaches around, paws at the ice cube and then slides off the edge.

I pick up the glass and squint at it, holding it toward the frosted glass window of the main door so I can get a least a little natural light into those fizzy brown depths. And I see something that shouldn't be there, something that is about the size of a Reese's Peanut Butter Cup, only it's flailing, which makes me think it might be drowning, or maybe it was that hand and the fact that appendages hang off it like legs and they're kicking weakly.

I'm not sure if I'm grossed out or intrigued, but either way, I'm not drinking more of that Diet Coke. So I lower the glass a little so I can still see what's under the surface, then stick the straw back in and push it against the side of the glass, underneath the kicking Reese's Peanut Butter Cup. The thing stops moving for a half-second, then leans forward and, I swear to God, wraps its appendages around the straw.

Okay, I admit, I actually had one of those moments, y'know, the kind you see in Lit-Raht-Shure, where the protagonist knows she's making a choice that could go one way or the other. (See, Mrs. McG? I learn. "Protagonist," not "hero." Heh.)

I know I could use the straw to keep that Peanut Butter thing underwater (underCoke?) but I don't. I haul the whole straw-Peanut Butter thing up with one hand while I'm setting the glass down with the other. Then, as the straw bends under the thing's weight, I slip my hand underneath it (half afraid that I'm grabbing a spider) and lift it the rest of the way.

The Peanut-Butter thing looks like one of those disk-like kid's toys. You know the kind. The round toys like a coaster or a gigantic coin, but with arms and legs and little white shoes and little white gloves where the hands are and a tiny round head perched on top.

The Peanut-Butter thing looks *like* one of those things, but it isn't one of those things. First off, it's squishy, not rubbery. Squishy like a frog, you know, the kind of squishy that means you could shove your fingers through it and do some serious damage.

Second, it's got a neck. Just a little one, and the head is like giant gumball, with round plastic-looking eyes that have a little too much black in them and a perfect circle of…well, not white, exactly, more like a really pale green. It doesn't have a nose, but it does have two little black dots above a big mouth. The thing is gasping and spitting out Diet Coke, and the top of its torso (disk?) is flapping like ducts on a bad heating system.

Third, it's not wearing shoes. It has arched green feet with three long toes. It's not wearing gloves either. Its little hands are clenched into fists.

I'm both queasy and fascinated. I look around the Watering Hole to see if anyone else notices, but I'm the only person in the place at the moment. Mom isn't even behind the bar. She's probably doing the accounts in the back or something. She probably even told me to holler for her if someone came in, and I probably ignored her.

I don't think this little guy (and God knows why I think it's a guy, but it's giving off guy energy, and no, Mrs. McG, don't ask me to explain that) counts as "someone." Mom would probably scream at it and squash it with a plate or something.

"What the hell are you?" I ask, not expecting an answer. I was asking it the way you ask some kind of bug crawling across the table what it is. You know, rhetorically, or just to hear your own voice.

"What the hell are *you?*" the thing snaps back.

I push away from the bar, startled, and nearly spill the Diet Coke all over my tablet. Okay, now I'm beginning to think I'm either crazy or dreaming.

I decide to go with dreaming.

"I'm…ah…human?" I say sounding a little unsure, because when have you ever had to identify yourself by species? I mean, I never have before (or since, to be really honest), and I certainly didn't expect to do it in my parents' bar.

"Are you a human or aren't you?" the thing snaps. Jeez, I don't like its tone. The little thing is beginning to piss me off. (And Mrs. McG, I already figure you're going to mark me down for language, so just deal, okay?)

"I'm human," I say a lot more decisively, "and I asked first. So what are you?"

It makes a sound between a sneeze, a gargle, and someone choking to death. Then it adds, "But I would suppose you can call me a Glorp."

"Oh, well, thank you," I say, as sarcastically as it was. "Let me ask again. What the hell is a Glorp?"

"Me," it says.

I roll my eyes. It's like talking to my three-year-old sister. "So, are you a bug, or what?" I ask, still going with the dream.

"Bug?" it repeats. Then it grins as if it's suddenly understood. "Oh! *Insect.* No, I'm not. I'm…." It sighs and sounds just a little annoyed. "I guess you would call me a…a…a fan."

"A *fan?*" I ask. "Of what?"

"*Little Women,*" it says, and now I *know* I'm dreaming. "We came to see the house."

"The…house?" I ask slowly.

"Orchard House?" The Glorp-thing is frowning, which is really weird because those round eyes now have corners, and there's a line that runs from the top of its gumball head to those two little black dots.

"This is the Watering Hole," I say, and then realize that we might be having language issues, so I add, "It's a bar."

"A bar. A tavern," it says. "For libations."

"I guess," I say.

"Well, direct me and my friends to Orchard House, and we shall depart," it says.

"Friends?" I ask. I hear a chittering sound, and see two dozen of these little Glorp-things standing on the bar. I hadn't noticed them land, although as I'm watching, two more haul themselves over the lip of the bar, using the water gun as leverage.

I look at the one Glorp in front of me. The SpokesGlorp, I guess.

"What is this, some kind of invasion?" I ask.

"No," it says, sounding offended. "We're on a tour of famous literary sites throughout the galaxy. We have opted for the ship-to-planet excursion, Literary Women in Modern America, and we expect to see Orchard House, a few Civil War battlefields, and the historical sites around Concord. We understand that the battle of Lexington/Concord belongs to some other arcane war, but Louisa mentions it in her papers and—"

I wave my hands, shutting the SpokesGlorp up entirely. Then I sputter. I mean I really can't get any words out in any sensible fashion.

Finally, I take a drink of the Diet Coke before I remember that the SpokesGlorp had floated in it, and I spit the liquid back into the glass. Okay, I'm grossed out and annoyed, and confused, which helps me find my voice.

"Okay, you're telling me that there's literary tourism for aliens, and you have come for *Little Women* because…you like that book?" And okay, Mrs. McG, full disclosure here: I'm having more trouble with the fact that there's a gigantic universal fan base for *Little Women* than I am with the fact that there are maybe thirty Glorp on my parents' shiny bar top.

"Of course, we like the book. It is a window into your society," the SpokesGlorp says. "We understand that the book is something you call *fiction*, but that there are elements of truth to it, and we sincerely hope that the truth does not involve Beth's death, but rather the existence of Marmee and Jo and—"

"They're made up," I snap. "They're sanctimonious and made up and I hate them."

The SpokesGlorp sits down. Or rather, it plunks down, as if the force of my words has knocked it over.

It reaches out a hand, and one of the other Glorp grabs it, pulling the SpokesGlorp to its tiny feet. It dusts itself off, or rather, wipes itself off, since it fell in a puddle of condensation from the Diet Coke glass.

"Well," the SpokesGlorp says. "Clearly the book can't be *fiction* as we understand it, since you feel so passionately about it. Surely untruths would not provoke such passion in any creature, even the overly emotional human variety."

There's so much wrong with what the SpokesGlorp says that I don't even know where to start. I sputter some more, and before I can manage some real words, the SpokesGlorp takes a step closer to me.

"Since we've clearly ended up in the wrong location, please give us directions and we shall leave your establishment."

I stare at it. I can't help it. I have to ask. "How did you read *Little Women?*"

It straightens and raises its gumball head a bit, revealing a neck that actually has a tiny gumball inside it, like a tiny Adam's apple.

"I read 5,734 languages fluently," it says.

Well, goodie for you, I think. I have enough trouble with English. But I don't say that, because—well. Because.

Instead, I say, "I don't mean how did you learn English. Which, come to think of it, is a pretty good question. I mean, why the hell did you read *Little Women*? It's such a —"

"Such a classic," the SpokesGlorp says with reverence. "Filled with such important characters. Any species can write about its wars and its warriors, and most do, but to write about those who support them, those who love them, with such passion and heartache, well, we of the—" and then he made that sneezy gargly choky sound again— "Literary Society prefer works that make us cry to works that make us think. We do enough thinking already."

"You cry?" I ask, then realize that's rude. I'm about to apologize when it opens its little hands, in a what-can-I-say? gesture. At least, on a human that would be what-can-I-say. Who knows what it is for a Glorp.

"To answer your initial question as I understand it," the SpokesGlorp says, "all of us first read the book in our introduction to Backwards Earth Societies Literature class in what you would probably call university. We—"

"Excuse me," I say, "Backwards what?"

"Earth Societies," it says, being ruder than I was, and probably not even realizing it. "So many of your societies have evolved beyond the primitive, but some of you are delightfully unfettered still. And the emotions…"

It puts two fingers to its mouth, makes a kissing sound, and then says, "*Bellissima!* Truly."

I smack the heel of my hand against my forehead but that doesn't wake me up. It only makes my forehead hurt.

"How did you get the book?" I ask, because you know me, Mrs. McG. I ask too many questions.

"Oh," the SpokesGlorp says. "The Library of the Galaxy, of course. Where else would you take literature classes in obscure societies?"

"Where else," I mutter.

"Exactly," it says, and its mouth widens. I'm hoping that's a smile, because the thing has pale green teeth too, and they look like shark teeth. "So, point us in the right direction, and we shall march out your door, and never see you again."

"I dunno," I say, because I don't know. Alamaloosa is a weird place and I don't know all of it, and for all I know, Mrs. McG, you teachers have set up some shrine to Louisa May Alcott for reasons I'll never understand. "Where's this house exactly?"

"Orchard House," the SpokesGlorp says slowly, as if I'm the stupid one. "Where Louisa May Alcott lived. In Concord, Massachusetts, North America. I thought you studied this—"

"Massachusetts?" I ask. "You think you're in Massachusetts?"

The SpokesGlorp leans its head back, and I'm afraid it'll topple over. It looks top heavy. "Are we not?"

"No, you're not," I say. "You're barely in North America. You're on the wrong side of the continent."

One of the other Glorp (or Glorps. Who knows what the plural really is?) walks over and starts jibbering at the SpokesGlorp. They gesture and yell and spit and punch their little fists on the palms of their little hands and jump up and down a few times.

Then the SpokesGlorp turns back to me. "You are certain of this?"

"Um, e-yeah," I say. "I live here."

"But there was a sense of *Little Women* here," the SpokesGlorp says.

"Here? In the bar?" I ask.

"Here, in the community," it says.

I sigh. What, were we the only class in the country studying *Little Women* this week?

"I can't speak to that," I say.

The other Glorp spits and sizzles and jumps up and down twice. The SpokesGlorp nods, but whether or not that's an agreement, I'll never know.

"I guess we just got the coordinates wrong," it says. "We are arguing over fees now. Is there anything to see here?"

"Related to *Little Women*?" I ask.

"Yes," it says.

"No," I say, probably more strongly than I should. "But there's a Shakespearean theater about thirty miles from here."

"Ah," the SpokesGlorp says. "Stratford-on-Avon. We have that scheduled for our next excursion, and it will screw up our itinerary if we attempt that."

And it would screw up the rest of my afternoon if I try to explain to them that they're nowhere near Stratford-on-Avon. I guess, like most book people, book aliens are geography challenged as well.

"Wish I could help you," I lie, "but I can't. You should probably get out of here, though, before the dinner rush crowd shows up. They'll think you're appetizers, or maybe just some bar snacks."

"Bar…snacks?" The SpokesGlorp looks at me in horror. Apparently horror translates across our species. "Thank you. No. We are not bar snacks."

It turns toward the nearest Glorp and gestures. Then all of the Glorp face me, and bow at the same time. It's kind of glorious, in a Radio-City-Music-Hall kinda way. Little Green Rockettes, with gumball heads, bowing at the same time.

Then, one by one, they pop—and I mean *pop* like bubbles popping—out of existence.

Or at least, off the bar. They leave a bit of green goo behind, and some brown stuff that I'm hoping is something other than what I think it is.

I have to clean up the bar before Mom comes out, and I do, and later when she asks me if everything's all right, I ask her, because I can't help myself, "Do you like *Little Women*?"

"The book?" she asks.

"Yeah," I say.

She gives me one of those cautious looks she specializes in and then says, "It's a classic."

"Jeez," I say. "Obviously. For some reason I don't understand."

Mom gives me an indulgent smile. "Well, try to enjoy it," she says, "and remember: Older books can be truly alien to us."

I let out a snort. "No kidding," I say.

Then I work my way behind the bar and pour myself another Diet Coke. I carry the glass back to my spot, but before I delve back into my homework, I put a napkin on top of the glass.

I don't want anything falling in it.

In fact, I've put napkins on top of my glassware ever since. And that's the only lingering effect.

I did Google Orchard House after the Glorp left, but there was no report of an alien invasion. Although I did read about the tourist attraction, which sounds more interesting than the damn book. (Not that that is hard, mind you.) And I'd love to travel there, if only to get the hell out of Oregon, and stupid expectations and *classics*.

So, there you go, Mrs. McG. My failure of an essay. Even though it does exactly what you asked.

And before you tell me to redo this thing or to write about a different day with unusual events or give me an F or something, let me add one thing.

I don't usually have unusual days. (Okay, no one usually has unusual days, but you know what I mean.) Every day is exactly the same. *Exactly. The. Same.* With the exceptions I mentioned.

I can't wait to get out of this podunk town. I can't wait to have a real life. And I can't wait to get out of school.

So if you make me try another essay on the same topic, I still won't have anything to write about except this one day, and it really did happen, and it really is true, and if you can believe in Beth, and Jo, and Marmee, you can believe in little green aliens that call themselves Glorps.

Because I find them a lot more believable than the March clan.

Just sayin'.

Copyright © 2017 by Kristine Kathryn Rusch

R.D. Harris is a biomedical tech by day and a science fiction writer by night. His recent sales include Terraform, Liquid Imagination, *and of course* Galaxy's Edge.

COMFORT FOOD

by R.D. Harris

Y'all—a popular saying in an area called the South. My favorite human phrase if I had to choose one, despite the contraction.

The Southeast region of the United States also has a proclivity for high-calorie, high-fat foods. This I discovered after being employed at a seafood establishment—J. Edwards Seafood—in rural North Carolina. I was reassigned from board manufacturing to food service by the federally-regulated Retired Artificial Persons of America program for obsolete android models. My model, W-6, fell to retirement in the early years of the program.

"James," I said to the owner while cranking out hush puppies one night, "may I ask why humans consume detrimental levels of cholesterol, calories, and saturated fats?"

James Edwards sidestepped away from the deep fryers. He expelled saliva into what he called a spit cup before turning to answer me. "Guess 'cause it's comfort food, Dubya," muttered James behind the girth of the mustache he had grown. He was a kind, hard-working man of few words. James also did not mind an android working for him, unlike most Southern business owners.

"Comfort indicates an alleviation of pain or stress. I fail to see the correlation between food consumption and increased dopamine levels in the brain," I said. The restaurant business was quite new to me.

James mustered a slivered grin. "Humans, Dubya, are weird creatures. C'mon over here for a minute 'n look." I strode over to the wooden swing door that separated the kitchen area from the dining room. "See 'em?" He pointed a covert finger to the patrons. No customer in the establishment was alone. Groups of humans sat together and the decibel level was elevated.

"Yes, James. They are consuming food and engaging in conversation," I said.

"They look happy huh?"

I said, "Ninety percent of the patrons have expressions of joy, satisfaction—"

"People like food that fills 'em up. And I make damn delicious food, Dubya."

"What makes food delicious?" I asked.

James shuffled to the fish prep station. He motioned for me to join him. "Grab a filet," he said as a teacher would. I obeyed and grabbed a piece of catfish.

"Now, let it soak a few seconds in the milk 'n egg mixture 'fore coating it with the cornmeal in the next tub there."

If I were human, I think excited would have been my feeling at the time. James was allowing me to prep fish. He quietly observed my movements as I soaked and coated the off-white meat.

"Time to fry it. Jus' hold it on one end and ease it in there. Don't need grease flyin' everywhere."

Four minutes and eight seconds later, I removed the catfish from its fryer basket. Cooking oil dripped from the golden-brown crust of the filet. Gently, I placed the fish on a plate while James added coleslaw and french-fried potato wedges to the meal.

"The proportions of each item appear proper," I said to James.

"Been doin' this for twenty some-odd years. Hope I'm good at it by now," he pointed out. James plucked the plate from the steel prep counter. "Wanna take this to the customer? I ain't had you do that yet, but talkin' with a customer might help that hitch in your noggin' about comfort food."

"I will do that, James," I said.

In a deliberate motion, my boss handed the plate to me. "Table six, Dubya."

My CPU processed an amalgam of sounds as I trekked from the kitchen to table six in the dining area. The scraping of silverware on porcelain, rowdy laughter, and ice cubes cascading in clumps into drinking glasses were among the sounds percolating through my auditory gateways.

A middle-aged couple sat at table six. The two held hands, outstretched across the table.

"Enjoy," I said politely, resting the plate on the wood-laminate table.

"Thank you," they replied in broken unison.

I retraced my path back to the kitchen, having what humans call an epiphany.

"I now see the correlation between high-calorie, high-fat foods and feelings of comfort," I announced to James.

James wiped dirty hands on his soiled apron, turning away from the fryers. "Yeah?"

"It reminds people of fondness for each other. Perhaps 'love' is the word you would use."

"Maybe you're more human than you think, Dubya," said James with a squinty, hopeful smile. He patted me on the back.

If I could smile, I certainly would have.

Copyright © 2019 by R.D. Harris

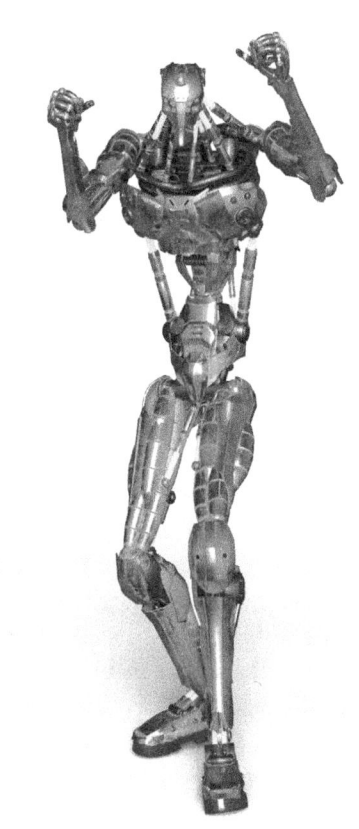

Eleanor R. Wood, who resides in England, has been published in Pseudopod, Daily Science Fiction, Deep Magic, *and* Diabolical Plots, *among other places. This is her second appearance in* Galaxy's Edge.

DOOMSDAY IN SPRINGTIME

by Eleanor R. Wood

He was in love with the girl from the apocalypse.

He had seen it dozens of times; immersed himself in her story until he knew it by heart. People called him a dreamer, an escapist, a fiction-lover with his head in the clouds. But they didn't know. They didn't know it wasn't fiction at all. And when he saw her, again and again, watching her world burn and crumple with angry seas and falling fire, her loved ones dead or dying or desperate to survive, his heart shattered. Every time.

He knew her whole life, from childhood on… her love of mischief, her flair for adventure. He'd grown up with her, living her life vicariously along with his own…her parents' divorce, her pursuit of the arts. He'd loved her from the moment he was old enough to realize that's what it was…her hair like liquid caramel, the way she adorned herself with color. He'd felt the tangibility of her, the essence of her, the reality of her very being. And she'd felt him in return.

He didn't talk about it anymore. Not to anyone except her. When he was little, they called her his imaginary friend. When he grew up enough to realize other peoples' imaginary friends left them at a certain age, he knew they meant something different. She never left him…even when he tried, during a brief period in his teens, to shake her. He almost convinced himself she was in his imagination after all. And then he read her story again, out of habit, or for old times' sake, or because it was still his favorite, or because there was a void in his chest where she used to be.

After that, he vowed to stay true to her always. He would never doubt again. She embraced his return with fervor and joy and the kind of love they said only existed in poems.

But the apocalypse still came, as inevitable as the lurch in his chest whenever she reached an invisible hand to his and found him, somehow, through the ether. He tried to warn her once, but she pulled away, not comprehending but frightened by his fear. He could reach her at any point in her life, and the times they shared were not lessened by the impending doom that only he knew was imminent.

Sometimes she would sense his anxiety, but she never asked him to elaborate. She simply offered him the gentle smile he could only see with his mind's eye, and told him she loved him.

How do you love someone, knowing how they end? The question plagued him whenever he thought of her. He forced himself to push it away when they were together. Over time, it made him angry. What was the purpose in knowing her death, in seeing the end of her world? He wondered, for the millionth time, what had brought them together. If she had taught him anything, it was that there was purpose in the universe. There was a reason he had discovered her story. A reason she had discovered his.

On the day the world ended for her, she reached for him. He knew it was happening from the raw panic that seared his mind. He witnessed it all over again, this time through her senses. Her confusion was a ball of white heat and jumbled debris, as disorienting as the quakes rocking her feet and the magma melting the ground. Her horror was a stake of ice through his heart as her family were burned and swallowed by the earth. Her pain was his pain when the embers struck her, inescapable needles of fire. Her terror was a flood of boiling ocean that bowled him off his feet even as she fled to high ground.

It was too much. He knew her death as intimately as his own life, but knowing and feeling were different degrees of trauma. He didn't want to experience it. He couldn't bear for her to.

He stood outside, his arms raised to the clear blue sky, feeling the soft breeze on his skin and the cauterizing heat on hers. He extended himself and covered her in the blanket of his own mind, willing her to feel his world's beautiful spring day instead of her world's crushing annihilation.

She still felt it. He knew the heat and chaos were too much to shut out. But he was muting them, and she clung to him, her anchor in the maelstrom. *Feel me*, he called. *I'm right here.* His awareness was her, and his world was merely his feet planted on firm ground. He could feel her pulling herself toward him along the guide rope of their shared consciousness. His eyes were closed. Something made him open them.

The blue sky was crystal, the cherries downy with blossom, birds sang to their rivals, and the air shimmered with some quantum change. A mirage of flood and fire shifted into his perspective, as though his brain had tuned to a new frequency. Flaming meteors plunged to the ground, evaporating into steam when they hit the swollen sea. He could still hear the birds. He smelled acrid sulfur and sweet cherry nectar. As her desperation breached the barrier, he saw his hands outstretched and felt his whole being reaching, pulling, tethering itself to hers.

The mirage rumbled and shook as buildings cracked and fell before his eyes, and he saw her—he *saw* her—reaching and crying and running to him... and then it was gone. The atmosphere rippled as the vision faded, and he fell to his knees on the grass, as devastated as if his own world had just split apart before his eyes.

But he was sobbing into her shoulder as she clutched him. Her skin was soft against his. Her hair was singed. She smelled of smoke and brimstone and fear, and she was alive.

Here.

With him.

He was in love with the girl from the apocalypse. And the apocalypse was the beginning of their world.

Copyright © 2019 by Eleanor R. Wood

Rick Norwood is a mathematician and writer whose small press publishing house, Manuscript Press, has published books by Hal Clement, R. A. Lafferty, and Hal Foster. Rick has been active in fandom since the 1960s.

LET A THOUSAND POPPIES BLOOM

by Rick Norwood

George David Abraham was the first president of the United States of America to use the words "God damn" in his inaugural address.

"America," he said, "is a republic, not a God damn democracy. If you don't know the difference, you have grounds to sue whatever school you went to. You've elected me your president. For the next four years, I intend to lead."

He got a standing ovation.

"How does he get away with saying things like that?" asked Press Secretary Andre Sanderson.

"He beat the Martians," said Chief of Staff Richard Sword. "He can say any damn thing he wants."

"And the people's gratitude will last?" Andre said.

"I give it another three days. Then we'll see."

The chief of staff and the press secretary were watching the speech on a television in the office of the chief of staff. Both men knew the speech by heart; they were listening to the audience reaction.

The president continued, "My grandfather on my father's side was a Jew. As a boy, he survived the death camp at Belzec. My grandfather on my mother's side was a Catholic, who married a full-blood Cherokee. I'm a Methodist. I have no use for prejudice, religious or any other kind. People are free to say what they think; that's as it should be. I hold governments to a higher standard. Any government whose official policy is racial or religious hatred will not find the United States a friend."

"They liked that," said Richard.

"They won't like this next bit," predicted the press secretary.

"In the past, the United States has attempted to come between warring tribes in faraway places. These attempts have been unsuccessful, as all such attempts must be. Peace comes from within, with freedom and prosperity. It cannot be imposed from without."

The audience, perhaps remembering the debacle in Iraq, did not applaud. It was a subject on which the nation was still deeply divided.

"As president of the United States of America, my foremost duty is to my country and its citizens. If any harm comes to American citizens, at home or abroad, my response will be swift and terrible."

There were ragged cheers at this, but not from everyone. These bellicose words seemed to make the crowd uneasy.

Richard Sword's secretary cleared her throat. Richard turned, saw General Lamont, Chairman of the Joint Chiefs of Staff, at the door. He stepped away from the television. "Hank, I wondered why you weren't up there on the platform," Richard said.

Without preamble, General Lamont said, "Five American peace-keepers in Afghanistan have been kidnapped by Saifur Rehman."

"Well," said Sword, "It didn't take long for somebody to put our new president's words to the test."

"This happened two hours ago. We've just now confirmed the reports."

"Wanda," Sword said to his secretary, "I'm going to need the vice president." Richard looked at his watch. "The president will be winding up his speech in about five minutes. Dispatch a helicopter to bring him straight back to the White House.

Andre said, "As soon as the news of this gets out, fifty reporters will all get the brilliant idea of a banner headline that reads, 'All Talk, No Action.' I know it."

He waited impatiently for the rousing but meaningless finale to this unusually short inauguration speech. He found himself smiling as the president got a standing ovation, but as soon as the president was off camera, he pushed star one on his pocket phone. "Mr. President. We have a problem."

☼

It was a hot January in Washington. Years had passed since snow last fell on the nation's capital. The air conditioning in President Abraham's jacket blew cool air up under his chin, but there was sweat on his brow. He slipped his phone into his jacket pocket and made his way to where the first lady

sat, in a Cadillac DeVille Touring Sedan, waiting for the presidential motorcade to start. Leaning on the car, he bent down and kissed her on the mouth through the window. "Duty calls. Will you wave to the good people who've waited all day in this heat for a glimpse of me?"

"Of course. I'll see you back at the White House in an hour or two."

"With these crowds, more like two." The president backed away from the car, allowing his hands to linger on hers for a few extra seconds before he turned and ran, bent over, toward the waiting helicopter.

The pilot handed him earphones and shouted, "We'll be there in five minutes, Mr. President." President Abraham put the earphones on and the roar dropped to a dull throb, which he felt in the seat of his pants. The helicopter tilted forward and rose rapidly.

The president looked down at the crowds lining Pennsylvania Avenue, at the broken stub of the Washington Monument and the dead Martian War Machine still standing in the Mall. The helicopter lurched, and began to spin slowly. It was losing altitude. The president gritted his teeth, and let the pilot do his job. There was a shock, a scream of torn metal, the slap, slap, slap of the rotor beating against something solid, sending vibrations through the wounded bird, and then all was quiet.

"Airman, report," snapped Abraham.

"These birds weren't built to take this heat. Sorry, sir. I don't know what happened. We crashed into the War Machine. We're about fifty feet off the ground. We seem to be stable."

The president looked out the shattered, tilted window of the helicopter. Yellow sands, surmounted by a heat haze, swept to the horizon. Men in desert camouflage, their shadows stretched out behind them, were running toward him. "This isn't happening," he thought. "This happened a long, long time ago."

His phone was vibrating. He took it out of his pocket and held it before his face. Both phone and hand were invisible. Instead, he saw dirty gray smoke, flecked with black soot, pouring past the broken window. He closed his eyes. He could hear Sword's voice. "Mr. President!"

"Richard, you're not going to believe this."

"I'm watching it on television, Mr. President. Are you all right?"

"I'm OK. Airman?"

"They're bringing a cherry picker to get us down from here, but they're having trouble getting it through the crowds. They say twenty or thirty minutes."

"I mean, are you all right? Are you hurt?" the president asked.

"I'm fine, sir."

"Look at me and tell me what you see."

"You…your eyes seem a little out of focus, sir. You may be in shock."

"I wouldn't be surprised. Carry on, Airman. Richard!"

"I heard. Thank God! Just hold on, Mr. President," Richard said.

"I haven't got time to just hold on. Right now there are a dozen reporters ready to characterize me as accident prone. Remember what happened to poor Gerald Ford? I need to give them something else to chew on. Get State and Defense and get the vice president."

"He's here, sir."

"Stu, I want you to get on the horn to some bright boys who know everything there is to know about Saifur Rehman. In particular, I want to know how to hurt him, badly—but not fatally—in the next three hours. I want three plans and I want them by the time they get me down from here."

"Yes, Mr. President."

"Here's one idea. I'm just going to toss it out for what it's worth. He's got a lot of workers and a lot of bodyguards and he lives a life of luxury. He's got to have a large cash flow and a lot of that has to be in either currency or bullion. How can we cut off his money supply, at least temporarily. Now, get busy."

"Yes, Mr. President."

Abraham squeezed his eyes shut. When he opened them, he still saw the yellow sand dunes, a flashback to his first helicopter crash in Iraq, forty years earlier. His phone was vibrating again. "Come on."

"You do have a way of getting yourself into fixes," said Tiffany Abraham.

"Tiff! Where are you?"

"I'm right underneath you. I'm looking up at you."

"Well, get out of there. It isn't safe."

"You always take things so literally. I'm about fifty yards off. But I can see you clearly. That War Machine looks like a praying mantis, which casts the helicopter in the role of its mate. It's a good thing it's dead."

"Tiff, I swear."

"You killed it, David. You killed it. David and Goliath. You're going to be all right. You're going to be all right." She was close to tears.

"Of course I'm going to be all right. I'll be down from here in no time. What's that?"

"It's a news helicopter."

"Idiots! I can feel their backwash. It's shaking us. I've got to call Richard. I'll be all right! Don't worry!" He pushed star two. "Richard, call Dulles International air traffic control. Have them tell that news helicopter to get the hell out of here. It's rocking the boat. Better yet, shoot it down."

"I'll take care of it, Mr. President."

"You do that."

His eyes still saw smoke, desert, and men dying. It was as if he was in two places at once. He rubbed his eyes, but could think of nothing to do about the strange disorientation, so he ignored it. "What's your name, Airman?"

"Lieutenant Griggs, sir."

"All right, Griggs. It looks like we're going to be here for a while. Is there anything we need to do or can do?"

"Not that I can think of, sir."

"All right, then. We'll just relax. I don't suppose you brought a deck of cards?"

"No, sir."

"Or a flask of whisky?"

"No, sir."

"Carry on."

While he waited, he turned over in his mind options for dealing with Saifur Rehman. His phone vibrated. "Richard," he said.

"We've got some ideas, Mr. President. Vice President Marshall got in touch with an old friend at Johns Hopkins, Dr. Conner, who probably knows more about drug lords in Afghanistan than anyone else alive. We've got those three plans to run by you."

"Good. I was getting bored. Put him on."

"This is Stewart, Mr. President."

"I hear you've got something for me."

"Yes, sir. We've got three ideas—just rough ones, but a start. First option, spray the poppy fields with Agent Orange. Kill their cash crop."

"No good. I've got plans for that crop. Next option."

"You were right about the cash flow. His personal compound is north of Mazar-i-Sharif near the Uzbekistan border. The branch of the Azizi Bank in Mazar-i-Sharif sends an armored car to his compound once a week."

"Is a car leaving today?" the president asked.

"Not for two more days," the vice president replied.

"If we take out the bank, we've got civilian casualties."

"Yes, sir."

"Even if we give them a warning?"

"Civilian casualties are still probable."

"Put that plan on hold. What's plan number three?"

There was a horrible crunching noise, and the weight of the helicopter shifted.

"Mr. President! Mr. President! David! Are you all right?"

"I'm still here, Stu. I think we were just settling. Go on with plan three."

"My God, David, how can you—"

The president interrupted him. "Plan three."

Vice President Stewart Marshall said, "Weapons. We have reason to believe that Saifur Rehman is expecting a large shipment of weapons—weapons, ammunition, and maybe half a dozen helicopters—some time in the next week. That means the shipment is already en route."

"Where?" the president asked.

"We don't know."

"Who's he buying them from?"

"We think the Costigan Group handled the sale. We're not certain."

"Stu, I want you to get me the CEO of the Costigan Group on the phone. And I want Saifur Rehman on the phone."

"I don't know if Saifur Rehman wants to talk to you."

"I'm the president of the United States. He'll talk to me. But get me the CEO first. What's his name?"

"John Conway."

"As quickly as possible."

"Sir," the vice president said.

"Lieutenant Griggs. You hanging in there?" the president asked.

"I'm fine, Mr. President."

"Any news on that cherry picker?"

"They're saying twenty minutes to half an hour."

"That's what they said twenty minutes ago."

The president took out his phone and touched star one. "Tiff."

"David!"

"Just wanted to touch base with you, let you know I was all right. How are you holding up."

"I'm fine, David. I'm just so scared."

"I think I may move the Oval Office up here." He looked out over the yellow sands. "Great view. Listen, I'm kinda busy, but I wanted to hear your voice. Take care. Gotta go."

He took a deep breath. The air conditioning in his suit was still blowing cool air under his chin. He squeezed his eyes shut to block out the glare of desert sands that were miles and years away.

He had just been a lieutenant then—his first taste of combat. Tiffany was the girl back home. He was twenty-two. It was hard to believe he had ever been twenty-two. That was two worlds and three wars ago.

He still felt a weight on his soul when he thought of the Martians. Was there any way he could have kept even one of them alive and still beaten them? Maybe, but it was too big a chance to take. They were smarter than humans, or at least they had better technology. They wanted our planet. They didn't have any use for us. Our only advantage was that there were so few of them, and all in one place.

When he had been appointed commander-in-chief of Allied Earth, General Abraham had delegated defense to subordinates. He knew a defensive war was a losing war. He had concentrated all of his energy on offense. He surrounded himself with smart people and listened to them.

The Amor asteroid 2011 FH was their best bet. Essentially abandoning Earth to the mercy of the remote-controlled Martian War Machines, Abraham had thrown all available resources into a mission to 2011 FH.

The men who had piloted the asteroid down to Mars, following the radio traffic in, all died. He had given the order that sent them to their deaths. He had known at the time that if the Martians had taken the elementary precaution of routing their radio signals through a distant relay, the war was lost. Thank God the Martians had underestimated the human race. Their overconfidence killed them. All of them. The crater was more than one hundred kilometers across.

"If only I could have kept one of them alive, somehow. If only we could have talked to them." His phone interrupted the president's memories.

"John Conway here, Mr. President."

"John. Good to talk to you. I'm going to ask you for a favor, and I want you to think about whether you want me for a friend or for an enemy. This is a one-time thing. Nobody will ever know how I got the information. There's an arms shipment on its way to Saifur Rehman. I want to know exactly where it is right now."

There was a long silence—but not too long. Conway did not get to be CEO of Costigan without being able to make quick decisions. "The shipment is aboard the freighter, Jorge Álvares, Portuguese registry. I can get you the coordinates in a few minutes.

"Good. I'm going to put the vice president on the line. I owe you one, John. Stu, you there?"

"Yes."

"I'm hanging up. As soon as you have those coordinates, get back to me."

It was a matter of several minutes before Stewart Marshall was back on the line. "We've got the coordinates, Mr. President."

"Take the freighter out. Use all available resources. Time is of the essence. I want the Jorge Álvares at the bottom of the sea before I talk to Rehman."

"Yes, Mr. President."

He touched star one. "Tiff."

"Hello, David," said Tiffany Abraham.

"I've got more blood on my hands," the president said.

"You could have retired."

"Sometimes I wish I had."

"I don't. Because I can't think of anyone in the world who could do this job as well as you."

"See you back at the White House."

"I'll be waiting."

President Abraham's head ached. He closed his eyes and stretched his neck, waiting for the call.

"Mr. President."

"Yes, Richard."

"Target is destroyed."

"Have you got Rehman on the line."

"I do, Mr. President."

"Patch him through. Wait! Does he speak English?"

"He does."

"OK, go ahead."

The voice on the other end of the line made Abraham's flesh crawl. Without preamble, Rehman said, "Are you ready to negotiate, President Abraham?"

"Rehman. This is the president of the United States of America. I have just sunk the freighter Jorge Álvares with all of your weapons on board. In one hour, if all five Americans are not released, I will destroy the Azizi Bank in Mazar-i-Sharif. One hour after that, if the Americans still are not released, missiles will target your personal compound. A United Nations helicopter is on its way now to your compound to pick up the hostages. That is all."

Abraham broke the connection. The phone vibrated.

"Did you get all that, Richard?"

"Yes, sir."

"Make it happen. I think I need a little rest."

President Abraham was in the Oval Office with his chief of staff and press secretary. As soon as he had climbed down from the helicopter into the big bucket of the cherry picker, helped by the pilot, his vision returned to normal. Back at the White House, he gave the first lady a long hug, then got back to work.

"Andre, I want you to play down the whole helicopter thing. Make it sound like a fender bender. No big deal. Put a bright coat of paint on the release of the American hostages. That's the news story. I'll meet the press corps tonight at six p.m.. Richard, get that bastard Rehman on the line. And be polite to the asshole!"

A few minutes later, the chief of staff handed the president of the United States a telephone.

"Saifur. President Abraham. You did the right thing. Listen, I'm buying next year's opium crop. All of it. My offer is five hundred million dollars. That offer is firm and non-negotiable. If I don't buy the crop, I destroy the crop. Notify your usual customers you won't have anything for them next year. Or any year. You'll be notified of the details in about a week."

Abraham handed Richard the phone. "I feel like I need to wash my mouth out with soap just talking to that slime. Set up an office to buy up the rest of the opium in the world before the word gets out and the price goes up. We're offering about half what they would get otherwise, but it's an offer they can't refuse. Try to buy eighty, maybe ninety percent of the world's supply. Same terms—sell it or lose it. What's the world's production?"

"About five-thousand tons."

"So I've just committed the United States to spend—what?—about a billion dollars on drugs. As Citizen Kane said, at this rate I may run out of money—in about one thousand years. Set up an office of—hell, call it the Office of Drug Enforcement—that sounds good."

"I hate to tell you, Mr. President," said Richard Sword, "but you don't have a billion dollars in the budget to buy drugs."

"Sure I do. Look under 'War on Drugs.' This will be the first victory in that war—ninety percent of the heroin off the street almost overnight."

"If you don't mind me asking, what do you plan to do with the opium?"

"Turn most of it into medicine, opiates. Give a lot of the medicine away to Africa, where the need for pain killers is critical; sell what's left of the medicine at a thousand percent profit. Call John Conway and see if he'd like to handle the sale. The rest of the opium we turn into heroin, sell that to developed countries for use in their maintenance clinics. We can make a large profit and still sell it to them for half what they're paying now."

"And in America?"

"Short supply means a high price for all the heroin that slips through. Which means all of the illegal heroin goes to high-end clients, which means—Stu?"

The vice president finished the president's thought, "Which means fewer new addicts. We break the cycle of addiction."

"Tell our maintenance clinics to stock up on methadone—if they continue to be too squeamish to give addicts the real thing. Then comes the hard part," the president said, "convincing the American people that sane drug laws really are a good idea."

The president of the United States leaned back in his chair and propped his feet up on his desk. "Not a bad first day on the job, if I do say so myself."

Copyright © 2019 by Rick Norwood

Nancy Kress is a multiple Hugo winner and a six-time Nebula winner.

ALWAYS TRUE TO THEE, IN MY FASHION

by Nancy Kress

Relationships for the autumn season were crisp and casual, following a summer where fashion had been unusually colorful and intense. Enkia liked wearing the new feelings. They were light, allowing her a lot of freedom of movement. The off-hand affection made her feel unencumbered and graceful.

Cano wasn't so sure.

"It's boring," he said to Enkia, holding the pills in his hand. Boxes from the couture houses were stacked around their bedroom. Enkia, of course, had done the ordering. Cano had on his stubborn look. "Love isn't supposed to be so boring. At least the summer fashions offered a few surprises."

"Too heavy," Enkia said. She dropped a casual kiss on the top of Cano's head. "Come on, Cannie, at least give it a try. You have the body for crisp emotions, you know. They look so good on you."

This was true. Cano was lean and loose-jointed, with a small head on long neck: a body made for easy carelessness. Standing in the middle of their apartment high in Alliani Tower, he already looked unstudiedly commanding: an Edwardian aristocrat, perhaps, or one of those marvelously cool American riverboat gamblers who couldn't be bothered to sweat. The environment helped, of course. Enkia always did their V-R, and she'd chosen straight, oyster-white curtains, terra cotta tiles, clean-lined sofas in a perfect off-white, restrained but not severe. Casual. But she'd left the windows natural. That, too, was perfect: too nonchalant about the view to bother reprogramming its ugliness. Only Enkia would have thought of this touch. Their friends would be so jealous.

"Come on, Cano, try the feelings on." But he only went on looking troubled, holding the pills in his white, long-fingered hand.

Enkia began to feel impatient. Cano was wonderful, of course, but he could be so conservative. He really hadn't liked the summer fashions—and they had been so much fun! Enkia knew she looked good in those kinds of dramatic, highly-colored feelings. They went well with her voluptuous body and small, sharp teeth. People had noticed. She'd had two passionate adulteries, one knife-fight with Kittery, one duel fought over her, two midnight reconciliations, and one weepy parting from Cano at sunset on the edge of the sea, which had been V-R'd into wine-dark roils for the occasion. Very satisfying.

But the summer was over. Really, Cano should be more willing to vary his emotional wardrobe. Sometimes she even wondered if she might be better off with another husband…Sendi, maybe, or even Jastinder…but no, of course not. She loved Cano. They belonged to each other forever. Cano was the bedrock of her life. If only he weren't so stubborn!

"Have you ever thought," he said, not looking at her, "that we might skip a fashion season? Just let it go by and wear something old, off alone together? Or even go natural?"

"What an idea," she said lightly.

"We could try it, Enkia."

"We could also move out of the towers and live down there among the starving and dirty-mattressed thugs. Equally appealing."

Wrong, wrong. Cano turned away from her. In another minute he would put the pills back in their little bottle. Enkia decided to try playfulness. She twined her arms around his neck, and flashed her eyes at him. "You are vast, Cano. You contain multitudes. Do you really think it's fair, mmmm, that you deny me all your multitudes, when I'm so ready to love them all?"

Reluctantly, he smiled. "'Multitudes,' is it?"

"And I *want* them all. All the Canos. I'm greedy, you know." She rubbed against him.

"Well…."

"Come on, Cano. For me." Another rub, and after it she danced away, laughing.

He could never resist her. He swallowed the pills, then reached out his arms. Enkia eluded them.

"Not yet. After they take effect."

"Enkia…"

"Tomorrow." Casually, she blew him an affectionate kiss and sauntered toward the door, leaving him gazing after her. Cano wanting her, and she crisp and insouciant.

It was going to be a wonderful autumn.

⟡

The next day was unbelievably exciting, more arousing even than when she'd walked in on Cano and Kittery in the summer bedroom and they'd had the shouting and pleading and knife fight. This was arousing in a different way. Enkia had strolled in to the apartment in mid-morning, half an hour late. "There you are, then," she'd said casually to Cano.

He looked up from his reader, his long-limbed body sprawled across the chair. "Oh, hello."

"How are you?"

He shrugged, then made a negligent gesture with one graceful slim-fingered hand.

Enkia draped herself across his lap, gazing abstractedly out the window. Today London looked even uglier than usual: cold, gray, dirty.

"Do you mind awfully?" Cano said. "I'm in the middle of this article."

"And so absorbed that you don't notice me, mmm?" Enkia rubbed against him.

Cano smiled, pecked her cheek, and gave her a careless nudge. "Off you go, then." He returned to his reader. Enkia stood and stretched negligently.

The rush of blood to her nipples and thighs startled her. He really was indifferent to her! She would have to actually work at getting him interested, winning him from his casual reading…God, it was exciting!

She would succeed, of course. She always did. But why hadn't she ever realized before how much more interesting the victory was when she'd had to struggle for it? She hadn't been this aroused in years.

"Cano…" She leaned over him and nibbled on his ear. "Sweet Cano…"

He tilted his head to look up at her, eyebrows slightly raised. The drugs had done something to his eyes; they looked lighter, more opaque. Enkia laughed softly. "Come on, it will be so good…"

"Oh, all right. If you insist."

He rose from his chair, turned to pick up the dropped reader. Leisurely, he nudged an antique vase a quarter inch to the right on a Gadella table. Enkia took his hand, and they ambled toward the bedroom.

And it was wonderful. The most interesting show in years. Really, the fashion designers were geniuses.

☼

"Cano, Fala and Sendi have invited us to a water fete at their tower on Saturday. Do you want to go?"

He looked up from his terminal, where he was working the New York Stock Exchange. He didn't even look annoyed that she'd interrupted. "Do you want to go?"

"I asked *you.*"

"I don't care."

Enkia bit her lip. "Well, what shall I tell Kittery?"

"Whatever you like, love."

"Well, then…I thought I might fly to Paris this weekend." She paused. "To see Guillaume."

He didn't even twitch. "Whatever you like, love."

"Cano—do you care if I visit Guillaume? For an entire weekend?" In the summer, a threat to visit Guillaume, a fiery former lover, had produced drama that went on for sixteen straight hours.

"Oh, Enkia, don't be tiresome. Of course you can visit Guillaume if you want." Cano blew her a casual kiss.

She charged across the room, seized his hand, and dragged him away from the terminal. His eyebrows rose slightly.

But afterward, as Cano lay deeply asleep, Enkia wondered. Maybe he'd actually been right, after all. Not that it hadn't been exciting to work at arousing him, but…she wasn't supposed to be working. She was supposed to feel just as detached and casual as Cano. That was the trouble with fashion—no matter what the designers said, one bloody fashion never did fit all. The individual drug responses were too different. Well, no matter. Tomorrow she'd just increase the dose.

Until she, and not Cano, was the more casual. The sought after, rather than the seeker.

The way it was supposed to be.

☼

"Cano…Cano?"

"Oh, Enkia. Do come in."

He sat up in bed, unselfconscious, unruffled. Beside him, Fala emerged languidly from the off-white sheets. She said, "Enkia, darling. I *am* sorry. We didn't expect you so soon. Shall I leave?"

Enkia crossed the room to the dresser. This was more like it. A little movement, for a change—a little action. Really, casual was all very well, but how many evenings could one spend in desultory conversation? Almost she was grateful to Fala. Not that she would show it, of course. But Fala was giving her the perfect excuse to put on an entirely different demeanor. She had rather missed changing for dinner.

From the dresser top she picked up a string of pearls and toyed with them, a careful appearance of anger suppressed under the appearance of sophisticated control. "Cano…how could you?"

Fala said, "Perhaps I *had* better leave, hadn't I? See you later, darlings." She activated a V-R dress from her necklace—easy unconstricting lines in a subtle taupe, Enkia noted—and left.

Cano said, "Enkia—"

"I trusted you, Cano!"

"Oh, rot," he said. "You're making a fuss over nothing."

"Nothing! You call—"

"Really, Enkia. Fala hardly matters."

"'Hardly'? And just what does that mean?"

"Oh, Enkia, you know what it means. Really, don't make yourself ridiculous over trifles." And Cano yawned, stretched, and went to sleep.

To sleep.

Enkia thought of waking him. She thought of pounding on him with her small fists, of dumping him on the floor, of packing her bags and leaving a note. But really, all those things *would* look rather ridiculous. People would hear about it, snicker…and even if they didn't, even if Cano kept her bad taste to himself, there was still the fact that the two of them would know it had happened. Enkia had lost her relaxed control. She had been as embarrassing as Kittery, the season Kittery showed up at a geisha party dressed in the crude emotions of a political revolutionary. Even if Cano kept this incident private, Enkia winced at his thinking her as capable as Kittery of such a major fashion faux pas. No, no. Better to let it pass.

Cano snored softly. Enkia lay beside him, fists clenched, waiting for winter.

☼

The new fashions were out. Enkia went to Paris for the pre-season shows, sitting in the first row at each important couture house, exultant. She saw, and was seen, and was happy.

The designers had outdone themselves, especially Suwela for Karl Lagerfield. The feeling was tremulous, ingenue, all the tentative sharp sweetness of virgin love. Pink, pale blue, white—lots of white—with indrawn gasps and wide-eyed sexual exploration. Ruffles and flowers and heart flutterings at a lingering look. Mallory House showed a marvelous silk, flowing biocloth abloom with living forget-me-knots, accessorized with innocence barely daring to touch the male model's hand. At Ano Tharian, the jackets were matched with flounced bonnets and a blushing fear that a too-passionate kiss would lead… where? The models' knees trembled with nervous anticipation.

Enkia wanted everything. She spent more money than she ever had before at a pre-seasonal. She could hardly wait for the official opening of the season. Cano and she, thirteen again, with everything new and sparkling and fraught with sweet tension…. While she waited, she had her hair grown long, her hips slimmed, and her eyes widened and colored, to huge blue orbs.

Maybe they could give a party. Everyone keyed up with anticipation and virgin hopes…wasn't there something called "spin the bottle"? She could ask the computer.

It was going to be a wonderful winter.

✿

"No," Cano said.

"No?"

"Oh, don't look so crushed, love. Well, maybe, then. I mean, what does it matter, really?"

"What does it *matter*?" Enkia cried. "Cano, it's the start of the season!"

He eyed her with amusement. But under the amusement was something else, the now-familiar feeling that he found her faintly distasteful, casually ridiculous. God, she couldn't wait to get him out of those wretched autumn fashions.

Enkia made an effort to speak lightly. "Well, if it doesn't matter, then there's no reason not to go for a bit of a change, is there?"

He flicked negligently at a speck of dust on his sleeve. "I suppose not. But then, love, no reason to go for change either, is there? This suits us well enough, don't you think?"

Enkia tried not to grind her teeth. "Well, perhaps, but one wants some variety, all the same…"

He shrugged. "I don't, actually."

She cried, "But, Cano—!"

"Oh, Enkia, don't get so worked up, it's quite tiresome. Can't we discuss it later?"

"But—"

"I have a lunch with Seldin. Or Kittery. Or somebody. Care to come? No? Well, suit yourself, love."

Casually he waved to her and sauntered out.

✿

She couldn't budge him. He didn't resist her; he just wasn't interested. Careless. Indifferent.

Opening day came. Enkia stood in the bedroom, biting her bottom lip. What to do? Everything was ready. She'd programmed the room for pale pink walls with white wood molding, filmy curtains fluttering in the breeze, a view of gardens filled with lavender and June roses and wisteria and anything else the computer said was old-fashioned. The scent simulator was running overtime. Around Enkia were the half-unpacked boxes of flouncy silks and sweet girlish slip-dresses and little kid slippers. Plus, of course, the white jackets and copper-toed boots for Cano. Who had glanced at the entire thing with amused negligence, and then gone out somewhere for a stroll.

"But you can't!" Enkia had cried. "It's opening day! And you're still dressed in…*that*."

"Oh, love, what does it matter?" Cano had said. "I'm comfortable. And all this stuff is a bit…twee? Isn't it, now?"

"But Cano—"

"I rather like what I'm used to."

"You're not used to it!" Enkia had cried in anguish. "You can't be! You've only had it for a season!"

"Really? I guess so. Seems longer," Cano said. "See you later, love. Or not."

Now Enkia scowled at the pills in her hand. There was a real problem here. If she took them, she would be garbed in the gentle sweet tremulousness of youth. Gentle, sweet, tremulous—and ineffective.

That was the whole point. Ingenues were acted upon, not actors. But without the whole force of her will, could she persuade Cano to stop being such an ass?

On the other hand, if she didn't take the pills, she would be dressed wrong for the occasion. She pictured showing up at the Donnison lunch in the Berlin Towers, at the afternoon reception in the Artificial Islands, at Kittery's party tonight, dressed badly, shabbily, in last season's worn-out feelings… no, *no*. She couldn't. She had a reputation to maintain. And everyone would think that she had lost all her money in data-atoll speculation or some other ghastly nouveau thing…damn Cano!

He came back from his stroll, whistling carelessly, a few hours later. The vid was already crammed with "Where are you?" messages from their friends at the Donnison lunch. Breathless, ingenue messages, from people having a wonderful youthful time. And there was Cano, crisp and off-hand in those detestable boring clothes, daring to *whistle*…

"Where have you been?" Enkia said. "Don't you know how late we are? Come on, get dressed!"

"Don't whine, Enkia, it's terribly unattractive."

"I never whine!" she cried, stung.

"Well, then, don't do whatever you're doing. Come lie down beside me instead."

It was the most assertive thing he'd said in months. Encouraged, Enkia lay with him on the bed, trying to control her anger. Maybe if she were sweet enough to him…

"You haven't dressed yet, either, have you, love?" Cano said. He was smiling. "That isn't the tentative embrace of an ingenue."

"Would you like that?" Enkia said hopefully. "I can just change quickly…"

"Actually, no. I've been thinking, Enkia. I don't want to get all tricked out as some sort of ersatz boychild, and you don't want to go on wearing these casual emotions. So what about what I suggested at the end of last summer? Let's just go naked for a while. See what it's like."

"No!" Enkia screamed.

She hadn't known she was going to do it. She never screamed—not she, Enkia! Except, of course, when fashion decreed it, and that didn't really count…. What was she thinking? Of course it counted, it was the only thing that kept them all safe. To go *naked*

in front of each other. Good God, what was Cano thinking? Civilized people didn't parade around naked, flaunting their natural attributes!

Or lack of them.

She struggled to sound casual. And she succeeded—or last season's pills did. "Cano…I don't want to go naked. Really, I don't think you're being very fair. We had it your way for a season. Now it should be my turn."

A long silence. For a moment Enkia thought he'd actually fallen asleep. If he had dared…

"Enkia," he said finally, "it's my detached impression that you always have it your way."

It hurt so much that Enkia's legs trembled as she climbed off the bed. How could he say that? She always thought in terms of the two of them! Always! Quietly she went into the bathroom and closed the door. Shakily, she leaned against the wall, and accidentally caught sight of herself in the mirror. Eyes wide with surprised hurt, lip trembling, like a young girl suddenly cut to her vulnerable heart…

And she hadn't even yet taken the season's pills!

Cano would have to come around. He would simply *have* to.

✿

He didn't. Enkia argued. She stormed. She begged. Finally, after missing three days of wonderful parties—irreplaceable parties, the season only opened once, after all—she dressed herself in the pills, and after that she pleaded with him tremulously, weeping delicate sweet tears. Cano only laughed affectionately, and hugged her casually, and went off to do something else off-hand and detestable.

She dissolved the pills in his cabernet sauvignon.

It bothered her, a little. They had always been honest with each other. And besides, it was such a scary thing for a young girl to do, her fingers shook the whole time she broke open the capsules and a single shining crystalline tear dropped into the glass (how much salt would one tear add? Cano had a keen palate.) But she did it. And wide-eyed she handed him the glass, her girlish bosom heaving with unexpressed emotion. Then she excused herself and went to take a long, scented bath in pink bubbles and to do her hair in long drooping ringlets.

By the time she came out, dressed in a simple long white dress, Cano was waiting for her. He held a single pink rose, and his eyes met hers shyly, for just a moment, as he handed it to her. They went for a walk before dinner along the beach, and the stars came out one by one, and when he took her hand, Enkia thought her heart would burst. At the thought that he might kiss her, the V-R waves blurred a little, and her breath came faster.

It was going to be a wonderful winter.

"Enkia," Cano said, very low. "Sweet Enkia…"

"Yes, Cano?"

"I have something to tell you."

"Yes?" Emotion thrilled through her.

"I don't like cabernet sauvignon."

"What—"

"I didn't drink it. But I did run it through the molecular analyzer."

She pulled away from his hand. Suddenly, she was very afraid.

"I wouldn't have thought it of you, Enkia. I believed that whatever fashion said, we at least trusted each other."

"What…" she had trouble getting the words out, damn this tremulous high-pitched voice. "What are you going to do?"

"Do?" He laughed carelessly. "Why do anything? It's not really worth making a fuss over, is it?"

Relief washed over her. It was last season's fashion. He was still wearing it, and it was keeping him casual about her betrayal. Unaffected, off-hand. Oh, thank heavens…

"But I think maybe we should live apart for a bit. Till things sort themselves out. Don't you think that would be best?"

"Oh no! No!" Girlish protest, in a high sweet maidenly voice. When what she wanted was to grab him and force her body against his and convince him to change his mind by sheer brute sexuality…but she couldn't. Not dressed like this. It would be ludicrous.

"Cano…"

"Oh, don't take it so hard, love. I mean, it's not the end of the world, is it? You're still you, and I'm still me. Be good, now." And he loped off down the beach and out the apartment door.

Enkia turned off the V-R. She sat in the bare-walled apartment and cried. She loved Cano, she really did. Maybe if she agreed to go naked for a season…but, no. That wasn't how she loved Cano, or how he loved her, either. They loved each other for their multiplicity of selves, their basic and true complexity, expressed outwardly and so well through the art of change. That was what kept love fresh and romantic, wasn't it? Change. Growth. Variety.

Enkia cried until she had no tears left, until she was completely drained. (It felt rather good, actually. Ingenues were allowed so much wild sorrow.) Then she called Sedlin, at home, on a shielded frequency.

"Sedlin? Enkia."

"Enkia? What is it? I can't see you, my dear."

"The vid's malfunctioning, I have audio only. Sedlin, I've got some rather awful news."

"What? Oh, are you all right?"

"I'm…oh, please understand! I'm so alone! I need you!" Her voice trembled. She had his complete attention.

"Anything, love. Anything at all!"

"I'm…" Her girlish voice dropped to a whisper drenched in shame. "I'm…enceinte. And Cano… Cano won't marry me!"

"Enkia!" Sedlin cried. "Oh my God! What a master stroke! Are you going to keep it going all season?"

"I'm…I'm going away. I can't…face anyone."

"No, of course not. Oh my God, darling, this will just *make* your reputation!"

Enkia said acidly, "I was under the impression it was already made," realized her mistake, and dropped back into ingenue. It wasn't hard, really; all she had to do was take a deep breath and give herself up to the drugs. She said gaspingly, "But I can't…I can't face it completely by myself. I'm just not strong enough. So you're the only person I'm telling. Will you come see me in my shame?"

"Oh, Enkia, of course I'll stand by you," Sedlin said, boyish emotion making his voice husky. Sedlin always took a dose and a half of fashion.

"I leave tomorrow," Enkia gasped. "I'll write you, dear faithful Sedlin, to tell you where to visit me…" She'd get a holo of her body pregnant, custom-made. "God, he just abandoned me! I feel so wretched!"

"Of course you do," Sedlin breathed. "Poor innocent! Seduced and abandoned! What can I do to cheer you up?"

"Nothing. Oh, wait…maybe if I know my shame won't go on forever…but, oh, Sedlin, I couldn't ask you what follows this season! I know you'd never let out a peep in advance!"

"Well, not ordinarily, of course, but in this case, for you…"

"You're the only one who I will let see me in my girlish shame. Everyone else will simply have to play along with you."

"Ahh." Sedlin's voice thickened with emotion. "I'd do anything to cheer you up, darling. And believe me, you'll love the next season. After a whole season away, everyone will be panting to see how you look, every eye will be trained on you…and the look is going to be a return to military! You're just made for it, darling, and it for you!"

"Military," Enkia breathed. Sedlin was right. It was perfect. Uniforms and swords and guns and stern, disciplined command breaking into bawdy barracks-room physicality at night…Officers pulling rank in the bedroom…*That's an order, soldier—Yes, sir!* The sexual and social possibilities were wild. And Cano would never skip two seasons of fashion. She would come back from a season's exile with everyone buzzing about her, and then Cano in the uniform of, say, the old Royal Guards…and herself outranking him (she'd find out somehow what rank he'd chosen, bribery or something), able to command his allegiance, keeping a military bearing and so having to give away nothing of herself…

It was going to be a wonderful spring.

Copyright © by Nancy Kress 1997. First appeared in Asimov's Science Fiction, January, 1997.

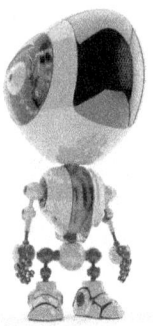

Auston Habershaw is busy making a name for himself with his science fiction novels, which include The Iron Ring, No Good Deed, Dead But Once, *and others. You can find him online at aahabershaw.com.*

WHAT THE PLAGUE DID TO US

by Auston Habershaw

I was going to be one of the survivors. Seven days into the apocalypse, I'd already outgrown civilization, you know? Me and my AR-10 had kicked some serious zombie ass and had plans to kick some more. I wasn't going down, no sir. Not like my parents had.

I had been forced to kill them. They were trying to bite me, to infect me. Pure them-or-me shit, right? No shame in that.

That was the moment, I thought. The moment when I went from shit-for-brains suburban burnout to badass survivor. I grabbed Dad's rifle from the basement and blasted them both away—blam, blam, blam. Headshots. Didn't even hesitate.

A week later, it was me and a couple other people—those who made it out of the city as it began to implode. We were slick, mean. Had a chick with a crossbow, big dude with a wood axe, kid who knew how to use a chainsaw. Woe betide the undead scum that crossed us, right?

That day—day seven—a supply run. Gonna bust into a big box store and see what wasn't looted yet. Expecting to find company. We gear up—football helmets, machetes, garbage can lids we'd spiked with nails. I'm sporting five clips of ammo I boosted from a place on day three. My rifle—Wanda, I call her—she's cleaned and oiled and ready to go, her steak-knife bayonet duct-taped in place.

Long story short, the raid goes wrong. It's zombie central, right? We're surrounded by, like, fifty of the bastards. Wanda's jammed and I can't seem to clear it. Fuck fuck fuck. They reach for us, their pale, bloody hands grasping. The moans. The drool.

Crossbow chick shoots a zombie in the chest. He falls backward. Wood axe dude is down, screaming.

The jam clears. I shoot the closest zombie.

The sound of gunfire makes all the zombies jump. They freeze.

Wait…they *jumped*?

Like, in surprise?

It's like time stops for a second. The zombies aren't coming for us anymore. It's…it's like something changes in the air. I can't describe it.

A zombie—a girl in a blood-slicked greeter vest, nametag that said "Kim"—coughs a bit. She blinks. Her eyes—so vacant a second ago—they seem clearer. Focused, like somebody waking up. "Hey… what's…what's going on?"

We—zombies and survivors—stare at each other. It gets, like, *awkward*.

Zombies start rubbing their eyes. One little girl zombie starts crying that she's been bit by a dog. A big fat zombie rubs his bald spot, sits down, and pulls out a battered cell phone. "Jesus, I feel like shit. Hey…anybody got bars?"

"Kim" looks down at the zombie I just shot. "Oh God! Frank! Are you okay?"

I clear my throat. My voice squeaks. "What the fuck?"

Kim looks up, cradling zombie Frank's head, blood still running down her chin from her last victim, her skin still sallow. "You *killed* him!"

I didn't know it at the time, but this same scene was happening all over the metro area.

They got better. It was crazy. So crazy. The plague, turned out, ran its course in about a week, give or take a day or two. They all needed water, medical attention, *rest*, but…they were okay. Just like they'd come down with…well…

…with a virus. Like the flu.

They were just sick. Not undead. Sick.

And me and my crew had killed them. We killed them when they were sick. I killed twenty-five people.

I…

I murdered my parents, you guys. I just…just saw Mom's eyes all glassy and saw the bite marks on Dad's face and I…just…

Jesus.

Twenty thousand people died. Most of them were "zombies." A lot of them died from exposure, dehydration, stuff like that. The rest were killed by people like me. By people who thought they were already dead.

And, like, it wasn't like we hesitated, right? We just started bashing away, right off. See your roommate groaning and staggering, his eyes way off somewhere, and you just crushed his head with a bowling trophy and didn't look back. It was our moment to shine. To show the world we were tough enough to survive. To prove how badass we were.

But then the world didn't end. It, like, wasn't over. Was never *going* to be over. If we'd just holed up in our houses like the government said—like so many people did—it all woulda blown over.

But we didn't.

We're a bunch of murderers. Bloodthirsty psychos. Sure, sure—there was an amnesty issued. A time of panic, they said. Totally understandable. But people know. You still get the looks. They showed some of the funerals on the news—the weeping, the anger, all over what we did. I get on the bus, and it's like there's a bubble around me—a bunch of ex-zombies, not wanting to get too close. Like they can see their blood on me still.

Turns out I'm no survivor at all.

I'm the thing they all survived.

Copyright © 2019 by Auston Habershaw

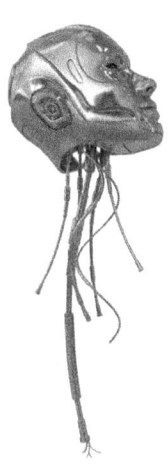

Robert Jeschonek is a prolific author of short stories and articles, and has four novels to his credit, including the recent National Literature Award winner My Favorite Dance Band Does Not Exist.

AN INFINITE NUMBER OF IDIOTS

by Robert Jeschonek

In every community on our world, which we call The World, there's a statue of an alien idiot, which we call The Idiot. And once a day, all the people in the world take turns pissing on these statues. We call this *praying*.

As in *praying* that The Idiot and his moron buddies never come back to The World—at least as long as we The People still live here.

That's the kind of impression that The Idiot—otherwise known as Captain Crap—and the crew of the Fartship *Excrement* made when they dropped by on their illustrious visit a while back.

In case you're wondering, yes—the names of The Idiot, his morons, and their ship have been changed to disrespect the indecent. But the rest of the story is true, or my name isn't Foca Zi Za.

And no, I don't normally talk like this, in words you'd understand or expressions for which I have no frame of reference. But I thought I'd switch on the Voice Box translator left behind by Crap so I can be sure I'm getting through to you.

Because I think it's very important that you know what happened with the *Excrement*, that you know the whole story.

Otherwise, it might not make a lot of sense that I'm carving you up like a piece of meat right now.

How *smoodgy* is too *smoodgy*? That's a tough one to answer since there's no good word for *smoodgy* in your language.

But that day, it was just *smoodgy* enough in my part of The World. The skeletal towers were blistering hot under the blazing white suns, the air swirling with crackling driftweeds and dustdemons. The parched ground was cracked and scattered with jagged bone shards and mummifying corpse shreds that gave off a sweet, musty smell. The dry air echoed with the shrieks of the dying in the Death Pits, crying first for mercy and then for release.

Does all this seem perfect and beautiful to you? It did to me that day, as I rolled along on my way to the nearest pit. It was just about as *smoodgy* as you can get, a true *paradise*.

If only the air in front of me hadn't started to sparkle just then.

It was enough to stop my central mass (and the spherical arrangement of thirty multi-articulated arm/legs radiating around it) from spinning. I crashed to a stop in a jumble of bony limbs, barely avoiding the four figures that solidified amid the jumping sparks.

My first thought when I got a good look at them was, *Only two arms and two legs apiece?* But the skins were a shocker, too—pink on three of them and a kind of pale pinkish green on the other. I was so used to The People's bright white skins (with the black blots constantly shifting under the surface in response to our emotional states) that these strange solid colors seemed unnatural.

Then there was the clothing, which at first I thought was part of the visitors' skins. One wore a red top, two wore pale blue, and the one in front wore gold. All of them wore the same color bottoms—plain black. On a world where no one wore clothes of any kind, it made for a very alien-looking group.

When the gold-topped one in the middle started talking, that impression was even stronger. The droning sounds he made with his single-channel voice (why not *triple*-channel like the voices of *The People*?) were like *nothing* I'd heard before, and they made no sense.

At least until he held up an oblong black device hanging from a slender black strap around his neck. (Identical to the one I'm wearing now, see?) The device had a silver mesh grate on its face and emitted familiar sounds when he switched it on. "Greetings." Somehow, I was able to understand what he was telling me as if he were speaking my language. "We come in peace."

As I untangled myself and restored my standard spherical configuration, other People gathered to take in this bizarre scene. One of the first to arrive was my mate, Vira Vo, who rolled up and parked at my side.

"Ugly things." The words came softly from her central mass, suspended within her lattice of arm/legs. "Bad feeling."

"Give them a chance," I told her, or words to that effect, even as gold-top droned on.

By then, he'd told us his name and the name of his ship, which weren't "Captain Crap" and *Excrement* at all (but let's keep it simple and go with those—they seem more fitting). He said he was on a mission of exploration and wanted only to have a look around. Who could argue with that?

We The People, that's who! We should've argued with that right from the *start*! It would've saved us a lot of *trouble* if we'd thrown those bums off The World right then and there instead of trying to be nice and showing them hospitality! We wouldn't have had to listen to more of their *bullshit* or put up with their *meddling*.

And we wouldn't have missed out on so many righteous *slayings* in the *Death Pits* either. We wouldn't have offended our almighty *gods* by depriving them of numerous *sacrifices*. We wouldn't have to make up for lost time now, offering up a steady stream of people like you. (Yes, *you*. Sacrificing *you* to the gods is the whole point of the carving and the altar and the screams, after all.)

A lot of things would have gone differently if I'd stood up to Crap that day…but no. Instead of driving off the newcomers, I introduced myself and Vira and agreed to act as their guide.

Which makes me think, looking back, that *Captain Crap* wasn't the *only* idiot in this story.

✿

Sightseeing on The World can be a wonderful experience. We've got the bone towers, of course, and the quicksilver fountains…the fuzzcanos and pop-up jungles…the Dung Mountains and the Footprints of Enormity. In the interest of goodwill, we showed Captain Crap and his *Excrement* bunch around these and more, telling them all the stories of how these landmarks and monuments came to be (when we could get a word in edgewise with motor-mouth Crap always blabbing).

But all *they* cared about were the *shrieks* from the Death Pits! Can you imagine?

What's with all the screaming, Foca?

Where's that screaming coming from, Foca?

It sounds like somebody's screaming for help out there, Foca.

And I just wanted to say, *Where are your manners? You're getting the grand tour! Why can't you shut up and enjoy it?*

But I didn't say that, and neither did any of the other People trailing along after us. Vira did the next best thing, though. Slipping away at the Coughing Cliffs of Hacknonymity, she rolled off fast to the Death Pits and got the clerics there to wrap up the sacrifices for the rest of the day. No more shrieking, problem solved.

Or so we thought.

"And now you know why we call these the Steps of Indignation." As I concluded another tale of one of our landmarks, I saw Vira roll up and give me a signal that all was well. Not for the first time, I thought about how lucky I was to have her as a mate.

"You truly have a magnificent world here." Crap looked around and nodded with a twinkle in his eye. "And a…*quiet*…one, as well. *Now*, at least." He was onto us and letting us know it.

But I didn't care, as long as he and his bunch stopped nagging about the screams. "I'm glad you like it, Captain. Right this way, and I'll lead you to the feast being held in your honor."

"Already?" said the blue-topped male introduced by Crap as Dr. Meh. "You folks sure know how to throw a party together fast."

"Your timing is good," I told him. "This is our holiday season."

At that instant, one last errant shriek escaped the Death Pits. "Some holiday," said Meh.

"There's just one thing." Captain Crap turned to his colleague with the pinkish-green skin and the pale blue top. "Mr. Suck here noticed some anomalous readings from—that way, wasn't it?" Crap pointed in the direction of the Death Pits.

"Correct." Mr. Suck had pointy ears, which suited him because he came across as such a humorless prick. Like Crap and the others, he spoke with the aid of a Voice Box device hanging from a strap around his neck. "The readings indicated violent activity or bloodletting which has since abated." He stared at the screen of a black-shelled device in his hand, then turned his gaze on me. "Was some sort of battle transpiring in the indicated area?"

"No battle," I said, bouncing nervously.

"Perhaps we could see what lies in that direction anyway," suggested Mr. Suck. "There might be someone in need of aid."

"There isn't." I rolled in a little circle. "No doubt you detected the slaughter of an animal to provide fresh meat for the feast."

"But the *high level* of activity suggests otherwise," said Mr. Suck.

"Not to mention the *screaming*," added Dr. Meh.

"Excuse me." I stopped bouncing. "Are any of you *from* here?"

Suck clasped his hands behind his back and stared down his long nose at me. "Obviously, we are not. And yet…"

"Then trust me, we local folk know better than you about a thing or two." I said it firmly to cut off any arguments. "Now who wants to go to the big celebratory feast?"

Crap raised his hand. "That sounds like a marvelous idea…just as soon as we've had a closer look at wherever that screaming was coming from."

"Perfect!" I spun around and bounced, and many of The People in the entourage did the same. "Feast it is! Right this way, my friends!"

With that, I, Vira, and the others led Crap and his companions away from the Death Pits and headed for the feasting place in the heart of the bleached, baking bone towers.

☼

Let me just say, you haven't lived until you've been to a feast on The World. We really pull out all the stops—dried tumblepups, sandsquito salad, rockhog marrow, headwing fritters, bonegoat marrow. And to top it all off, the very best aged elixirs of mudblood and mite sweats.

But I guess you'll never know what it's like; too bad. Even if you were invited, you couldn't enjoy the experience anymore, not with so many parts of you missing.

But I hope you won't let the bad news get you down. After all, your sacrifice helps keep the gods

happy, which keeps The World turning, the suns blazing, and the bones dry and crisp.

Without you and those like you, our little paradise might all fall apart, and The People would have to give up their joy. I think that's worth screaming in pain and missing out on a few feasts, don't you?

☼

How would you like it if you threw a party, and the guests of honor wouldn't eat anything? (All because Dr. Meh claimed it was poisonous to their systems!) Then, on top of that, one of the guests kept *coming on* to your *mate*!

That's how the big feast for the *Excrement* group went. Every time I turned around, Crap had Vira cornered and was saying things like, "Do you believe in *quantum entanglement*?" and "I have so many *questions* about your *biology*." The complete lack of physical compatibility between them didn't put him off at all; he kept leaning in closer and closer, brushing his fingers over her arm/legs and making suggestive comments about her bones and central mass.

I was so busy watching out for Vira, I didn't notice that the number of *Excrement* guests got smaller as the feast went on…at least until it was too late.

We reached *that* point long after the suns had gone down, just as the swear dance was starting up. I was explaining the symbolism behind the intricate obscene gestures in the dance to Dr. Meh when suddenly the air filled with a piercing shriek…a piercing *Excrement* person's shriek.

It was enough to finally tear Crap's attention away from Vira. When the shriek erupted, he stopped flirting with her and leaped into action, looking around for the other members of his party.

"Where's Mr. Suck?" Crap's voice was all business. "And Security Officer Dork?"

"No idea, Captain," said Meh. "I didn't see Suck that long ago, though."

Crap grabbed a small silver device that was clipped to his belt and flipped open the cover. The device warbled, and Crap spoke into it. "Mr. Suck? Officer Dork? Please respond."

Crap waited a moment, but there was only silence from the device—and then another scream from afar.

Crap whirled and stormed over to confront me. "All right, Foca. Take me to my people, *now*."

"They should all be *right here*," I told him. "At the feast being held in their *honor*, not roaming around our private sacred places *unaccompanied*."

Another scream cut through the blistering hot night. "That's one of my people!" said Crap. "Does it *sound* like he's at the party right now?"

"Perhaps he's just having *a really good time*?" I suggested.

The next scream was louder and more agonized than the rest. Crap leaned closer and narrowed his eyes. "Take me to them *now*, Foca. I'm out of *patience*."

I hesitated. The truth is, I knew the screams were coming from the Death Pits—and I also knew nothing should be happening there since Vira had put a stop to it earlier. So I had a bad feeling about the whole thing and didn't want Crap anywhere near those pits.

Unfortunately, someone else got *that* ball rolling. "I've got a fix on their life signs." Meh was staring at the glowing screen of the boxy black device in his hands. "Thataway." Meh jabbed a finger toward the Death Pits.

"Let's go!" Crap ran from the feasting plaza with Meh in his wake.

I just wanted the whole mess to go away but fell in behind them with Vira just the same. As we charged among the bone towers, and the shrieking grew louder, I racked my brain but could think of no good plan to resolve the situation in The People's favor.

✧

Would you say the Death Pits are a dump? Or is it more of a cultural thing?

Everything's relative, right? What looks like a dump to you and your people looks like a *showplace* to me and mine.

When I see these vast pits bubbling with red-and-green sludge, each rimmed with spiked bone altars under chandeliers of mummified central masses and tendons, my heart-like organs skip three beats apiece. As I gaze around at the spinal domes and the pale, waxen walls carved into relief sculptures of clerics slashing sacrifices and dumping their corpses into the pits, I feel uplifted.

But *you* don't get it, do you? It's all a horror show to people like you, an abomination against everything you believe.

You primitives just refuse to see the *bright side* of agony, death, and decomposition in the name of remorseless gods who demand unending sacrifice to satisfy their monstrous hungers.

To make matters worse, you don't understand how to show proper respect when walking in on the sacred sacrifice of your lucky, screaming friends. I witnessed this bad behavior firsthand on that fateful day when Crap and Meh barged into the Temple of the Death Pits.

✧

There are many great reasons for calling Captain Crap an idiot. One of those is his habit of shooting first and asking questions later (or never).

For example, as soon as he ran into the Temple of the Death Pits, following the signal from Meh's device, Crap drew the handheld weapon from his belt and started shooting.

Bright yellow beams flashed from the tip of the gun, lancing across the temple toward a cleric on the far side of an enormous, bubbling pit. The beams missed, and the cleric went on with what he was doing, which was methodically slicing somebody up on a spiny altar slab.

"Get your hands off him!" Crap let loose another series of beams while running full-tilt around the rim of the pit. "Stop what you're doing!"

But the cleric continued to ignore him. He pulled a dripping green heart from the sacrifice's chest and raised it overhead, chanting a prayer with his eyes pinched shut.

"I said stop!" Crap sounded almost hysterical as he continued to run and fire, run and fire.

Though I didn't run, I did call out from across the rim. "Cleric Oodwa! Please halt the ritual!"

Oodwa's answer was to toss the green heart over the altar into the Death Pit, where it dissolved with a wisp of pale steam. Then, just as Crap was closing in, he pulled a lever on the altar, tipping the slab on its side and sending the heartless body splashing into the muck.

Even as Crap tackled him to the ground and pummeled him with blows from his fists, I said a secret prayer to the gods, begging them to bring good things to The People of The World. Why waste a good sacrifice, even if it *was* unscheduled?

"Dear God." Was Meh praying, too? "You people just *murdered* Mr. Suck."

"'Murder' is a strong word," I said.

"I hated his guts, but he didn't deserve *that*," said Meh.

"Don't worry," I told him. "He's not gone."

"What's *wrong* with you?" Meh glared at me. "Did you not just watch him *dissolve* in that corrosive pit?"

"I'm telling you, he's still with us," I said.

Meh waved me off. "You know what you can do with that spiritual mumbo-jumbo, don't you, son?"

Meanwhile, across the pit where Suck had been dumped, Crap was shaking Cleric Oodwa so hard, the black blots in his bone-white skin were scattering. "You *maniac*! That man was my *best friend*!"

"What about Officer Dork?" Meh shot another glare in my direction. "What have you done with *him*?"

"How should *I* know? I've been at the feast all evening!"

"Where *is* he?" Crap gave Oodwa the roughest shake yet. "Where is my *security officer*?"

"He is closer than you might think." As always, Oodwa's voice was serene. "He has not left us."

"*I* have a question for *you*, Captain Crap," snapped Vira. "What were your people doing *here* to begin with? This place is *off limits* to outsiders."

Suddenly, a deep, familiar voice resounded through the temple. "Perhaps *I* can provide the answers to your questions."

✧

Everyone turned at once to look toward that voice. A solitary figure in a blue shirt and black pants emerged from an arched doorway across the temple.

"Mr. Suck!" Captain Crap leaped to his feet, letting Oodwa fall to the ground.

"You're *alive*!" shouted Meh.

"Told you so," I said.

"Indeed." Suck nodded. "I commend you all for your keen powers of observation."

Meh rolled his eyes. "That's him, all right."

"But how?" Crap sounded suspicious. "How did you come back to life?"

"Quite simply, I did not," said Suck.

"But you're standing right there!" said Meh.

"The point is, I was *never dead*," said Suck.

"But we saw your heart torn out and your body dumped in *there*!" Crap pointed at the Death Pit.

"That body was *cloned*," said Suck. "As was Officer Dork's. Apparently, *his* clone was disposed of before you arrived."

"Cloned?" Crap shot a look my way. "You people sacrifice *clones*?"

"We don't speak of this with outsiders," Vira said before I could answer. "The secret, manifold rituals are reserved for The People alone."

"Then why the *hell* did you clone and sacrifice *our* people?" barked Meh.

"We can't tell you that," I said, "because we don't *know* what happened." That was only partly true. Actually, I thought I could make a pretty good guess about it.

"We were investigating the screams and violent activity I'd detected earlier," explained Suck. "When we entered this place, however, we were quickly apprehended and subdued."

Another voice spoke up then, from another doorway not far from Suck's. "We fought back, but they overpowered us." The man in the red top stepped out, looking most definitely not dead.

"Officer Dork!" Crap sounded thrilled. "*You're* alive, too!"

"Glad to be here, sir." Dork smiled. "Though I could've done without the roughhousing from that guy and his buddies." He pointed at Cleric Oodwa, who was still sprawled on the ground. "They tied us both up and threw us into some kind of electrified booths. The next thing we knew, we had *identical twins*."

"Clones," corrected Suck. "Which were promptly led away by the cleric. Officer Dork and I struggled to break free and pursue them, but breaking out of the booths took longer than we expected."

"The booth walls were stronger than they looked." Dork raised a clenched fist. "But I got a burst of adrenaline once I heard my own voice *screaming* in *pain*. The voice of my *clone*, I mean."

"They grew adult clones *that fast*?" said Meh.

"These people are *remarkably* adept at the cloning process," said Suck. "I am at a loss to explain how they were able to generate full-grown clones of us in such a short time."

"Which they then proceeded to carve up and dump in a pit of corrosive sludge." Meh sounded disgusted. "Why bother?"

Suck looked my way. "Correct me if I'm wrong, but I surmise *cloning* is the primary means of *reproduction* in this society."

Meh turned and ran his device over me, tweaking controls and watching the glowing screen. "Wrong, Suck. Near as I can tell, this fella has a perfectly functioning reproductive system with all the right parts for a male of his species. No need for clones for the purpose of procreation."

"Perhaps the people of this planet prefer a higher degree of control over expressed characteristics," said Suck. "Perhaps they prefer a specific assortment of forms that have proved to be most durable and beneficial in the past."

"Is that so?" Meh scowled at me. "Then what about all the *screaming* we've heard since we *arrived* on this planet? I assume that's been coming from sacrificial *clones*?"

"It has," I told him.

"So why *sacrifice* these clones if they're so damn *beneficial*?" asked Meh.

"Why not?" Crap walked back over to stare down at Oodwa. "If they can make an unlimited number of copies, they can *afford* to use a few to keep the gods happy. Am I right?"

Cleric Oodwa shivered and said nothing.

"When life is *cheap*, it's *easy* to throw it away." Crap spun on his heel and glared over the pit at me and Vira. "But *mercy* is the truest mark of an advanced civilization. The greatest cloning technology in the *galaxy* isn't worth a damn if you're incapable of showing *mercy*. *Especially* to *guests* who go astray."

"Why *did* you people sacrifice clones of *our* people?" asked Meh.

"You'll have to ask the clerics that one," I told him. "Though I *can* say they can be…*overzealous* at times."

"Well, I hope those particular sacrifices were enough to hold your gods *over*," said Crap. "Because the bloodbath is going to *stop*."

"Correct," I said. "The Death Pits are closed for the night, and no sacrifices will be conducted until tomorrow at—"

"That's not what I meant." Crap strolled over and stood face-to-mass with me, eyes narrowed and jaw set. "What I'm saying is, all further sacrifice of sentient beings on this planet—cloned or otherwise—will hereby *cease*, effective *immediately*."

☼

The Idiot never got it. Even as he stood with his companions before The People the next morning under the blistering white-hot suns and gave a dramatic speech (in the halting, affected cadence I'd come to expect—and despise—from him) about the virtues of not killing clones, I could tell he didn't understand.

"For what better measure of a man can there be… than how he treats his fellow beings?" Crap cast his steely, self-righteous gaze over the crowd, pausing as if he expected applause. It didn't come, and he continued. "And how can we, and you, in good conscience…reach out to other species in friendship…if we cannot respect and preserve *our own*?"

As I watched from the front of the audience, I had the distinct feeling he wasn't really giving the speech for *our* benefit. It seemed to me the performance was more about *him* and *his people* than *us*. As if he were stroking his own colossal ego or trying to justify what they were about to do to us…or both.

Whatever the reason for it, his words meant nothing to me or any of us. We just listened politely because the only way to get this all over with was to let the big blowhard have his say.

"We, and those like us, are committed to the advancement of *all* lifeforms…throughout the universe." Crap nodded proudly. "We are pledged not to intervene…in the natural course of development of other species. But wanton *slaughter* in the performance of sacrificial *rites* is surely not *natural*. It cannot be considered *civilized* behavior…or the actions of a species worthy of joining the interstellar community. Therefore, I am doing you a very great *favor*."

"You mean you're finally going to shut up?" whispered Vira, just for me.

I couldn't help laughing to myself.

Crap spread his arms wide as if to take in all of us. "I am going to *free you* from your old, barbaric ways. I am going to *free you* from the curses of *cloning* and *blood sacrifice*…in the name of a *brighter* and *more enlightened* tomorrow!"

Again, he seemed to be waiting for applause that never came.

"Dr. Meh and Mr. Suck assure me your species will be able to continue to procreate via natural, biological means. You don't *need* cloning to survive… but *ending* the practice will restore the balance of genetic diversity among you. And ending the self-destructive brutality of blood sacrifice…will restore the balance of compassion in your *souls*."

With that, he plucked the silver communication device from his belt, flipped it open, and raised it to his lips. "And now, I give you back your *freedom*… your *dignity*…and, yes, I will even say your *humanity*. For though our peoples come from worlds apart, we are not so *different* as you might imagine."

He gave a signal over the device then, and the bombardment began. Colossal twin beams of golden energy blazed down from the sky, screaming from the guns of the orbiting Fartship *Excrement* into the district of the Death Pits behind Crap.

"Your brave new world starts here and now!" Crap shouted over the noise of the energy beams. "When *these* pits are demolished, our ship will move on to destroy *all* such sites around this planet."

The ground rumbled and shook. Dust and smoke filled the air as the bone and rock walls of the temple collapsed, burying the cloning pods and the vast vats of corrosive sludge.

Just like that, our way of life disappeared. Centuries of faith and tradition were buried in minutes.

All because of one Idiot who was convinced he knew what was best for People he'd only met a few days ago. An Idiot who had the power to change The World on a stupid whim.

And he never *did* get it.

Not that we bothered trying to make him understand after that. He and his people stayed on The World much too long for our liking, trying to guide us in changing our ways after the loss of the Death Pits. We just wanted the lot of them gone, so we told them what we thought they wanted to hear—how we'd all seen the light and were grateful and ready to make our world a better and more civilized place.

When it seemed like they might *never* leave, we even put up *statues* of The Idiot in every community around The World, supposedly paying tribute to his greatness. We didn't even *piss* on them at first.

Eventually, they *finally* said goodbye. They thanked us for our hospitality, congratulated us on the progress we'd made, and the air sparkled around them. They were gone…and still, I knew they didn't *get it*.

They didn't understand that the Death Pits weren't that easy to get rid of. With enough determination, we could dig them up and rebuild the temples around them.

They also didn't understand that the cloning had *nothing* to do with reproduction. That had just been Mr. Suck's theory, with no basis of any kind in our reality.

For The People, cloning is *all* about sacrifice…and *punishment*. Making the lives of those who offend us miserable. Bringing the people we hate back to life again and again and making them *suffer*.

In other words, *hurting* people like *you*.

Can you still hear me? Hello?

Oh, good. Your one remaining eye just opened. I'm so glad somebody's still paying attention in there, because I'm not quite done yet, my friend.

You finally get it, don't you? There's a *reason* I've been carving you up like this, on the bone altar in the newly-restored Temple of the Death Pits, sacrificing you to the gods of The World in the name of The People who love and fear them.

It's because you look just like *him*—Captain Crap, The Idiot who came on to our mates (Vira and *so* many others in the time before he left)…who lectured us as if we were children…tore down our most beloved institution…and jeopardized our favored status with the gods by denying them sacrifices for so very many weeks. It's because there's nothing more satisfying than cutting up his identical clone and dumping the body in the pit to dissolve into steaming goo.

And then doing it *again and again and again*.

You see those others lined up over there? The ones who look just like *you* and just like *him*? They're *next*. They're waiting for me to finish with you, waiting to be led by the clerics to the altar for their turn under the knife.

And there will be plenty *more* where they came from. An *infinite* number of *Idiots*, born in the clone pods, dying in the name of the very gods who were once scorned by your predecessor, the template for your line.

And if we ever get bored with *you*, we can churn out clones of the rest of Crap's motley landing party. We'll *never* run out of Craps and Sucks and Mehs and Dorks to kill. We collected *plenty* of genetic material from them before they finally left to spread their nonsense elsewhere in the unsuspecting galaxy.

Oh, hush now. Enough with the ear-splitting shrieks. I mean, you've got to appreciate a little poetic justice, don't you? And you've got to admit, there's a lot of *black humor* in the situation.

Shhh. Settle down now. I'm finally done. I think it's safe to say you finally understand.

It's time for your bath in the pit, but I wouldn't worry. I've heard it doesn't hurt all that much as it melts your flesh and bones into bubbling sludge.

Or if it does, it won't last long. Though everything's relative, as your ancestor learned during his time on The World. One man's murder is another man's sacrament.

Perhaps, from your point of view, it will seem to last an eternity.

Kevin J. Anderson is a Hugo nominee, the author of more than fifty national or international bestsellers, and is the publisher of WordFire Press.

TWENTY THOUSAND YEARS UNDER THE SEA

by Kevin J. Anderson

He dreamed of tentacles again.

The battered *Nautilus* cruised listlessly through uncharted waters, its engine struggling, pumps and pistons wheezing like an injured man trying to catch his breath. The hull seams showed the strain of the recent battle, and some rivets leaked water, preventing the armored sub-marine boat from diving deep.

But the dreams of her captain were darker and more restless than the seas around them.

In his stateroom, Nemo's bunk was padded with fine cushions, and he tossed under silken sheets that were fit for a caliph—*stolen* from the corrupt caliph, as was the *Nautilus* and everything else.

In the nightmare, he fought alongside his loyal crewmen against the slimy, thrashing tentacles. Though Nemo's true war was against evil men and their unquenchable thirst for slaughter, the giant squid was a mindless beast of nature. The squid had tried to crush the armored hull in its suckered embrace, and Nemo and his men fought it with cutlasses, harpoons, and daggers, covering the deck with foul-smelling slime and a gushing of black ink like a shadow made out of acid. A well-placed harpoon blinded the monster's eye and penetrated its rudimentary brain, then the wounded creature released its death grip, slipping away from the sub-marine boat and into the sea, taking four crewmen with it.

Captain Nemo and his surviving sailors tended their injuries. The men already had many scars from years of engineering slavery at Caliph Robur's prison camp of Rurapente. After escaping in fire and blood, Nemo had declared his own war on war. Nature, however, didn't care about their battle or their pain—the giant squid proved that.

Nemo would not be deterred by storms or by attacking monsters. He tried to rest while Mr. Harding and his engineers repaired the motors. Others caulked and welded hull breaches, reinforcing the seams on the wounded vessel. The navigator steered through the night, looking for some sheltered place where they could put in and complete repairs.

Exhausted and sore, Nemo tried to rest, if only for a few hours, but nightmares of that soulless tentacled creature granted him no peace. Even in sleep, Captain Nemo continued his battle….

Thus, it was a relief when Mr. Harding tapped on his cabin door. "Sorry to disturb you, sir, but we found an island. Looks uninhabited."

Nemo climbed from his bunk, disentangling himself from the silken sheets that reminded him too much of tentacles. "I'm on my way."

☼

Nemo was amazed his navigator had been able to find this bleak and rugged island. With its crescent-shaped cove bounded by black walls that plunged down to the waterline, it reminded Nemo of a claw.

When they encountered the giant squid, the *Nautilus* had been stalking naval battleships in the southern seas, eager to eliminate the bloodthirsty soldiers before they could prey upon innocents. Nemo left any merchant vessel unmolested, but French, British, or Spanish warships were sunk to the bottom of the sea. No mercy. The sailors aboard would have shown no mercy to those they preyed upon: innocent women and children who became pawns in political power plays, like Nemo's own wife and son, like the families of the other engineering prisoners from Rurapente.

Because the seas were so rough south of Terra del Fuego, few sailing vessels wandered far afield for the pleasure of exploring. Now, damaged and limping along, the *Nautilus* had blundered upon a bleak no-man's land not far from the untouched shores of the Antarctic continent. This isolated, never-inhabited island was surrounded by mist and freezing drizzle.

The sun was only a pale, gray fuzz swathed in mist when Nemo emerged from the hatch with Mr. Harding and engineers named Louart and Fallon. He inspected the glistening hull for traces of slime or pools of blood, but the spray of rough waters had washed the *Nautilus* clean.

Nemo inhaled the salty, mist-laden air, but there was a sour, rotten taint to it. Louart asked, "What's that smell, Captain?"

"This is a sheltered cove," Harding suggested. "Maybe a school of fish…"

Fallon said, "I remember each year when the alewives would die off and wash ashore. Made the whole port stink."

Nemo did see numerous fish floating belly up on the surface of the cove. "But these are all different species. They wouldn't have died off at once."

Harding got down to business. "No matter, Captain. We're here to make repairs and be on our way."

Nemo gazed up at the sheer cliffs. Seabirds wheeled about, not the usual gulls but black ones that looked like bats. As they hunted in the shadowy mist, their screeches were haunting.

In some trick of the warming dawn, the mist thinned, and hazy light dappled the surrounding cliffs and the mountains inland. Nemo saw more than just boulders and outcroppings: the cliffs were scattered with blocky geometrical shapes, graceful pillars, magnificent but crumbling towers. Even from this distance, with details blurred by fog, the structures looked unspeakably ancient.

"They're ruins, Cap'n!" Fallon cried.

Nemo frowned. "We're off the coast of Antarctica. No civilization ever existed this far south. Even the savages in Terra del Fuego have nothing more than huts."

Louart pointed toward the mysterious city inland. "And yet, Monsieur Capitan—they exist."

Nemo turned to his second-in-command. "Mr. Harding, I'll let you continue the repairs. I intend to see that city."

Harding never argued. "Suit yourself, Captain. We have plenty of work to do." His bearded face was smeared with grease and his hands were dirty. "I spent hours in the engine room. We'll have to take the motors apart, replace one of the screws. That squid did us a lot of harm."

"Can you fix it?" Nemo asked.

The other man raised his eyebrows. "Of course, we can fix it—we built the boat in the first place. It's just a matter of time."

"Time to explore, then."

Joined by five companions, Nemo took a boat to shore, searching for a safe landing spot against the cliffs. At last, they encountered a cleverly hidden road cut at an angle down the rock, all but invisible except when approached face-on. The wide path was paved with moss-slick flagstones cut from black obsidian. The carved steps were at the wrong height for human legs.

Inland, the strange, bleak island was littered with ruins, white stone structures with trapezoidal doorways that were too low and too wide for an average person. The streets spread out in unsettling angles, and the walls were constructed with a disorienting obliqueness that made Nemo feel as if he were falling when he faced them.

Temples or observatories crowned outcroppings, and huge columns rose high, but many were broken, strewn about like the bones of prehistoric animals. Boulevards led across a high plateau and then plunged over a cliff edge. Rounded arenas had once hosted some kind of unknown sport or spectacle.

On the lintels of collapsed buildings and an altar of what must have been a temple of worship, or sacrifice, Nemo saw a repeated dot pattern that seemed familiar to him, but he couldn't place it.

Standing tall, dark stone obelisks were covered with strange glyphs unlike any alphabet Nemo had ever seen—a mixture of runes, hieroglyphics, and squiggles. He had learned many languages in his life, and after years of oppression at Rurapente, he was fluent in reading and writing Arabic. His engineers understood the language of mathematics. The language of the ancient engravings seemed an amalgam of all those things.

Even in the gray cold mist Nemo smelled brimstone, and a pall of old smoke seemed hung in the air. These ruins reminded him far too much of Rurapente….

He had been selectively captured in the Crimean War along with other scientists, engineers, and visionaries. The evil Caliph Robur forced them to work in his isolated prison. As the ambitious French engineer de Lesseps carved a channel across the Suez Isthmus that would connect the Mediterranean to the Red Sea, the caliph had commanded Nemo and his fellow workers to build him a warship unlike any the world had seen: an armored vessel to prey upon trade ships that came through the new Suez Canal. He could become the world's most accomplished pirate, the greatest leader, the master of the world.

For years Nemo and his comrades had toiled in slavery. They were rewarded with wives whom they learned to love, even families that gave them a spark of solace in their captivity. Caliph Robur had made the *Nautilus* his fortress, until Nemo and his men overthrew and assassinated him during a test voyage, stole the armored sub-marine boat, raced to Rurapente to save their families. But they were too late. The caliph's political rivals had already marched upon the secret base and slaughtered everyone….

Nemo could never burn away the images of his return to Rurapente. The foundations of buildings stood like blackened stumps of teeth. The smelting refineries had been caved in, windows smashed, bricks crumbled. The living quarters had been burned to ash and slag. Everything…destroyed.

The oppressive silence had been broken only by a faint whistle of wind. As he stood there, Nemo had thought he heard the shouts of raiders, the crackle of flames, the clang of scimitars against makeshift weapons, or against soft flesh, hard bone. Screams of pain and pleas for mercy from the desperate slaves, the women, the children—everyone who had endured life at Rurapente. All dead.

And was this place any different?

He and his companions found weathered statues hewn from lava rock, details blurred by time and something more. Together, two crewmen pried loose a stone figure that had toppled face-first into the crumbling gravel and frozen mud. When they lifted it up, Nemo saw not the figure of any man, but a creature with a face that was a hideous mass of tentacles, and eyes that even in the pitted and eroded stone looked as empty and unimaginable as the universe.

Louart paled and made the sign of the cross, though he had not previously demonstrated any penchant for religion. "It must be one of their gods," said Fallon.

"Or one of their demons," Nemo said.

They continued to explore, studying friezes that depicted the daily life of a civilization inconceivable even to the most fevered opium dream, populated by barrel-like creatures with starfish heads. None of the men spoke, uneasy, awed, and intimidated.

The sour smell of rot was more pronounced as he led the way to the steep path down to the cove. The sun ducked behind the mist again, and gray shrouds thickened around them.

Mr. Harding was on the upper deck of the *Nautilus* waiting for the captain. "Those are ruins even greater than the city of Pompeii," Nemo told him.

The gruff second-in-command scratched his bearded chin. "Then you'll be even more interested in what we found in the cove, Captain. There's an even larger ancient city submerged under the water." His lips quirked in a small smile, "And this one's intact."

✧

When the *Nautilus* had fought its way to the shelter of the natural harbor at night, no one had been looking deep below. As Nemo peered into the deep cove, he could see the shimmering fever-dream architecture of the sunken city. "That city down there has waited a long time for us. It might have been submerged for twenty thousand years or more."

"I don't intend on staying here anywhere near that long, Captain," Harding said. "We'll get to work."

Nemo picked Louart and three other men to don exploration suits and join him. The Rurapente engineers had designed the suits for Caliph Robur, after he lied that he wanted to explore the bottom of the sea; in truth, Robur had needed those suits so his underwater army could augur holes in the hulls of helpless ships.

Nemo gathered the waterproof leather suit, the weights, the buckles, the helmet, and the wrappings that sealed all the seams. As he and his team fastened their helmets and attached the breathing hoses to tanks so they could inhale the stale compressed air, he thought again of his war against war.

The *Nautilus* could have been an unprecedented means of exploration, a boon for science. Before being captured in the Crimea, Nemo had seen much of the world, dared many adventures, but thanks to the smoke and the misery of Rurapente, his spirit of curiosity had been snuffed out like a bright ember under a bootheel. Now, though, this ancient and mysterious underwater city intrigued him.

He sank slowly and gracefully toward the bottom. The pressure of the water closed around him like a squeezing fist, but the reinforced suit protected him. His weights pulled him down until the *Nautilus* was only a strange angular shape that eclipsed the rippling daylight. The other men spread out as they drifted down and landed with slow gracefulness. Together, they turned on their galvanic lights, shining yellow into the gloom.

The buildings of the sunken city were similar to the ruins up above, but here they were better preserved. The walls stood upright and arches gracefully framed entryways into ominous temples.

Taking the lead, Nemo walked with his armored boots on the silty floor, sending up puffs of murk to expose broad flat flagstones. They passed titanic facades, statues, obelisks covered with markings, friezes that depicted the creatures with the barrel-bodies and starfish heads, and another species that were formless conglomerations of bubbles or masses of pseudopods that seemed to be servants or guardians to the starfish-headed creatures. And more images of the tentacle-faced creature from the toppled statue. The arches and rune-encrusted pillars again bore that familiar dot pattern. Perhaps it was something from a book Caliph Robur kept inside the *Nautilus* library.

They spread out to explore, and their galvanic lights bobbed along. The sunken metropolis carried a weight of ancientness, a weariness of years that extended far beyond the twenty thousand years he had suggested. Perhaps these buildings had been erected long before humans had ever populated this planet.

A golden glow flared and then died down, but the suit made Nemo sluggish, and the hazy glow had faded by the time he turned. He felt a chill. He had encountered many predators under the sea, had fought off sharks and a giant squid, but this fear was different and inexplicable.

Louart approached him, signaling with a gloved hand. The two men pressed their face plates together so that Louart's voice echoed through the thick glass. "Notice, mon Capitan. No coral, no seaweed, no rubble."

Nemo indicated a cluster of perfectly placed sea anemones and a large fan of corral, but Louart shook his head inside the helmet. They touched panes of glass again. "Those are intentional—decorations. Something is *tending* this city."

Nemo realized the other man was right. Always when he ventured to the sea bottom, the marine flora was scattered and lush: sponges, shellfish, anchored kelp, and waving fronds of seaweed. Here, though, the cove appeared sterile. He realized that he hadn't seen any fish.

The group spread out again, wary. Nemo shone his light around, found a line of imposing arches that seemed to guide him on. He walked under the first span, and the second, until he saw a domed and thick-walled structure ahead, sealed and armored like a bunker…or a crypt.

Nemo felt drawn to it, as if compelled. The vault door was barricaded with a complex stone mechanism…clean, smooth stone. Any normal ruins would have been encrusted with marine growth and cemented shut by coral, but the lines here were razor sharp and clear of debris.

He shone the yellow galvanic beam to illuminate the door. It was covered by a stylized bas-relief that showed a creature with the smooth dome of a skull and baleful red eyes that glowed with inset phosphorescent jewels. The lower half of the creature's face was covered with twisting, curling tentacles.

Though the thing was frightening, Nemo felt a tantalizing tug on his heart that ignited his anger. This thing with the tentacled face symbolized Nemo's own hatred toward those who wrought violence, and it seemed to possess a power to eradicate war. This was something far more deadly than the *Nautilus*, if only he would set it free….

With great difficulty, he pulled himself away and withdrew beneath the looming arches. He could hear his breathing in the helmet, and his heart was pounding like drums. He looked around for his companions.

One figure, Louart, stood close to a tall, ethereal spire of rock carved into delicately balanced segments. The man studied the carvings, then pulled himself to a higher section to see.

Although the sunken ruins were perfectly preserved, they were still fragile with unspeakable age. As Louart placed weight against the joints, the segmented spire wobbled and bent. He pushed himself backward and out of the way as the stone sections collapsed.

The galvanic lights flashed in random directions as the other men backed away from the tumbling stone. Suddenly, the golden glow appeared at the edge of Nemo's vision, brightening and rushing forward. He caught only a glimpse out of the curved helmet.

A swarm of light and bubbles erupted along the corridors of the ancient city. It was a mass of living spheres, like gelatinous blind eyes clumped into a sentient form. All the spheres turned forward, as if targeting the intruder who had knocked down the spire.

Louart saw the thing coming and flailed away. The bubble mass moved so swiftly that it reached the man before the last spire block had tumbled to the ocean floor. The shapeless amoeboid swarmed over Louart. He fought with his arms and legs, but the bubble creature surrounded him and *squeezed*.

Nemo and his companions hurried to Louart's defense, but they were too slow underwater. The ocean was so incredibly silent. Nemo and one other man had spears; the others carried scimitars. The bubble thing continued to contract around its victim, and a sudden splash of red exploded in Louart's helmet, filming the faceplate.

Nemo hurled his harpoon, and it glided through the water, sizzling into the amoeboid thing, puncturing several of the spheres before it disappeared into the mass. But the formless creature rearranged itself, extending pseudopods in other directions. By now Louart was surely dead, perhaps even half digested. The other crewman threw his spear, to no effect.

The bubble thing squirmed along and retreated among the empty buildings of the sunken city. Nemo knew that it could have killed the rest of them, but the creature had retaliated only against the one man who had caused damage.

The other men were panicked, and Nemo pointed upward. His four comrades tore off their weights and floated upward to the waiting *Nautilus*.

Nemo remained in the ancient city, warily looking around. He glanced back toward the tantalizing, armored tomb that he hadn't had the nerve to explore, then he, too, released his weight belt and swam up to daylight.

☼

Even without Louart's body, the *Nautilus* crew held a solemn funeral for him. Afterward, Harding came to stand in the doorway of the captain's quarters. "We've lost too many crew already, Captain."

Nemo sat at his small desk, but did not nod. "We would all be dead if we'd stayed at Rurapente. This way, at least we can keep fighting."

"Fight against what, Captain? A giant squid? Some primordial monster in an ancient city?"

"The world is not a safe place, Mr. Harding, and there are other kinds of wars besides the one we chose. We can either give up, or we can continue our fight. This is a setback, but it is not a defeat."

Nemo stared at the books on the shelves, ancient Arabic tomes that Caliph Robur had considered essential—military strategy reports and treatises about the use of bladed weapons, instructional manuals on methods of torture (some of which masqueraded as medical texts). But he thought he remembered seeing something....

"When will the repairs be completed?"

His second in command stood in cold silence for a moment before answering, "Tomorrow, sir."

"Then let me read tonight."

After hours of paging through documents, he found the volume that contained the familiar dot pattern he'd seen on so many of the ruins. It was a thick handwritten book bound in a curious pale leather. The text inside had been penned in a dark brown ink; all the words were scribed in a trembling hand, as if the author were afraid to put into words the nightmarish thoughts that consumed his brain. *Necronomicon*.

After years as the caliph's prisoner, Nemo was fluent in Arabic, but this writing seemed to be an odd archaic dialect, written by a man named Abdul al-Hazred. Pages and pages of speculations seemed utter gibberish, something concocted in the hashish houses of Cairo or scrawled by a man dying from a madness plague.

According to the mad Arab, the dot pattern was a sign of the Old Ones, creatures from beyond time and space that had settled Earth soon after its formation, long before any natural life had emerged from the ooze. He saw drawings of the starfish-headed things depicted in statues in both the above-ground ruins and the sunken city. The *Necronomicon*'s ravings told how the Old Ones had found a way to traverse the airless chasms of open space, how they had created and enslaved a race of shapeless sentient clusters of protoplasm called Shoggoths that were their servants, their guardians, their caretakers.

The preposterous imagined history laid out a march of epochal events, how a race of tentacle-faced beings—immense and powerful strangers from beyond the stars—had engaged in a great war against the Old Ones, nearly wiping them out, but the Shoggoths and the Old Ones fought back, defeating the octopoid creatures, at least for a time. And the Old Ones had retreated into their cities beneath the sea.

Nemo thought the ruined city on this mysterious island might have been one of those ancient and impressive dwellings of the Old Ones. And the shapeless bubble thing that had attacked Louart—was that a Shoggoth?

The bas-relief carved in the doorway of the armored crypt was much like the octopoid race. The *Necronomicon* named the beings in a word written in blocky letters, as if al-Hazred had dared himself to write the word: CTHULHU.

He closed the book. Rationally speaking, Nemo didn't believe any of it. And yet in a primitive and easily frightened corner of his mind, he thought he knew the answers.

✦

Mr. Harding delivered the welcome news that repairs were nearly completed and the *Nautilus* could be under way by nightfall. The crew let out a ragged cheer. After the death of Louart, the oppressive anxiety that hung over the abandoned island and the ruined city had begun to seep into their psyche like mildew in a dank tomb.

Nemo, however, heard the report from his second-in-command as if it were distant background noise. He wasn't yet finished with this ancient sunken city. The tales from the *Necronomicon* had inflamed his imagination, caught hold of him like an incurable fever.

If he had read the ravings of the mad Arab in the camp of Rurapente, he would have discounted it all, but after what he had seen, not just the statues and cyclopean buildings, but the appearance of the murderous—protective?—Shoggoth that had killed Louart, he knew it had to be real. And that thing sealed in the armored tomb pulled on him like the inescapable current of the fabled maelstrom off the coast of Norway.

"I'm going back down there, Mr. Harding." He raised his voice and glanced at his crewmen at their stations on the bridge. "I'd like three volunteers to accompany me—but I won't require it." He didn't speak further, because he didn't want to be challenged to explain what he was doing or why.

Harding looked skeptical, but he held his tongue. The crew were terrified, knowing what had happened to their comrade, but they were Nemo's men and they would do anything for him. In the end, he had more volunteers than he needed.

As he suited up, Nemo felt preoccupied, his thoughts focused on what he knew was down there. In his life he had fought pirates, been shipwrecked, crossed Africa in a balloon, fought in the Crimean War, and suffered years of imprisonment under a murderous caliph who wanted to be the master of the world. But he doubted he would ever face anything as nerve-wracking as this. His obsession went beyond fear.

In their weighted underwater suits, the four explorers plunged to the bottom of the cove, shining their galvanic lanterns into the murk. They were all more wary now, seeing movement in every shadow, alert for the golden glow of the lurking Shoggoth. The men each carried a spear in one hand and a cutlass in the other, although the previous day's encounter had shown that such primitive defenses were ineffective against the Shoggoth.

This time, Nemo was pulled by an invisible force, like a questing tongue drawn to a broken tooth. He felt a call of that other being whose very image and name exuded awe. *Cthulhu.* The crypt seemed to contain more power than Nemo would need to win his war against war.

The four galvanic beams shone out, illuminating the arches that led to the squat armored building. The circular walls were like low battlements surrounding the sealed temple—or was it a tomb?—of an elder god.

The other men spread out, holding their spears and cutlasses, on guard for the swarming mass of one of the Old Ones' guardians. But Nemo faced the graven image of the cosmic creature. This being was different from the builders of the ancient sunken city; it might have caused the destruction of the starfish-headed Old Ones. But if so, why would

they build a temple to it here? Why honor Cthulhu with such an impressive and elaborate tomb?

He ran his gloved hands along the complex locking mechanism that sealed the crypt door. The stone components were carefully carved and arranged like a puzzle, a mystic trigger built by minds immeasurably superior to his own.

This mechanism was a problem unlike other engineering challenges he had faced in Rurapente, but his hands had their instincts. He applied his mind to the problem, sliding the components sideways, then down, then back into a different interlocking configuration. Something seemed to be guiding him. He felt the stone door thrum beneath his fingertips, as if an energy inside were building, awakening.

Next to him, the men scrambled backward, and Nemo turned to see if the Shoggoth were coming, but his companions were staring at him, at the temple…at the door cracking open. What seeped out was not a golden glow, but the opposite—an emptiness of light, a shadow that sucked at the beams of their galvanic lamps.

The water grew suddenly colder, penetrating even his thick undersea suit. The stone door spread wider, and darkness boiled out, along with an ominous emerging figure—a titanic looming shape that seemed much too large to have been contained within the structure.

A current blew Nemo backward like a howling storm wind as the crypt burst open, and the enormous thing with baleful eyes and facial tentacles emerged. The statues had conveyed only a hint of the overwhelming cosmic *presence* of what Abdul al-Hazred had named Cthulhu.

Then Nemo realized what he should have known from the start—that this was not a temple or a tomb…but a *prison*.

One of his men thrashed in a frantic effort to swim away, but the reawakened Cthulhu turned a horrible maddening gaze upon him—and the man's struggles immediately ceased. He drifted motionless, struck dead by the mere sight.

The galvanic lamps flashed wildly in all directions as the other two fled. Nemo was stunned and tumbling, trying to reorient himself in the water. He slammed into one of the stone walls and held on for balance. Nemo's mind couldn't contain the immensity of the emerging Cthulhu, a being that had been locked away for twenty thousand years or more beneath the sea.

What have I unleashed?

The water around him suddenly glowed, frothing golden as if illuminated by an unknown and insane source of light. Through his faceplate, he saw a roiling blob of bubbles, a conglomeration of translucent spheres that might or might not have been eyes—it was the Shoggoth returned to continue its attack.

But the formless thing did not pursue Nemo or his companions; instead, it confronted the horrific elder god. The light in the water continued to grow, and another Shoggoth streaked in from a separate part of the city. Then a third—and four more!

The Old Ones may have been long extinct in this isolated city, but they had left these shapeless but somehow faithful creatures to maintain their cursed metropolis. The Shoggoths did more than just maintain the buildings, arches, and sunken gardens; they were also here to keep the Cthulhu thing imprisoned.

Nemo and his men tried to find shelter behind the enormous facades, unable to do anything but watch. In their scramble away, they had dropped cutlasses and spears. Nemo's eyes were so blasted that he could barely see details in the glaring light, the masses of bubbles, the thrashing tentacles, and a defiant roar that vibrated through the fabric of the universe.

The Shoggoths swept in and surrounded the powerful, unspeakably evil creature that had emerged from its millennial prison. The formless creatures showed no vengeance toward the *Nautilus* men, but regarded them as utterly beneath notice.

Nemo and his companions tore away their weighted belts and clawed their way upward, rising toward the distant surface while expecting to be struck dead at any moment.

Below, the battle continued with all the fury of an active undersea volcano. The emerging Cthulhu tore Shoggoths to pieces, ripping the masses of bubbles, but the spheres reconverged. The Shoggoths were many, and they had been placed there for the sole purpose of guarding this monster. In a hurricane of golden light and swirling pseudopods, they drove the Cthulhu thing back, unable to destroy it—how

does one kill a godlike being that has existed since before time?—but at least the Shoggoths could contain it. They surrounded the ancient monster in a cocoon embrace, and pushed it back toward the tomb chamber.

Nemo finally broke the surface of the water, and he detached his helmet, gasping. The muffled sounds suddenly grew louder; next to him, the men couldn't stop screaming. Nemo's own throat was raw, and he knew he must have been screaming as well.

Careless and terrified, they dropped their helmets into the water and climbed the rungs to fight their way aboard the imagined safety of the *Nautilus*.

Mr. Harding stood watching them, surprised and alarmed. "Engines are ready to go, Captain, but what—"

Below, the supernatural storm continued to unleash explosions of light and inky shadows. "We must depart immediately!" Nemo said. "Now!"

Harding didn't argue. Seeing the expressions of absolute terror, not just on the other sailors but on their brave captain as well, the sailors moved more swiftly than they ever had in their lives.

When he spoke, Nemo's voice was torn and hoarse. "Take us away from this island. Far, far away."

The repaired engines hummed, and the submarine boat lumbered forward, picking up speed. Beneath them, the cove's deep water looked like a storm of lights and fire, inconceivable colors in a simmering battle that Nemo himself may have triggered…but one in which he could do nothing to fight on either side.

"What was down there, Captain?"

"Nothing I could understand, Mr. Harding."

The second-in-command gave a small nod, then focused on business, intent on more than cosmic monsters, elder gods, or vanished alien cities. "The *Nautilus* is in prime condition again, Captain. Engines at full power. Hull integrity, ramming blades, and reinforced bulkheads all check out. We can continue our mission."

Nemo stared ahead through the dragon's eye portholes. The *Nautilus* left the mysterious island behind and cut across the water into dark and uncharted seas. His own war against human hatred and bloodshed was an all-consuming struggle, a war so big that he knew it could never be won…still, the battle had to be fought.

Yet, the war he had just discovered between the Old Ones and Cthulhu was so much vaster, so much more ancient, so much more inconceivable that his own puny struggle against the evils of man seemed laughably trivial in comparison.

But it was his struggle, and it was all Nemo had left. "Yes, Mr. Harding, we will continue our war." He lowered his voice. "Even if it doesn't matter to the rest of the universe."

The *Nautilus* cruised away from the nightmarish island, toward the normal trade routes, continuing the hunt.

Copyright © 2015 by WordFire, Inc.
Originally published in The Madness of Cthulhu, *ed. S.T. Joshi, Titan Books, 2015.*

Richard Chwedyk, our new reviewer, sold his first story in 1990, won a Nebula in 2002, and has been active in the field for the past twenty-nine years. We're pleased to welcome him to the team.

BOOK RECOMMENDATIONS

by Richard Chwedyk

Fall; or, Dodge in Hell
by Neal Stephenson
William Morrow
June 2019
ISBN: 978-0062458711

The mind is its own place, and in it self Can make a Heav'n of Hell, a Hell of Heav'n.

—*John Milton*
Paradise Lost, *Book I, Lines 233-4*

Hard to believe, at least for a not-so-old-timer like me, that it's already been twenty-six years (or thereabouts) since Neal Stephenson first made a splash in the sf world with *Snow Crash*. I remember seeing him accept a Hugo Award a few years later for *The Diamond Age*, looking understandably pleased, but somewhat aloof as well, like he wanted to be *of* this world of science fiction without *really* being a part of it. Over the years, his works have been rightly honored by the science fiction community, even when his publishers carefully make sure to leave the sf label off the covers.

But you can't fool science fiction readers.

This latest novel proves it admirably with a fascinating premise, one that has long intrigued other writers in the field: death and what comes after.

Multibillionaire Richard "Dodge" Forthrast dies suddenly during a routine medical procedure. As per the orders in his will (liberally interpreted), his brain, his neural networks and such, are scanned and preserved in the cloud (or perhaps we should say *a* cloud) until technological advancements permit him to be revived into a virtual environment, a "Bitworld," which is as much a creation of its digital inhabitants as it is of the living designers who made it possible.

In more than a sense, it's a new universe, a new reality, which invites comparison to the Genesis myth—an invitation Stephenson enthusiastically accepts.

As in the original and its many retellings, what begins as Paradise does not remain so. Stephenson's tale proceeds with wit and energy, his extraordinarily phantasmagorical imagination set free. His ability to summon up Bruegel-ian imagery and make it tangible to readers is breathtaking.

As any reader of Stephenson's earlier works might expect, at its core are deep existential and metaphysical questions, and that core rests upon an even deeper question: the nature of identity. If that sounds daunting or dull, don't worry. This may be his most accessible novel in years, written with admirable clarity and attentiveness to its audience.

In explaining what, on a practical level, is the engine that turns this story, I kept returning to this passage:

> Sometimes tech advanced by gradually creeping up on things. Other times it did so by saltation: suddenly leaping forward. She [the character Zula] had heard an argument that those two couldn't really be teased apart, because in the case of an exponential creep-up, like Moore's Law, the bend in the curve could look like a jump if you took your eye off the ball at the wrong time.

If it walks like science fiction, if it talks like science fiction, if it flaps its wings like science fiction…

It's a fine novel, his best in years. And Mr. Stephenson needn't worry. I'll never disclose his secret: he's one of us.

✧

Atlas Alone
by Emma Newman
Ace Books
April 2019
ISBN: 978-0399587344

I'm not a gamer, which may be just as well, but I'm also more than a little fascinated by the allure of gaming. Perhaps I'm also jealous because it seems to me (an admitted outsider), good gaming, no matter the kind, resembles (or is) good storytelling.

Over the years, I've asked my writing students how much their interest in gaming has had an influence on their writing. At the start, they told me that gaming was gaming and writing was writing and never the twain, etc. Then, not long ago, one student told me, "If it wasn't for my interest in gaming, I don't think I'd be able to write at all."

The balance has shifted. Gaming "plays" an increasingly greater part of our reality. And Emma Newman's *Atlas Alone* addresses this shift with considerable, and thoughtful, insight.

Admittedly, my jumping in midstream to her "Planetfall" series affects my reading. The good news, for me at least, is that *Atlas Alone* can be approached as a standalone novel—quite well, in fact.

The protagonist and our narrator, Dee, is the kind of person we can implicitly trust even when she is skeptically weighing the evidence of what she is participating in. She is a person looking for answers, especially to the matter of who approved a nuclear strike that destroyed Earth (which you must admit is damn big question), but who doesn't accept easy solutions.

Newman places us not only in the midst of a space-faring society (lucky for us, since Earth is no more), but one in which gamers can inhabit a sort of virtual reality, called "mersives" (I love that word) which, at their best, are hard to distinguish from objective reality, whatever that is. That point becomes more than a metaphysical speculation when Dee discovers that a man she has killed in one of these mersives shows up dead in that objective "real" world. That this person may have played a significant role in the nuking of our home planet is no mere red herring.

What is most effective, at least for me, about this novel is how well its objective, external "mystery" plot reflects the subjective, internal struggle of Dee. In much good fiction, what makes the external conflicts and nemeses so powerful lies not in what they represent in some concrete sense, but in how they play to the internal weaknesses and strengths of our protagonists. The fault lies not in our stars, etc.—not even for a spacefaring society. "My face is a mask, in front of a mask," Dee tells us when she learns that her virtual murder has a real victim.

Years ago, Ursula K. Le Guin wrote that the depiction of VRs and mersives in fiction poses a challenge for writers because writing is a kind of VR in itself, and defining the borders between one sort of virtuality and another is no easy task.

One of the things I found most gratifying in this novel is how well Ms. Newman rises to the challenge without oversimplifying the situation. We are all gamers, in a sense, and often live as we game, and game as we live.

Even when you're not a gamer.

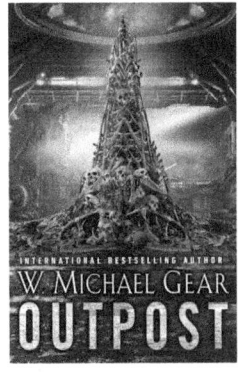

Outpost
by W. Michael Gear
DAW (mass market paperback)
February 2019
ISBN: 978-0756413385

The recent mass market paperback release of this novel permits me the apparently rare opportunity to hop on board a series of novels with the very first volume. Since becoming a book reviewer, I have two "TBR" piles—the first one is "To be read," and the second, "To be reviewed." The third book in Gear's series, *Outpost*, currently rests in the first pile, and after reading this one, will unreservedly jump to the second.

I haven't read anything by Gear in a while, and nothing written without his longtime collaborator, Kathleen O'Neal Gear, so I was intrigued to see how he did in a solo effort.

Authors of recent seem to be fascinated with gritty worlds, failed colonies, dens of iniquity populated by beings that are not so much amoral as selective in their choices of moralities. In such a milieu, the danger for an author is to well around in the muck without regard to those distant lights that may lie somewhere up ahead.

What makes Gear's novel a cut above the usual foray of this sort is that he doesn't forget we need that light to define the dark, and vice versa, and to do so with a grim but effective sense of humor.

Gear maneuvers a varied cast and a detailed world of murder, greed, and cunning with practiced facility. Our ostensible heroes navigate through deceptions and madness. Our villains are motivated by nearly-coherent aspirations, even when these evildoers are certifiably psychopathic.

It is one thing to create an engaging jungle to lead us through, with multiple protagonists and multiple conflicts, but quite another to do so by way of *story*, weaving these plotlines to add up to something bigger.

Gear never loses sight of his story, of his world, Donovan, the Port Authority colony, and all the characters willingly or unwillingly tied to it.

This novel may be first in a series, but it holds together in a self-sustaining way that old buzzards like me can truly appreciate.

✧

Finder
by Suzanne Palmer
DAW
April 2019
ISBN: 978-0756415105

Reading this novel reminded me of a favorite quote from a favorite author, Nelson Algren, and in a good way: "No book was ever worth the writing that wasn't done with the attitude that 'this ain't what you rung for—but it's what you're damned well getting.'"

Readers want one thing, and publishers want to give them that thing. It's how readers stay happy and how publishers make a living.

But writers want something too. They want to add to that simple formula. Readers should be happy, they know; publishers should make a living (that's how writers make a living, at least in theory). But to that "something" that makes the world go round, writers want to add one more word: "else." As an old mentor of mine put it, "A good story is something and something else."

This novel provides "else" to max without committing excess. Readers of space adventures will get just what they ordered: a hero, Fergus Ferguson (first off, any novel with a hero named Fergus Ferguson goes to the top of my first "TBR" stack without argument, period) a "finder"—he finds things, like starships, and brings them to whoever pays him, even if he has to steal them; they will get a far-off world like Cernee, a gas giant harvesting colony, full of deceit, treachery, grimy dens of grumbling miners, inadequate technology, all on a short fuse tied to the threat of civil war.

We even get a map (beautifully drawn by Francesca Baerald).

Will things go as Fergus planned? Of course not. Will there be chaos and confusion and impending doom? Of course. That's what we paid for.

And Palmer is willing to give us what we pay for. I've read enough of her short fiction to know that not only does she know her away around a sentence; she knows her way around a *plot* (ably proven in her Hugo-winning novelette, "The Secret Life of Bots"). This may be a first novel (and I had to keep reminding myself of that), but we can trust her to bring this wild ride to a satisfying conclusion (and she does, far as I'm concerned).

So, what is the "else"?

It consists, so I see, in a consciousness that every character, from Fergus Ferguson on down, is invested in a collection of conventions, of an existence in a story that is their reality. Not the only reality, but their reality. This consciousness comes with expectations—somewhere out there, in this great universe, there is an audience, waiting for these characters to do things.

To say more risks spoilers. I'll only add that Palmer brings to the space adventure an extra dimension and an awareness of the form that adds to any reader's delight in this tale.

And that "else" comes free of charge.

✧

L. Ron Hubbard Presents Writers of the Future Volume 35
Edited by David Farland
Galaxy Press (trade paperback)
April 2019
ISBN: 978-161986-6041

With any collection of short fiction, I feel back on home turf. Circumstance and preference return me to short stories, novelettes and novellas. That I remember the *first* volume in this series dates me—*carbon* dates me—but that's still good news.

Over the years, Writers of the Future, the contest and the anthology, has garnered a well-deserved reputation. Heck they've even chosen a couple of my students to appear in recent volumes (and another one who appeared as an Illustrators of the Future winner), so they must be doing something right.

If for no other reason than to gain a copy of Bob Eggleton's wondrous cover (who doesn't love robots these days? And this robot is irresistible), this volume is a keeper. Eggleton is a painter of the old school, and the old school houses depths the new school is still learning to pursue.

Always included with the winning stories are essays and other writings—one called "Tips for Embryonic Pros" by Mike Resnick, a name with which you may be familiar—that are all entertaining and informative, even if you have no aspirations toward a career as an ink-stained wretch of the fiction-writing or illustrating variety.

And two extra short stories: "Lost Robot," by Dean Wesley Smith, inspired by Eggleton's cover painting, and Rebecca Moesta's "Yellow Submarine,"

no doubt at least partly inspired by another submarine of a certain hue.

The winning authors here may be new names, but their work is of a quality that would make any editor of a year's best anthology proud. In many ways, these stories give me even greater hope for the future of fantastic literature than what I regularly find in those annual "best" compilations.

Perhaps this statement from David Farland's introduction helps explain why I feel this way: "I'm not looking for authors who recognize *problems*; I want authors who are bright enough to see *solutions*. I want authors who are not only capable of talking eloquently about problems, but who can ultimately, if they desire, have a positive effect upon the world."

That these stories are here, in this volume, is in itself a positive effect. Maybe not an earth-shaking effect, but a good start.

✿

Castle of Days
by Gene Wolfe
Tor (trade paperback)
1995 (check your libraries or used book venues)
ISBN: 0-312890427

My choice this time for an "older" book with which you might want to acquaint or reacquaint yourself is this omnibus of two even older and more obscure volumes, *Gene Wolfe's Book of Days* and *Castle of the Otter*, along with another little book's worth of extra material—essays, columns, speeches, introductions and more on writers, writing, and reading, all of it demonstrating Mr. Wolfe's extraordinary voice and even more remarkable mind, wit, charm, and humanity.

We lost Gene Wolfe this April 14, and I mean "we" most emphatically, even if you've never touched one of his novels or collections, much less read them. There's a good chance that any, even many, of the authors whose works you do embrace count him as an inspiration. A truly great writer shapes more than the work coming out under that author's byline. Mr. Wolfe shaped the field in ways we can only now begin to assess.

Impressive as his reputation as a novelist may be, his gifts as a writer of short fiction border on the miraculous. Several of the stories in *Book of Days* will leave you wondering at first, "Wait, what? Isn't there something missing here? And then, when you least expect it, you'll find that "missing" element in the place you least expect to find it, staring you square in the face.

Each story is tied to a particular commemorative or holiday or otherwise special occasion. My picks for ones not to miss are "How the Whip Came Back," "Forlesen," "The War Beneath the Tree," "How I Lost the Second World War and Helped Turn Back the German Invasion," and "Car Sinister." Pick your own favorites.

And don't pass over the introduction. Just…don't.

Castle of the Otter can be considered something of a guide or compendium for anyone who has braved the four-volume *Book of the New Sun*. Unlike similar volumes offered from more academic perspectives, these little articles and essays can be informative, enlightening, and hilarious, often simultaneously. They are not, however, essential to one's enjoyment of Mr. Wolfe's best-known series. They just add an extra angle from which to view an already multifaceted masterpiece.

Perhaps because I'm a teacher (allegedly), and a teacher of writing (also allegedly), not to mention an impassioned reader (without equivocation), I find myself most taken by the pieces in the collection's final section. In an introduction to one of the *Writers of the Future* anthologies (see above) he advises a young writer (who can be all young writers, no matter their age) on why his or her story was not chosen to be in the book: "You didn't really *do* much with your idea. You unconsciously assumed that because it was such a fine, strong, sleek, and even potentially dangerous idea, it could run the story by itself."

His Guest of Honor speech at Aussiecon and his Nebula Awards speech should be required reading, full stop.

And when I pulled this book from the shelf, in solace, upon learning of Wolfe's passing, this summation to his address at an academic conference especially struck me with profound resonance:

"Fantasy, it seems to me, is a much larger thing, and a much more influential thing, than you as a group are willing to concede—the only thing in the world that is bigger than the world, and a thing that touches upon virtually every area of thought, influencing and illuminating physics and biology as well as history and sociology, testing the borders of everything in the curriculum. It is not a small and safe area of academic specialization like the Medieval Lyric, and you owe it to the rest of us to give us a clearer indication of that. It is the living hand of the past—and of the wildest and strangest parts of the past at that—upon the reins of the future, and we are all passengers in its chariot, lurching and rattling faster and faster among the stars. We can hardly be blamed, I would say, for shutting our eyes now and then. But there is among us one small group that must never do so. I leave it to you to name that group.

"What is it that you call yourselves?"

None of these pieces are to be missed.
Only Mr. Wolfe himself is to be missed, alas.
Farewell.

Copyright © 2019 by Richard Chwedyk

Gregory Benford is a Nebula winner and a former Worldcon Guest of Honor. He is the author of more than thirty novels, six books of non-fiction, and has edited ten anthologies. He has been our regular science columnist from the get-go.

A SCIENTIST'S NOTEBOOK

by Gregory Benford

FROM HERE TO ETERNITY

Until lately, only science fiction writers thought about the truly distant future—beyond, say, ten thousand years. Now government is getting into our act.

In earlier columns I described the Pilot Project to bury nuclear wastes in a salt flat in southern New Mexico. I was a consultant for the Department of Energy on the far future prospects of such a nuclear tomb. The biggest aspect of the question is the final, big markers which will warn future generations, all three hundred of them, about what lurks over two thousand feet below their bootheels.

I asked a computer-whiz friend how he thought we should mark the site, and he had a quick answer: "Scatter CD-ROM disks around. People will pick them up, wonder what they say, read them—there you go."

After I stopped laughing, he said in a puzzled, offended tone, "Hey, it'll work. Digitizing is the wave of the future."

Actually, it's the wave of the present. This encounter made me think of our present fascination with speed and compression as the paradigms of communication.

I imagined my own works, stored in some library vault for future scholars (if there are any) who care about such ephemera of the Late TwenCen. A rumpled professor drags a cardboard box out of a dusty basement, and uncovers my collective works: hundreds of 3.5-inch floppy disks, ready to run on a DOS machine using Word Perfect 6.0.

Where does he get such a machine in 2094? Find such software? And if he carries the disks past some magnetic scanner while searching for these ancient artifacts, what happens to the carefully polished paragraphs, duly digitized on those magnetic grains?

Ever since the Sumerians, in communications technology we have gone for the flimsy, fast and futuristic. To them, giving up clay tablets for ephemeral paper—with its easily smudged marks, vulnerable to fire and water and recycling as a toilet aid—would have seemed loony.

Yet paper prevailed over clay, so that though Moses wrote the commandments on stone, we get them on paper. Paper and now our trusty computers make information cheaper to buy, store, and transmit.

Paper isn't for eternity. But even tombstones blur, and languages themselves are mortal. How to talk across the ages, to call out a warning? How to even get their attention? We have to learn to write largely, clearly, permanently. And largely may be most important of all.

Buildings of religious, emotional or memorial impact tend to fare well. Cemeteries, for example, hold their own against urban encroachment. One of the striking images as one approaches Manhattan is the broad burial grounds, which remain after centuries, despite being near some of the world's most valuable real estate. In Asia and Europe, temples and churches survive better than the vast stacks of stones erected to sing the praises of more worldly power.

Of course, often they were better built, but as well communities are hesitant about knocking them down. Often, new religions simply adopt the old sites. The Parthenon has survived first as a temple to Athena, then as a Byzantine church, later a mosque, and now it stands as a hallowed monument to the grandeur of the vanished Greeks who made it.

Sometimes conquest destroys even holy places, as when the Romans in AD 70 erased the Temple of Solomon. Perhaps some conqueror thousands of years from now would pass by the Pilot Project monoliths, berms and buried rooms (if, indeed, the rooms haven't been exposed, turned into a tourist attraction…). Seeing them as tributes to a society now vanquished, a general might order them all knocked over, buried, their messages defaced.

Something comparable happened many times over as the Europeans moved across the planet a few hundred years ago, rubbing out the religious and literary past of whole peoples. The Mayans wrote on both paper and clay, but nearly all of their work is gone.

✿

Our charge from the Department of Energy was to consider inadvertent *human* intrusion into the Pilot Project. An important adjective.

I personally do not think the human species will remain intact for even the next thousand years, much less the next ten thousand. Unless we soon halt progress in biotechnology, and don't recapture the ability to tinker with our own genes, I expect that variants on our Cro-Magnon theme will appear.

Other post-human species will have ways of thinking quite different from our own. Still, even if they have extensive physical modifications (one finger like a screwdriver? a stomach which can digest cellulose into sugars? a better designed back?) I expect they will share the deep programming we primates picked up far back there on the African veldt.

Among that ancient legacy is a set of preferences for particular landscape features. Universally, we share likings because they were adaptive. Such "landscape archetypes" may well be so strong because Darwinnowing for them covered many hundreds of thousands of years as small hunter-gatherer bands made their way across rugged terrain.

Developing consciousness got imprinted while the whole mind-body integration proceeded with dazzling speed. Tied every moment to weather and the wiles of other species, our ancestors sensed themselves as part of a living unity, the wonderful oneness of nature. Our enormous emotional ties to that view are a form of nostalgia, no less powerful for its distant origin.

Pre-humans who preferred the savannah prospered; those who liked swamps or highlands did less well. These "hard-wired" preferences have little survival value today, but in our cerebral cortex, the past shouts and the future can only whisper.

The biologist John Appleton believes three types of cues rewarded pre-humans who could pick them up: hazards, prospects and refuges. Hazard-rich images or smells reach right into the brain, arousing anxiety that can only be resolved by taking action: the flight-or-fight response.

Taking action relaxes us, dissipates energies, may even bring pleasure. People heavily into this go to scary movies or ride roller-coasters, and get a genuine, evolution-ordained kick out of it. Most of us simply prefer landscapes we recognize, that balance prospect (views) and offer refuge. It's also intriguing if the places invite exploration, i.e., aren't boring.

This kind of thinking goes further, into mythic consciousness. Presumably our evolutionary record is written into our basic internal stories, because once these tales were true. They sit down in the unconscious, ready to spring out and make surrounding events coherent.

Candidates for these are father, mother, authority, self, childhood, femininity and masculinity, gathering food, eternity, circles and squares (Plato's divine forms, somehow useful back on the savannah), devil/evil, god/goddess/good (note the similarity of these words even in as advanced a language as English), sleep, pain, death, communion. I would add number, space and time—but then, I'm a mathematical physicist. These may be the very substratum of human experience, how we construct meaning, whether it be in myth, language, religion, art—or artifacts.

Joseph Campbell became famous for popularizing the species-wide myth-themes: virgin birth, the great mother, the creation of All from a chaos of nothing, the fire-theft, the plentitude of Eden and the beauty of paradise, the return of chaos in flood or deluge, the land of the dead, the dying and resurrected hero/god, the great quest journey, the sacred versus the profane, redemption through suffering and sacrifice.

We extract these stories from our environment because we are hard-wired to "see" them popping out, patterns which spontaneously order a chaos. The argument here is that what seems to us to be meaning *in* the world is in fact our projection of meaning *into* the world. But all this came from the utility of such filters, which sort out a savannah-like plain into easy categories.

✿

There are four classes of knowledge to convey at the site: simple ("humans made this"), cautionary ("danger!"), basic ("this is old and technical") and detailed ("radioactives—leave alone"). The first is essential, because the others emerge only if the site is clearly artificial.

Seen from eye level the whole pattern should strike one in a single glance. (The huge stone circle at Avesbury, not far from Stonehenge, fails to do this. It is not widely known because its stones are small compared to the circle, so one can stand in it and not realize the whole design.) Further, the site will compete with a plethora of all present monuments and an undoubted plentitude to come: statuary from the Civil War and wars to come, stumps from old freeways, the carcasses of banks and stadiums.

Most monuments proudly announce that the great Kilroy was here, so pay respect. The Pilot Project is self-effacing: we were here, so stay away. How can we get that message through, when posterity will by habit expect the usual one?

Some basic designs emerged. To honor important people or events we erect beautiful, soaring monuments which mirror our aspirations—the pyramids, Cleopatra's Needle, the Washington Monument, even the monolith in *2001*. The waste site has to send the opposite message, straight into the collective unconscious, drawing the eye yet repelling the spirit. Perhaps we could learn from the Holocaust memorial in Berlin—zig-zags, its hard edges offering no comfort or nobility.

Consider the Black Hole: a black basalt slab, unbearably hot from accumulated sun's heat. Laced with thick, crazy-quilt expansion joints like cracks in parched plains, it forbids farming or drilling.

Or the Rubble Landscape: the local stone, dynamited and bulldozed into a crude square pile covering the whole Project. It rears above the landscape, hard to hike through, a place destroyed, not made.

With a bit more trouble, Forbidding Blocks: that same broken stone, cast into mixed concrete/stone blocks twenty-five feet on a side, dyed black, irregular, distorted. They define a square, with chaotic "streets" five feet wide between blocks.

But the streets lead nowhere and no one could live or farm there. The blocks get very hot, and the whole crudely ordered array massively denies use. Some granite blocks stand out, covered with inscriptions, warnings.

The Plain of Thorns sprouts eighty-feet high basalt spikes, erupting from the ground. They jut at all angles, which can cause cracking and faster erosion. To offset this, perhaps use a Fiend of Spikes, perfectly vertical, interspersed among the Thorns. If the Thorns can't fall and damage the Spikes, eventually only the Spikes remain, in a field of rubble.

The favorite of many panel members was fifty-foot-high Menacing Earthworks, all radiating outward from the bare site center. These are lightning-shaped, jagged, crowding in on the tiny traveler, cutting off views of the horizon, chaotic. At the open center is the existing Pilot Project concrete hot cell, going to ruin.

Beside it, a vast walk-on world map of all repositories of waste. Also, a map of New Mexico showing this site. The map is of granite and slightly domed, so sand blows off, rain can't pool. A room buried beneath holds details about what lies in the salt bed below, as do four smaller buried rooms beneath the largest earthworks. Inscribed "reading walls" of granite appear throughout the site.

The common ideas here are irregular geometries and anti-craftsmanship. This contradicts human archetypes of perfection in our imperfect world, which circles, squares, pyramids and spires echo. Using crooked forms when plainly the designers knew "better" suggests a deliberate shunning of the ideal, a lack of value here.

People value craft too, so these designs are roughly made, of materials such as rubble and great earthen mounds that discourage workmanship. Yet they are large, important—suggesting that there is no pride or honor here.

✧

This theme should echo through the inscriptions. Awe, apprehension, outright fear—independent of language or culture. Human figures and especially faces, made clearer by using bas relief. A face with hands, sculpted in abject horror, as in Edvard Munch's well-known painting, "The Scream." Or perhaps an eloquent warped face, nauseated.

With the wind blowing through the monoliths, coaxing mournful resonances from their curves, a dissonant and wailing aura should surround the place. Whatever cultures come and go, they should inherit a legend of a spooky, disagreeable place—whether or not anybody knows exactly why it is that way any longer.

Details such as that await the intruder who digs. Each design had a buried room at the center. There would lie plenty of duplicate technical detail, from lists of radioactive elements in the site to a periodic table of the elements itself, for correlation with the notation on the walls.

The buried vault might be plundered, though. Here the Sumerians left us a valuable lesson. Around the third millennium B.C. they began writing on little clay tablets, letting them pile up in such numbers into the Christian era. This left us an unbroken line of hard documents with dazzling detail about religion, beliefs, economics, customs.

Similarly, we should seed the waste site with small, ceramic plates, carrying compressed warnings and information. This could offset vandals who wreck the big, imposing monuments, or natural disasters. As erosion changes, buried plates get exposed: time-released information.

If the locals can read them. But our current languages are not going to make it across the sea of millennia.

Languages change unpredictably. They are so complex that tendencies to simplify one part (say, in grammar, when English shed the masculine/feminine/neutral articles and verb forms) will quite likely trigger complication in another (in English, more irregular verbs). Historical accidents bring great change. The main reason that English differs so profoundly from its closest German relative, Frisian (spoken in the northern Netherlands) is that the Angles were invaded by French-speaking Normans, and the Frisians were not.

No artificial language can avoid this either. Esperanto, which once had about fifty-thousand speakers, was effectively killed when the U.S. and U.S.S.R vetoed using it as the working language of the U.N. However, there may well be no "natural" language emerging in isolation, as the great past tongues did. Our world is cross-linked by media and travel, so language evolution will be different, sophisticated. How? We can't tell, because we have no general theory of how our amazing verbal arts evolve.

So there will never be a science which predicts future languages, and the problem of writing in the Pilot Project markers becomes immense. After a few centuries, only experts can read even early forms of their own language; we can struggle through the original Chaucer, but forget Beowulf. If there is no great cultural discontinuity, probably a few antiquarians will be able to decipher English or any other current tongue. But antiquarians seldom consort with vandals.

The finders of these many buried messages might not be able to read the languages inscribed, but they might recognize a symbol. Our evolutionary legacy gives us some predispositions to seeing gestalt wholes, so we naturally group objects if they are enclosed by a line. We're sensitive to edges, and pick figures out of ground readily. Breaking down information from large chunks into bits comes easily to us.

Symbols should play to this. We like narratives, and proved so 11,500 years ago when the big explosion of human sign artifacts began with Spanish Levantine rock art. These were pictographs showing hunters, weapons, clothing, prey, sexes.

Similar simplified line drawings could show stick figures burying the waste, warning others away. Others could present people digging or drilling into the site, ground water flushing through the hole, and then people getting sick, falling down, dying, then others mourning them.

The story should unfold in different ways, touching on the great mythic stories where possible. The Bayeux Tapestry of twelfth century France, the Japanese scroll of the Mongol invasion and the Lakota Sioux picture story The Battle of the Greasy Grass (to us, Custer's Last Stand)—all gather their power through successive images.

Storytelling is itself a powerful current linking eras. Why not use the oral tradition of the region to carry our warning? The *Iliad* and the *Odyssey* of Homer made their way to us through millennia as purely spoken stories, after all. Even after they were written down in the sixth century BC, the final text did not settle down for four centuries. A great saga commissioned to lend mythic status to the Pilot Project might do just as well.

But of course, nobody can reliably order up mythic works. Even if the work survived, told and retold, it will evolve, maybe lose its essential warning function.

And experience shows that once oral traditions get written down, they fade as great tales. Books entomb storytellers.

✧

So we are left with a picture story. While a picture may be worth a thousand words, there's always the problem of knowing *which* thousand words are evoked. In the last century, the swastika went from a positive religious symbol of India to the hated Nazi emblem. We want to call across the millennia, "poison—radioactive materials—don't intrude."

The panel considered our most common symbol for radioactive materials, the "uranium" of three ellipses centered on a dot. But this merely describes, doesn't warn. And some people think it's a solar system.

The "radiation" symbol is international: a "trefoil" of a black circle with three vanes sticking outward. But it's not an icon, it's just an arbitrary design, and nothing about it that relates to the idea of radioactives. Some see it as floral or like a Japanese *mon*, a clan crest. One team member quipped, "Ummm—why are they burying all those submarine propellers?"

The skull and crossbones go back to medieval alchemists, who saw in it Adam's skull and crossed bones promising resurrection. Only later did it come to mean poison, and though it's international, it has problems. In an experiment with three year olds shown the symbol, they immediately shouted, "Pirates!" Put it on a bottle and they shouted, "Poison!"

There is, though, a certain basic horror built into the image of disembodied heads. Steve Harris, a UCLA research physician, pointed out to me that skull motifs evoke a primal primate fear, like fear of snakes. Chimps are alarmed by isolated chimp heads or other body parts. This is understandable in evolutionary terms, since animals that snack on chimps tend to leave such "markers" in their wake. Humans seem to share this. (In fact, I'm convinced that Shelley's "Ozymandius" derives some of its power from the great, isolated head image.)

Even if no symbol will probably last ten thousand years, perhaps a cluster of them would help. The "Mr. Yuk," a recently adopted poison warning, is a happy face reversed into a scowl, tongue sticking out, eyes squinting. Put that together, say, with a slashed circle, and X'ed out other symbols.

But what to X out? A drilling tower is easily mistaken for a monument itself. A pictograph of a stick figure digging doesn't hit the mark, because in fact nobody could reach the salt bed that way.

A big problem is that exposure to radioactive materials usually takes many years to do damage. One possible way to convey this is to tell a story, starting with a child figure encountering the waste (represented, say, by the trefoil). Then comes a panel with the symbol now on the figure's chest and young, short trees nearby. Next panel, the trees have grown and the child is an adult—lying down, scowling, feeling bad. Simple, direct—See Dick Run from Radioactive Death.

These may help convey meaning after all language connection with us is lost. A few antiquarians may know how to decipher the inscriptions, but wildcatters won't necessarily call on a distant university for help.

Some panel members felt that while the monuments should be discordant, to carry the essential threatening message, they should have aesthetic appeal. "Beauty is conserved, ugliness discarded," one said. The pyramids may have survived in part because they are striking—they alone endure, of the ancient world's Seven Wonders—and the same might prove a useful strategy for the Pilot Project markers. "A gift from our century to the future," one suggested. Another proposed commissioning artists for a large-scale environmental sculpture.

Trouble lurks here, I feel. So did panel member Jon Lomberg who, with Carl Sagan, designed some of the interstellar diagrams on board the *Voyager* spacecraft. Even if *we* think our markers are ugly, he said, "How can you be sure it won't be mistaken for art?"

Art is ambiguous. As a universal language it tells little of the artist's intent. Cave paintings of animals don't tell us why they were made. Representational art fares better than symbolic, but the marker designs were quite symbolic, as is most large-scale sculpture. Recall how often you've heard audiences puzzle over the intent of abstract painters.

Further, said Lomberg, "Even if we could commission some monument great enough to become a wonder of the world whose fame would be carried down through three hundred generations, the very fact that the marker was so impressive could lead to the belief that the purpose of the marker was artistic rather than communicative." A big, powerful sculpture isolated amid desert wastes could be seen as like Mount Rushmore, a spot with a sole, uplifting message. A tourist attraction.

Art often has no function; it is an experience, period. Even art trying to be ugly, as with the fearful faces, can miss its supposed target. Picasso's *Guernica* wasn't really warning us about the Spanish Civil War. It spoke of a more general horror and anguish.

Worse, art draws a crowd. "We want people to stay away from this site, not travel from distant places to see it," Lomberg remarked. Suppose it draws tourists, come to see the ancient wonder. They need a hotel to stay, which needs water, so it drills…

And does anyone expect that our government can commission great art? It has enough trouble agreeing on mildly interesting but intensely controversial photographers and performance artists. Lomberg remarked that for every successful commission there are a hundred failures, from the Prince Albert Memorial in London ("an architectural laughingstock") to the Airman's Memorial in Toronto, locally known as "Gumby Goes to Heaven".

Lomberg pointed out that much of the art world is anti-scientific, anti-representational, and favors detached, nihilistic work. He doubted that our present art community would be well qualified to create or even select a design that was informed about the many scientific and technical intricacies needed—aspects like encroachment of sand dunes, material durability, future technologies.

Announcing a grand competition for ideas virtually promises that something will be chosen, adequate or not. "They're likely to end up picking a giant inflatable hamburger to mark the site," Lomberg said, grinning.

Suppose further that this Pilot Project does turn out to be the model of future sites. Will the French or Chinese use a marker system—symbols, art and all—like ours? Or will national rivalry rear its head? Two thousand years from now, it will be hard to tell that these variously designed places scattered around the world have some common story to tell.

Thus the present, irascible humanity of us all could well propagate into the far, far future. The Pilot Project will not be filled and need marking until around 2030, but thinking about it has begun precisely because we need to mull our way into that inconceivable perspective—a time when not merely we will have vanished, but probably our entire culture. This is the first radioactive sepulcher in the world, and may set the standard for all others, nuclear or otherwise.

This is merely our first conscious attempt to communicate across the abyss of deep time. There will be others, and unconscious aspects of how we present ourselves may be our longest-lasting legacy. The people of that time may know us mostly by our waste—and our planning.

And maybe we'll throw in a few CD-ROMs, just for the hell of it.

Copyright © 2019 by Gregory Benford

Robert J. Sawyer is the Hugo, Nebula, Campbell Memorial, Heinlein, Hal Clement, Skylark, Galaxy, and Seiun Award-winning author of twenty-three science-fiction novels, including the trilogy of Hominids, Humans, *and* Hybrids, *which won Canada's Aurora Award for the Best of the Decade, and the No. 1 Locus bestsellers* Calculating God, Triggers, *and* Quantum Night. *Rob holds two honorary doctorates and is a Member of the Order of Canada, the highest civilian honor bestowed by the Canadian government. Find him online at sf-writer.com.*

DECOHERENCE

by Robert J. Sawyer

WHAT SFWA WAS SUPPOSED TO BE

My friend Lawrence Schoen has just announced his resignation from the Board of Directors of the Science Fiction and Fantasy Writers of America. This is nothing remarkable. In the last twenty years, at least fifteen SFWA board members have resigned. Starting with the most recent and working backward, they are: Lawrence, Maggie Hogarth, Justina Ireland, Catherynne M. Valente, Elizabeth Moon, Sheila Finch, Paul Melko, Catherine Mintz, Diane Turnshek, Sam Lundwall, Cory Doctorow, Derryl Murphy, Allen Steele, Edo van Belkom, and myself.

In his resignation letter, Lawrence wrote obliquely of the SFWA crisis *de jour* that led him to step down (about which more later) and ends by affirming his support of the mission statement for SFWA drafted and adopted in 2018 by the nine men and women who compose the organization's board:

We are genre writers fostering a diverse professional community committed to inclusion, empowerment, and outreach.

To which I say, Whiskey Tango Foxtrot?

Now, before anyone gets upset, I one hundred percent support diverse voices (and have the track record going back over twenty years as an editor to prove it). But the above is parsecs removed from what SFWA's function was supposed to be. Here's the description Damon Knight, SFWA's founder, gave on February 28, 1965, to the seventy-two charter members:

The purposes of this organization shall be to inform science fiction writers on matters of professional interest, to promote their professional welfare, and to help them deal effectively with publishers, agents, editors and anthologists.

See the difference? It was specifically and only an organization devoted to *improving the economic conditions of working writers.* A professional organization is, by nature, exclusive not inclusive. I cannot be a member of the American Dental Association, and this is right and proper. When I ceased decades ago making my living principally from writing magazine articles, I dropped out of the Periodical Writers Association of Canada as I no longer had skin in the game and therefore didn't deserve a voice in setting that organization's policies anymore.

SFWA is the only professional organization that has damn near one hundred percent of the rank beginners—people love to join for the bragging rights just as soon as they qualify—and maybe fifty percent of the working pros. It also has a metric ton of voting members who haven't made a dime off SF&F writing in over a decade.

When Damon Knight drafted SFWA's bylaws, he outlined his vision, which made active membership available only to *currently* publishing professional writers, and he demanded periodic requalification:

Any person is eligible to become or remain an active member of the Science Fiction Writers of America who has done any of the following:

- Had a science fiction story published, for the first time, in an American magazine of general circulation, or in a collection or anthology published by an American trade publisher, **within the previous two calendar years;**

- Had a science fiction novel published, for the first time, by an American trade publisher **within the last five calendar years;**

- Written an original science fiction radio play or teleplay broadcast, for the first time, in America **during the previous calendar y ear;** or

- Written a screenplay for a science fiction motion picture released, for the first time, in America **during the last two calendar years.** Any person who has done any of the things listed in Section 1, **but not within the time restrictions set forth** in Section 1, is eligible to become or remain an **inactive** member of the Science Fiction Writers of America.

If only. The crisis that led Lawrence to resign was precipitated by an unprecedented loosening of SFWA's membership credentials, undertaken by fiat by the board, allowing huge numbers of self-published authors to join. Hustlers by nature, some of them immediately organized a successful block-nominating slate to get self-published authors onto the Nebula ballot, hijacking the Academy Award of the science-fiction and fantasy fields.

Meanwhile, as I write this, my *other* professional organization, the Writers Guild of America, has just gone to war. It, too, believes in diverse voices, but that is not its *raison d'être*. It exists solely to make its members more money and to guard them against perfidy by engagers and agents. Damon Knight, who died in 2002, is surely smiling at WGA from on high.

On April 12, 2019, the WGA told virtually all of its members that they had to fire their agents because of blatant conflicts of interest perpetrated by those representatives. On April 17, WGA went further, launching lawsuits against the four largest Hollywood agencies.

Now, yes, WGA is a union and SFWA isn't. But SFWA was never intended to be just a club. Rather than a virtue-signaling oh-so-2018 mission statement, what's wrong with the one Damon Knight came up with fifty-four years ago?

Of course, times change; of course, publishing is different now than it was then. But in the thirty-six years I've been a member of SFWA, I've seen—and, indeed, foreseen—all the changes that people are talking about now and more (I was writing in 1998 as SFWA president about "the post-publisher economy").

For instance, it used to be that giant print runs were required to get economical per-copy pricing; that's no longer true. It used to be there were many thousands of bookstore accounts for publishers to service in North America; sadly, that's no longer true. It used to be that audiobooks were only made in eviscerated abridgments and only of the biggest print sellers; wonderfully, that's no longer true. And it used to be that the only effective way to publish a book was on paper. That's no longer true, either (and I've got a bunch of my own older titles out in self-published e-book editions).

Whatever you might think of these changes, every single one of them came with enormous cost savings for publishers, but no portion of that was ever passed on to the authors. I remember at one convention this decade hearing the late David G. Hartwell brag that Tor, the publisher he worked for, had just had its best year ever, while one of his authors—with Hugos galore—confided to me that he didn't know how he was going to heat his house that coming winter.

Among the most egregious things that have happened during my career: literary agents going from ten-percent commissions to a fifteen percent; publishers locking in a 3:1 split of e-book royalties—three dollars for them to every one for the writer; and publishers using print-on-demand and the mere notional existence of an e-book edition to keep from reverting rights to authors for titles the publisher is no longer promoting or selling in any meaningful quantity. SFWA rolled over on every one of these.

But never let it be said that SFWA is without achievements. They recently—and I'm not making this up—produced an official SFWA secret decoder ring. I didn't pony up to get one; I doubt Damon Knight would have wanted such a thing, either.

Copyright © 2019 by Robert J. Sawyer

Gordon Van Gelder is the publisher and past editor of the Magazine of Fantasy & Science Fiction, *as well as an editor of anthologies and novels ranging from mysteries to science fiction and fantasy. We heard from Mr. Van Gelder last month but he touched on so many interesting topics in his interview we just had to share more of it with you this month.*

Joy Ward is the author of one novel. She has many stories in print, in magazines and in anthologies, and has also conducted interviews, both written and video, for other publications. This issue's interview is with Gordon van Gelder, long-time editor and now publisher of the Magazine of Fantasy & Science Fiction.

THE *GALAXY'S EDGE* INTERVIEW

Joy Ward Interviews Gordon Van Gelder

PART II

Gordon Van Gelder: I really love the spring stage of gardening where you plant something and just watch it come out and grow and start to flourish. I really love that. And I love watching that with writers, too. I could rattle off the names of about a dozen writers who I may not have published their first story, but I was the fertilizer where their seeds took off and grew in. And I find that really rewarding.

I've also been an administrator of one award for twenty-some-odd years now and administrator of another award for four or five years now. I didn't put a lot of weight onto awards before being involved with them. After being involved with them, I put even less into them. They're bowling trophies. Each award is different. Some of them mean more than others. But they're very nice to have on the shelf. They've never meant more than having a work connect between a reader and a writer. That's what it's all about. It's not about who has the most Hugos standing on their shelf or who won this year's blah blah award or whatever. David Hartwell used to tell people, usually to comfort people who'd lost an award, he had a line that went, "You know, the books they give awards to are the ones that don't sell very well."

Especially in literature, I don't want to say awards are the height of vanity but they're really saying this work is better than that work and it's nothing inherent in the work necessarily. It's much more likely to be what standards are we using to apply, we who present the award, are applying to the works to decide which one deserves the award more. Does it do this better? Does it do that better? Those criteria change over time. They're fickle. The voters are fickle. I have two Hugos and two World Fantasy Awards I think. Honestly, the one that means the most to me was the first World Fantasy nomination I got. Because it was the same sort of thing. I knew I'd been doing a good job. They gave it to the coach because they couldn't give it to all the players. I knew I had a top-flight list. I knew I was putting out books that really mattered, that really meant something at least to me. When the award nomination came in, I felt like this is an indication that someone else has noticed what I'm doing and that it's actually having an impact.

The only awards I really care about nowadays are the juried ones. The ones that are done by a vote, some sort of popular vote, are indicative of what's popular, but does that mean it's good?

Joy Ward: How do we get away from that?

GVG: Probably not. I don't know that we should anyway. If we did away with the Hugo, the Nebula, any other award that we decide is no good right now, the World Fantasy Award, this pleases some people if we did away with that. Someone else would cook up something.

One of the things that you see as an editor, the awards always look different to the editors than they do to the voters. We see a lot of the works on the ballot before they've been published. We'll see a story, and I say we meaning a bunch of editors. Many of us will swap notes with each other over lunches and things like that. A story will show up on a ballot or win an award that we turned down.

I was going to say I don't think I ever turned down a book at Saint Martin's that went on to become a national best seller. Actually, I take it back. There was one I can remember. Most editors went through that though. It happened to me far fewer than most people. When it happens, we stop and say, "What did I miss about that? Was there something there that I failed on?" With the awards, it's a similar thing but in a sense it's less important. It's commercially less important. I can't think offhand of a story I turned down that went on to win an award but I'm sure there are dozens if not hundreds of them.

One of my first years in the saddle, I was in one of these conversations at the Nebulas before the banquet and somebody said, "How many of the stories in the ballot did you turn down?" I started looking over the ballot saying, "This one, this one, this one." He got very upset I was going through this list. He says, "Well, you turned down mine." I didn't even remember.

JW: We're seeing changes in fantasy and science fiction now. You're probably seeing it more than most of us are seeing it because you're on the front lines. What changes are you uncomfortable with or not happy about?

GVG: I'm happy to see a broader spectrum of writers getting into the field. Happy to see the field growing and changing in different directions. To go back to my gardening metaphor, it's great to see shoots and branches going off in different directions and watching them flower and develop. I do not want the metaphorical garden of the SF&F field to be what I…, I do not want to be the sole gardener of it. I think that would look awful. That's partly why I stepped down from the magazine. I felt like I had grown too predictable. As an editor, it means you're stale. When I started the process of stepping down, I was flying to England for a convention and I had two books with me. One was one of Mike Ashley's histories in science fiction magazines. The other one was a business book by Clayton Christensen on disruption. Reading Ashley's perspective on the magazines, and especially how Campbell got very stale in the 60s and passed on Delany, for instance, and how the magazine grew predicable, reliable, but not very interesting— at least from some perspective. In the meantime, reading Christensen on how big businesses are constantly disrupted by smaller businesses that come up like transistor radios doing in the old Philco mantel top radios. Even though they were inferior products, they were cheaper and they were more accessible and that was the main thing. There was nothing that the bigger companies could have done to stop it.

I was looking at this and looking at the state of the field and realizing that growing stale at F&SF was not going to make me happy, was not going to make the readers happy. It might have made us more salable in certain markets because you know what you were getting every issue but that didn't mean that was what I wanted to put out.

I never figured I'm going to make a million bucks publishing a magazine. I want to put out a product that I want to read every time it comes out. If I'm not doing that, that's my first failure as a publisher. You're almost literally putting on different hats and saying as a publisher, I got to do this. As the editor, I have to do this. I was looking and it was like as a publisher, I got to get a new editor because this editor is not meeting the standards I guess I set for myself, but compartmentalize it and say that I'm not meeting the standards that I look for as a publisher. I was falling short of my own personal marks.

JW: One of the things that we're seeing is, I've noticed, that there is not just the lack of interest in the older writers but there's almost dismissal of them.

GVG: I was just talking about it this morning with someone. It's frustrating to me because I spotted this a few years ago, quite a few years ago, and tried to do things to stop it and I don't think any of my efforts succeeded. To me, it looks like there's a big rift between people who grew up without the internet and people who grew up with the internet. I think people who grew up with the internet, and I hate to generalize too much—but just to make a broad point, there's a very strong anti-authoritarian sentiment that came with the internet from the early days. I saw it happen over and over where there'd be some discussion or other in any field you can name and a person who had worked in that field for a long time and knew what they were talking about were shouted down by newbies who wanted things to be different and better and didn't have any experience in it but they had idealism.

This is the way the internet works and I understand that now. I didn't understand it so well at the time. Growing up with this environment and with the internet as an available reference I think led a lot of people to develop an attitude that if it's someone from that era where the rules were different, they're not going to be of interest to me because the rules were so different. One example is a lot of people talk about entitlement. They weren't aware of their entitlement. I try to read their fiction and all I see is them exercising their entitlement. To me as a reader, it just doesn't speak to me. We're dealing with fiction here. We're not dealing with solid facts so it's perfectly reasonable for readers to react that way.

Like I said, I got frustrated because I could see it happening and couldn't figure out how to bridge that. I tried setting up, I'd have social dinners or lunches at conventions where I'd deliberately try to get what I consider some of the old guard writers and some of the young writers and they wouldn't interact really. It was just almost like they were speaking different languages.

JW: What's bad about that lack of understanding of the history of the field?

GVG: There's so many different things. One is that it's reinventing the wheel, which isn't the worst thing in the world. Two, is that it does mean you're losing a lot of valuable stuff. Who's it valuable to is arguable. Three, is that it does create an environment that tends to exclude the older guard, so to speak, in that they no longer feel like they're welcome in the playground of the younger generation. They're all friends, to me. I'd like them all to get along. It's frustrating when it doesn't happen. I don't expect all my friends to be friends with each other but I would like to see everyone playing comfortably side by side if not playing with each other.

It does hurt in a serious sense when you've seen these things develop. Like I say, it pains me not to have been able to do more to change it. But so it goes. On the flip side, the good thing is that the work is still there.

JW: What is it that we lose?

GVG: A sense of where the field has been. It's hard to have any idea where you're going if you don't know where you've been. That whole repopulation anthology, I did it because I came across the Garrett story and another story that was a one-off. I don't think I ever published another story. His name was Rex Jatko. The Jatko story I really like, it's very much of its time but I found it a really good read.

All these Cold War anxiety stories are not completely gone. In fact, they had a resurgence from what I've seen but I got attracted to them because they were essentially a dead shoot on the plant, to use the metaphor again. They were forgotten but you go back and look at them and they're fascinating in retrospect. There were so many gender issues being played out in them. There were two stories that were about gender reallocation, one by Marion Bradley and the other by Bob Shaw. These were stories in early and mid 60s. I think if more people read them now, I think those stories stand up in very interesting ways and say interesting things about then, now, and can still blow people's minds just as well as a story in the latest magazine of your choice. I think those are all valuable things to have.

JW: What kinds of stories are we not seeing that you wish you would be seeing?

GVG: I started reading after the New Wave had crested but was very influenced as a reader by the new wave. *Dangerous Visions* made a big impact on me and Harlan's work just to take one example. For me, if stuff isn't challenging on some level, I don't want to say it's not worth doing, but I really find the challenge appealing. I love a story that I don't agree with but it hits me on an emotional level and it makes me reconsider my own biases and perceptions. That's one of the things I have loved science fiction for because for so many years it was one of the few areas where you could tell these stories without getting in trouble.

One of these classic cases where…. Oh, Ted Sturgeon's "Affair with a Green Monkey" where he could not have sold it at the time as a mainstream story but by turning it into a science fiction story, there was an audience for it. You had to look past the screen that he put up to see what he was really talking about but the emotional impact was still there. I'm not seeing as much of that in the field as I'd like. That's one thing that I think is disappearing.

I'm seeing signs that it's going to come back, little shoots here and there. I find also at the moment that it's harder to publish and sell anything with an erotic element in the field. But I'm seeing that, especially in the magazines, shying away from sexual subjects.

I respect the attitudes of mothers and fathers anywhere who don't want their kids reading stuff. But I do think since then, and we've gotten into this period where there's so much fear of giving offense to anyone, that I think writers are shying away from edgier subjects which often includes stuff with an erotic element or stuff with a violent element. I understand the need for putting in trigger warnings. But I do feel like, and I have heard this from writers too, that they're shying away from topics that they think that they'd have a tough time selling and they'd have a tough time dealing with any fallout afterward. To me, that's like losing one branch in the field that I've always loved. I don't want stories that are only going to comfort me. I love comforting stories but I also want stories that are going to challenge me. If we're losing the challenging side, I feel like it's not a plant that's growing in a healthy manner.

You start to create a lopsided plant. If it gets too lopsided, it's going to fall over. I don't see the science fiction field in any danger of dying. It's always going to be changing so I'm not sounding a panic over it, but part of the reason I did that dystopia anthology was because I had an edgy idea for a story. I emailed a writer about it and said, "This seems like it's right up your alley." The writer got back to me and said, "I like the idea but I could never touch it. I'm too afraid that someone would actually take the idea and enact it and I don't want to go there."

I started thinking back again of *Dangerous Visions*. I don't want to be shying away from the stuff that's got a provocative, dangerous element. I think we need more of that. It's one of the things that led me to do the book.

I think science fiction is one of the genres that's set up best to be able to handle stuff like that. I've edited a good number of mysteries and I love that genre but a mystery almost always has a murder or a crime or something at the center of it and whoever did it either gets away with it or doesn't. The science fiction field has so much more potential and so much more freedom to it. To give up that freedom is like cutting off a whole section of the field and saying, "You guys can't play there."

For me, personally, I have a natural rebellion toward authority and so if somebody says, "You can't go play over there." My initial reaction is like, "Okay, if that's what you say, fine," and then to figure out a way to go and play over there. Damon Knight told me the best way to get a kid to read a book is to tell them they're not allowed to read it and then put it somewhere where they have to work to get their hands on it.

JW: What made you decide to buy the *Magazine of Fantasy & Science Fiction*?

GVG: That's pretty simple. For three years, maybe four years, I was editing for Saint Martin's Press and editing F&SF. Busy, yes, but manageable and I didn't want to give up either one. I liked being able to do books. I liked being able to do the magazine. Of the two though, I liked the magazine more. There was far less bureaucracy. One of the big things I could see coming, frankly, was that book publishing was about to institute a system, BookScan, where essentially every publisher has access to the same sales figures now. I really didn't like what I thought that was going to do. I'm afraid I was right about that. I didn't want to have to face that. The Fermans were looking to sell the magazine. You don't get that many opportunities in life to buy F&SF. So when the opportunity was presented to me, I did not think I should pass it up.

When I first bought the magazine in October of 2000, obviously I'd never published a magazine before. The Fermans were great but they were not overseeing things on a day-to-day basis. For the first time in my life I started having panic attacks.

I can remember sitting there looking at my computer screen, watching the little time clock numbers change every minute feeling unable to move because I didn't know what to do and got over it when I realized what's the worst thing that happens? I screw up totally. I run the magazine into the ground. It goes out of business. I destroy one of the field's mainstays, one of the great flowering bushes in this garden. That's it. And I probably have to work at McDonald's for the rest of my life and that's it. Nobody's life ends.

After I recognized that, I found publishing the magazine fairly rewarding. It's a steady job. I am my own boss, which has its good sides as well as its bad side. Those are the main things it does for me. It is nice to be able to look at the magazines and say, "Yes, I've done these." I asked a book publisher once what his proudest achievements were and he cited his biggest selling examples. "We did this one and sold this many copies." I didn't get into it for that reason. In fact, I don't think circulation has gone up since I took over more than one or two months in a row. It's been a pretty steady decline but I kept it going during one of the worst periods in magazine publishing.

So many of my friends in the field have died. It's up to the living to decide the legacy of the dead. If I die tomorrow and everybody in the field says, "Thank God that bastard's gone," I don't mind as long as some people still say, "He was a bastard. I couldn't stand him but he put out a good magazine."

Copyright © 2019 by Joy Ward

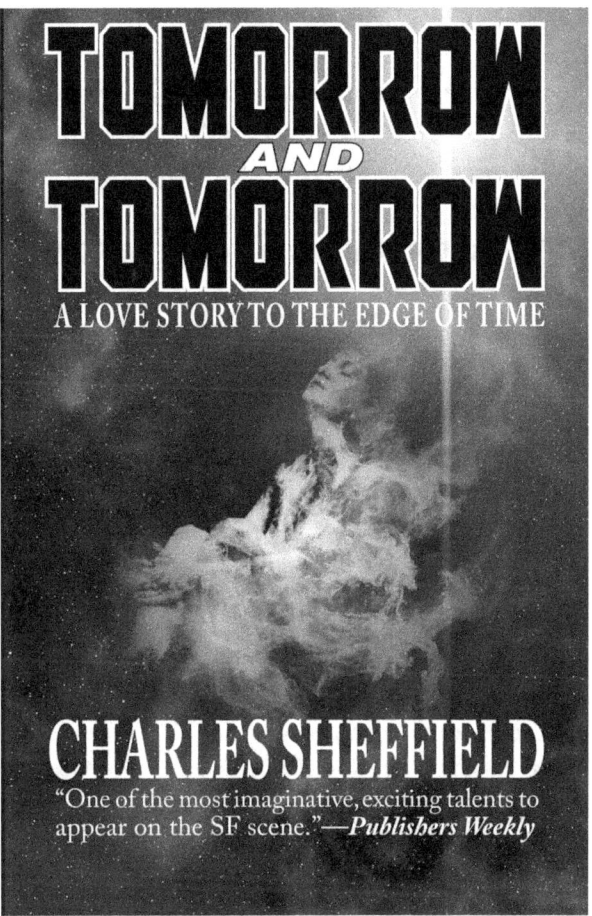

Charles was a Hugo and Nebula winner, as well as a Campbell Memorial Winner. He served as President of the Science Fiction Writers of America, and also put in time as Chief Scientist of the Earth Satellite Corporation.

TOMORROW AND TOMORROW

Charles Sheffield

23

"There's Trouble in the Wind, My Boys, There's Trouble in the Wind. Oh, It's Please to Walk in Front, Sir, When There's Trouble in the Wind!"

At last.

After hundreds of millions of years and a hundred billion tries, Drake and his team had something to work with.

Of course, the something made little sense. The group in the War Room was puzzling over eight copies of data records, all identical, that had been delivered through the caesura.

"It's perfectly consistent with the statistics," Cass Leemu pointed out. "There was a ten percent chance that we'd get exactly eight copies, but anywhere between six and fourteen is high probability. I'm afraid there's no sign of the ship that was orbiting Lukoris."

She did not need to say "the ship with Drake on board."

"The statistics may make sense." Tom Lambert was studying one of the displays. "But nothing else does. Look at this."

The record of the final minutes on Lukoris existed in two forms. One of them showed events as seen by the sensors scattered around the surface. The other was Drake's own perception as received through the mander embodiment.

According to the surface sensors, Lukoris was much the same as it had been in the previous year; or, for that matter, the past half million. Swamps, broken by clumps of scrubby plant life, stretched away flat and dull to the horizon, where mile-high scarps of rock loomed skyward. The sky above them was the unchanging sulfurous yellow of late summer.

But Drake's view....

"What is he *seeing?*" Milton said. "And what does he think he's *doing?*"

They were looking through the mander's eyes as it walked forward across a sward of healthy turf and spring flowers. Milton, who had never seen old Earth, was justifiably puzzled. But Drake, seated in the headquarters' War Room, knew where he was. He was having trouble answering Milton, because he also guessed what was coming next.

The mander embodiment had become human in form. It was walking barefoot on the Sussex Downs, one of Drake and Ana's favorite vacation spots. She had been standing by a hedgerow, admiring a thrush's nest. Now she turned at Drake's approach and smiled a greeting. Spontaneously, without a word, they embraced.

In that first ecstatic moment, Drake in the War Room forced himself to look across to the other display. The sensors showed the mander, unchanged in form, standing motionless before a foot-high bulbous plant with spiky silver leaves.

"Freeze!" Drake said urgently. And then, to the others, "You know the earlier records. Is that"—he indicated the little plant—"new to Lukoris, or to this region? I don't think I've ever seen it before."

"It appears to be new." The others, using the power of their composites, could answer almost at once and simultaneously.

"But what is the significance?" Par Leon asked. "It is nothing but a plant."

"I'm not sure. Look for more of them."

That analysis was also finished almost before the command was given. All of the Galaxy's computing power was available when Drake asked for it. With such resources the problem was trivial. Using the spiky-leaved plant as a template for a matching algorithm, the global database of Lukoris was scanned and analyzed, every day of every year since observations first began.

"They're all over the place," Cass said. "This size or smaller. But ten years ago there were none. They've all sprung up in the past few years. Do you think they are real?"

"I'm sure they are. It's the *other* scene that's a false reality." Drake hated to say that. He wanted what he had seen to be true, and he found it almost impossible to keep his eyes away from the image of Ana.

"I think the plant is able to create an illusion in the mind of an intelligent being."

"Why intelligent?" Par Leon asked.

"Imagination needs intelligence." Drake gestured again to the first display. The mander stood motionless before the plant, while other animals wandering the swampy surface apparently took no notice. "There must be a certain minimum awareness, a level of intelligence before a mind can be made to imagine something other than what it receives through its senses."

"Like hypnotism," Melissa said. "The subject sees what she is told is there."

Mel Bradley scowled. "Hypnotized by a *plant?*"

"Do you have a better explanation?" Drake zoomed in on the mander. "Look at me. Cass can probably suggest a thousand ways in which an electromagnetic signal, or a scent containing the right chemicals, could affect the functioning of the brain. Remember, the plant doesn't change Lukoris. It just persuades the subject to see an alternate reality."

"But *what* reality?" Milton sounded confused. "It surely can't impose its own reality on someone."

"No." It did not surprise Drake that he knew what was happening when the others did not. His understanding was exactly proportional to his pain.

"Not *its* reality," he went on. "*Your* reality. It allows you to see, and to imagine that you live in, the reality that you desire beyond any other."

He, more than anyone else in the universe, understood the seductive power of that vision. He would give anything to be that other Drake, kissing Ana in the quiet countryside. It was the siren call of the Shiva: *Stay with me, and receive your heart's desire.*

Drake tried to explain that to the others, but after a while he realized it was not working. They could not know the mind of the other Drake, and it was impossible for any of them to feel what he was feeling. They were merely asking more questions.

"How does it reach the planet in the first place?" Tom Lambert said.

"I don't know."

"Is that *it*, the whole thing?" said Mel Bradley. "You think the Shiva are nothing but little plants?"

"I don't know."

"And the planetary defense systems failing...."

"And their spreading between the stars, between the *galaxies....* How?"

"And moving more slowly where we *didn't* have colonies...."

"And the failure of the lost colonies to send any sort of message...."

"I don't know." Drake was longing to terminate this meeting, so that he could enjoy the vicarious pleasure of Ana embracing his other self—even if it was nothing but illusion, he wanted it.

"You're missing the point," he continued. "This doesn't prove that some spiky little silver plant is all there is to the Shiva. It doesn't tell us how the Shiva spread, or why. It doesn't say what happens to a world after they reach it. It tells us little about the Shiva themselves. But we still have a reason to celebrate. *We've had a breakthrough.* For the first time ever, we've been present on a planet when the Shiva took over. We've sent back information about what happened.

"We don't have an end. We barely have a beginning. Here's what we must do next. We must install organic copies of me on every planet along the front of the Shiva's spread."

Drake paused, realizing what he had just said. Those copies were going to disappear, every one of them. *He* was going to vanish, a million times over. But now there was a hope that some of the embodiments would not die. He might be transported to a personal Paradise—a dream life, but a perfect dream from which the copies might never waken.

"We also," he went on at last, "have to put arrays of independent sensors on every planet. We must install caesuras on or near each planet, ready to operate whenever a reality shift signals that the Shiva have appeared. We must install on a ship near the caesura the equipment to produce millions of identical copies of all data, with the equipment to feed those copies into the caesura at the first sign of trouble."

Equipment. That was one way to describe it. But the equipment would include copies of himself—and these copies, unlike the ones down on the planetary surface, were surely doomed.

"And when we've done all that"—Drake's gaze, beyond his control, was drawn back to the display; it showed his other self, still holding Ana in his arms—"when we've done all that, and we have recorded the information from a thousand or a million or ten million worlds, maybe we'll get what we need. Maybe we'll find a way to fight back."

Breakthrough.

Drake had called it that, but it was the wrong word. No torrent of information flooded in from other worlds on the path of the Shiva expansion. No sudden insight explained everything.

What came was a slow dribble of isolated bits and pieces, an image here, a paradox there; confirmation of a hypothesis, a measurement of sizes and rates and masses, calculations of galactic geometry, the cross-correlation of events from a million worlds as they were absorbed into the Silent Zone.

Drake could not perform that analysis. It was far beyond him, calling for the combined analytical power of a trillion composites. All he could do was sit at headquarters and record the disappearance of each copy of his own self. There was always the possibility that a caesura would deliver a copy of Drake back to headquarters, along with the packets of acquired data; but it never happened.

Data collection and analysis continued; the arc of the Silent Zone spread its darkness farther across the face of the Galaxy; nothing seemed to change. But one day, a day that Drake saw as no different from any of the billion that preceded it, his assistants appeared un-summoned in the villa headquarters.

"Drake, we must talk." Milton had been appointed as the spokesman. The Servitor's physical form was the usual one, but now Drake detected a weariness and a discomfort, a gray translucency to the presence. The tangle of wires on the whisk broom were in constant agitation.

"I'm listening." Drake looked them over, Cass and Milton and Tom, Melissa and Par Leon and Mel Bradley. They all displayed that same uneasiness. "Bad news?"

"Yes," Milton said. "But not what you might be thinking. Every composite in the Galaxy has been in full superluminal connection for the past few days. We finally have an integrated picture of Shiva activities. It is an inference derived from many trillions of pieces of data, but we are convinced that it is a correct one."

"That doesn't sound like bad news. Quite the opposite."

"In many ways you are right; but it introduces… complications. First, let me summarize for you our understanding of the nature and actions of the Shiva. Much of this you may already know or have guessed. Some of your original conclusions were, if I may suggest it, wrong."

Milton paused, and Drake laughed.

"Don't worry about hurting my feelings. I've been wrong more often than you can imagine."

"But right more often than any other being in the Galaxy. Let me continue. The Shiva are living organisms, unlike any encountered before. They have four distinct phases to their life cycle. Two of those phases are capable of two different forms of reproduction. The first phase, which we will call the adult Shiva, is immobile and enormous—one full-grown specimen can measure two hundred kilometers across its base, and stretches high enough for its top to extend beyond the atmosphere of most planets. The adult is invulnerable to normal predator attack, because of its size, and also because it is protected by a second form. We will call this second form the *warrior*, although it acts aggressively only in defense of the adult. The warriors are one form of offspring of the adults.

"It is important to note that the adult, in spite of its size, can survive only in certain environments. Atmospheric oxygen and water vapor must lie within tight limits. Most worlds of the Galaxy do not come close to satisfying that requirement. We will come back question later.

"And one other point, perhaps an obvious one: an adult, because of its size, grows, lives, and dies on a single planet. No Shiva adult can ever travel to another world.

"But when they achieve full size, the adults can send another form of offspring out into space. There is a mystery here—the propagation mechanism is not something as simple as dehiscence, an explosive projection of seeds. However, let us use the analogy and call this phase a Shiva *seed*. The seed is tiny and light, nothing like the warrior, and once in space its movement is assisted by two factors: radiation pressure, pushing it away from the planet's primary, and the galactic magnetic field. Originally, the seeds may have propagated only to other parts of the home world; but billions of years ago they became an interplanetary and an interstellar traveler; eventually, an intergalactic one. We do not know where the Shiva originated, but it was not in our galaxy.

"The Shiva seed is enormously tough and durable, able to survive extreme environments and a multimillion-year passage through space. There is another mystery which still waits an explanation: the seed motion is not mere random drift. Movement is preferentially toward other stellar systems. In the final stages, that implies movement *against* radiation pressure.

"Most Shiva seeds must end their lives on barren planets, or burn up as they fall into stars; but there are enormous numbers of them. Some small fraction will meet a world and drift down through the atmosphere to a surface on which they can transform to the next stage of the life cycle.

"This stage we will call the *worker,* though analogy with Earth's social insects must not be carried too far. It would be just as good to call it a *changer* or a *preparer.* The worker, like the adult, is a sessile form incapable of movement. It is the plantlike entity that we saw long ago on Lukoris. Like the seeds, it is tough and robust. Workers thrive on worlds that would quickly kill an adult. They also propagate like plants, and they do so very fast.

"We have debated whether the worker or the adult should be considered the mature form of the Shiva, and decided that the question is meaningless. As in cryptogams, the ferns of Earth, two forms are alternating mature phases of a complex life cycle.

"Much more important, from the human point of view, is the worker's other function. It is able, through a combination of generated fields and chemical diffusion, to affect the behavior of native animals on a planet. You have argued that only intelligent beings could be affected by the Shiva, since they alone are able to consider an alternate reality. It was then natural to conclude that the worker form of the Shiva must be intelligent.

"We now believe that those deductions are false. In our own galaxy, before the spread of humans, life developed on a billion worlds. Only five of that great multitude of forms achieved self-awareness. A life-form that *relied* on the presence of intelligence on every planet that it reached would surely fail. More-

over, the worker is not itself intelligent, and thus can have no concept of intelligence. Unable to move, it must somehow achieve its objective while remaining in one place. The objective is simple: the planet must be changed from its initial state to one in which an adult Shiva can thrive. Then, and only then, will the worker advance to its second form of breeding and produce not more workers, but *new adults.* Those will in turn grow, mature, and allow the Shiva to reach new worlds.

"The workers employ the native life-forms on a world as the unwitting agents for planetary change. Their breeding, their numbers, and their patterns of behavior alter under the workers' control, to make the world suitable for adult Shiva habitation. Some native species will become extinct. Some will thrive, some will evolve to other forms. When the planet is ready, the adults begin their growth. The workers disappear. The life cycle begins again."

Milton fell silent. The wiry head began to writhe more furiously than ever.

"That's wonderful." Drake wondered what was not being said. "Once you understand something, it's much easier to stop it. The Shiva are vulnerable. We can destroy their seeds as they reach a planet, or kill the workers as soon as the plants appear. If I hear you right, humans don't suffer their changed perception of reality until the workers begin to operate."

"That is correct."

"So let's get going. There's plenty of work to do."

Milton sat silent, and at last Tom Lambert said, "A ton of work. But there are a few more things that we have to talk about. First, we've been thinking all the time of the Shiva as *evil*—as deliberate, calculating destroyers. That just isn't true. There was no malice involved, no plan to achieve destruction. Changing human perceptions, even making the colonies use the defenses that we installed against us, was an accident. We believe that the adult form of the Shiva possesses some kind of intelligence and self-awareness, but the workers do not. They were simply doing what all life-forms do, trying to ensure their own survival and propagation. In the case of humans, Shiva propagation required the acceptance of a false reality that justified human actions."

"And, sooner or later, led to the human's death."

"True. But now that we know what's going on, we may find many ways to stop the Shiva. Peaceful ways. There will be no more wholesale destruction of our planets or theirs; no more firebreaks, devastating whole arcs of the Galaxy; no more use of the caesuras, casting ships and intelligences and worlds beyond the bounds of space and time. And there will be no need for certain other things."

And Drake, at last, saw what they were unwilling to tell him directly. "You mean, there will be no more need for *me.*"

"Yes. The service that you have performed for us is too great ever to be measured. We are eternally in your debt. When we thought that the Shiva were malicious and deliberately trying to destroy us, your presence and courage and mode of thinking were absolutely essential. Now, they are not. Of course, we would not suggest that you, or we, do anything at once. Many, many unknowns and potential difficulties remain. We hope that you will assist in their solution. But ultimately we see you as a hindrance to *peaceful* answers. You are too steeped in war, too much in favor of the crudities of combat." Tom Lambert ducked his head. "I'm sorry, Drake."

"That's all right." There was no point in explaining that he was not aggressive, that his instincts had always been toward peace. They would not understand. He had operated as commander in chief for many hundreds of millions of years. So far as the composites were concerned, a militant Drake had been summoned from electronic darkness to fight a battle, to rid the universe of the threat of the Shiva. And when that threat passed, Drake would be useless. Worse than useless—he would be an embarrassment, a source of violence, a reminder of the ancient and cruel ancestry of humanity.

"You don't need me now that the problem is solved and the war is ending, right? I understand, Tom. It's all happened before."

"It has?" Tom looked and sounded bewildered. "You have encountered a similar situation in the past?"

"Not me personally. But it's as old as human history. Remember the Pied Piper, and Tommy Atkins?"

They did not, and he didn't expect them to. There were blank looks on every face. Drake could imagine countless invisible composites, delving into fourth-

and fifth-level storage, trying to make sense of his reference. Maybe they would find it; or maybe he alone held that particle of early human folklore. Either way, it didn't matter. His own next step was clear.

"You say that you're in my debt. I agree. So do something for me. Return me to electronic storage and let me remain dormant. Keep looking for new ways in which Ana might be restored to me. And wake me again only when you make progress."

Drake anticipated no problem with his request. But again, he saw hesitation and embarrassment in the other's eyes.

"What's wrong this time? Come on, Tom, spit it out."

"There is one more difficulty. You have always refused to become part of any composite."

"I still do. You know why. I didn't survive for eight billion years, just to lose focus now. I can't afford to become part of a shared consciousness. I want to stay me. Think what shape you would be in if I'd chosen differently."

"We appreciate that. We know that we cannot change your obsession. But what you ask is impossible. You already exist in multiple forms. As the spread of the Shiva is halted, many of those forms will survive. Someday, they will return."

And of course, Tom was right. Drake had become accustomed to the idea that billion after billion copies of his personality had been created and sent as S-wave signals across the Galaxy. He knew that they had been embodied in native forms on a hundred million planets, and set to watch and listen on a billion ships along the Shiva frontier. Those innumerable versions of himself would be changing, absorbing new experiences, becoming quite different from the Drake Merlin who remained at headquarters.

He had learned to live with the idea that he was dying, daily, in endless different ways. What he had never considered was the time when an understanding of the Shiva was reached, and all the scattered copies were no longer doomed. As ways were discovered to deal with the Shiva, they would survive in increasing numbers.

"I get it. You can't handle one of me. How do you hope to deal with a billion?"

"We fear that we cannot. We want to ask your help—again. Many of the returning minds will be changed, many will be seriously damaged. You are the only being in the whole universe who can understand and help them. We will promise you unlimited resources from us, anything that we have, in performing your task. We ask only that you should avoid contact with our composites."

"You mean you want to lock me up, me and every version of me?"

"No. There would be no restriction of your freedom. You would travel as you choose, and act as you choose. The only condition that we ask is that there be a separation between us and you. You may find this ridiculous, but we fear your intensity—what is, quite literally, your single-mindedness in our universe of composites. If you agree, we promise in return continued research on the subject that most interests you: the return of Ana."

"Has there been progress?" Drake had hardly thought to ask that question in a hundred million years.

"Nothing of immediate value. It should be possible to re-create Ana at the eschaton, when the universe approaches final convergence. But that is far off. We promise to continue working on other possibilities, if you in turn will help us. What is your answer? Will you deal with the copies of Drake Merlin, returning in their broken billions from the Shiva frontier?"

What option was there? How could a man turn his back on his own self—especially on a damaged and troubled self?

Give me your tired, your poor, your huddled masses yearning to breathe free, the wretched refuse of your teeming shore, send these, the homeless, tempest-tos't to me.

He spoke more to himself than to the others, and their baffled faces showed that again they didn't understand. Drake turned away. The composites were digging into the historical data banks, seeking a reference, wondering what he had just said.

He knew, even if they did not. He had agreed to do what they asked. The war with the Shiva might soon be ending, but his own most difficult task lay ahead.

24

E Pluribus Unum

Trillions of bits, billions of pages; now it was all unnecessary. Drake surveyed the mass of storage that represented his private journal and reflected on a curious irony: The prospect of victory rendered his work irrelevant, as danger and defeat could not.

He had no cause to complain. He had known what was coming, the moment he said yes to Tom and the others in the War Room.

For all the years since first resurrection, he had kept strictly to himself. Originally it was because no one else understood his need or shared his quest for Ana. His solitude had seemed even more crucial when the Shiva appeared on the scene. His was the only consciousness in the Galaxy left over from humanity's early days, and he dared not become close to any composite—certainly, he could not consider a merger with the webs. He had even refused to share the contents of their data banks.

His obstinacy had caused trouble, a billion times over, but he had felt that he had no choice. Inefficient as it was to rely on others for most of his information, he must do it that way. He had to remain aloof. Someone must make the hard decisions. Someone had to be willing to sacrifice humans and composites and whole planets. No one but Drake would do that, and he dared not risk any dilution of his own will.

Drake glanced again over the long record of events. The composites must think that he had no heart and no soul; certainly, they believed he had no imagination. They could not see how else he was able to send out countless versions of *himself*, to face an uncertain end on the dark borders of the Galaxy.

They knew nothing of the effort that it had taken. And why should they? He had not said anything to them. He had done it, and that was the important thing.

When the Shiva were ascendant, it had been a one way process. Copies of him had gone out and never come back. But no longer. One week ago, the first copy had returned. *He* had returned.

The composites urged him to study that copy well before he attempted contact with it. They were worried because his returning self had been through what they felt was a "traumatic experience." There were also, they warned, a hundred billion more like it on the way.

A traumatic experience? You might say so.

Drake had checked the background, and this case was probably typical. Downloaded and shipped out eight hundred thousand years ago, as a superluminal signal to a ship in permanent orbit about a planet of a faint star on the other side of the Galaxy. Taken down to the surface of that world and embodied in an enhanced alien life-form of increased life expectancy. Left there to survive, endure, observe, and await the arrival of the Shiva.

Except that this one had been retrieved, without warning. The Shiva seeds were to land soon on its world. The composites were making special preparations there, as on a hundred million other planets, and they did not want an uncontrolled element disturbing their plans. They feared that this being, like the others that would be retrieved, might have "major instabilities."

"Traumatic experience," "study it well," "major instabilities." Bland, aseptic words.

Didn't they understand that anyone left alone for a million years *must have* instabilities? Didn't they realize that Drake had no need to study the returning copy, that he understood it perfectly already? That whatever came back from the other side of the Galaxy was not *it*. What came back was *him*, Drake Merlin.

A different him, certainly. That must be so, because the revenant had unique experiences. But it was Drake, nonetheless. And the composites were right about one thing: the returning Drake needed help.

He had stood apart from all others for so long, it was an ingrained habit. But how could he hold apart from himself?

He could not.

So, at last, Drake Merlin would become part of a composite. This, however, was going to be a unique composite—every element of it would also be Drake.

He had no idea how it would work out. The returning selves had been scattered far off through space and time. He had long ago lost count of their number. Some would be maimed or incomplete versions of a whole Drake Merlin; some would surely be totally deranged. Perhaps they would unbalance the whole.

No matter what happened in the long run, at first it was going to be total chaos. Each one of him, without exception, was going to be *different*. Time and events produce changes in form, in perspective, even in self-image.

It would be his job to understand, to assimilate, and ultimately—if he could—to integrate every part to a single being.

How? He had no idea.

He called on Ana to give him strength.

25

"Let Me Not to the Marriage of True Minds, Admit Impediments."

The first one is the most difficult.

As Drake repeated this to himself he tried to believe it. His revenant self had been dormant when it was retrieved from eight-hundred-thousand-year isolation. It still wore the snakelike organic form considered best for the surface of the planet Greenmantle.

Drake faced his first decision: Should he transfer the mind of his other self to electronic storage, before the interaction began? The technique to do it was routine, and information transfer would surely be easier and faster if they were both electronic. But would the change offer an additional shock that made the revenant's awakening harder to bear?

It was better to do it the other way around, at least for the first meeting. Electronic downloading and merger could come later. Drake arranged for his own transfer to the same snaky form. When he awoke he occupied the body of a legless animal with vestigial wings on its sides and a triplet of prehensile tentacles on the blunt head.

He gave the signal to awaken the other, and wondered: *What am I going to call him, whenever in my own mind I must distinguish us?*

Again, the answer was obvious. *If he is to suffer minimal shock, he has to be Drake Merlin. If anyone changes his name, I must do it.*

Slitted green eyes opened and stared at him.

"Hello." His own greeting came out as a complex waving of the three flexible proboscises.

The other Drake regarded him warily but said nothing. He felt sure he knew why. Drake Two was thinking, *Has the planet fallen to the Shiva? Is this some manifestation of them, designed to trick me and destroy me?*

"Drake, don't go by appearances. You are among humans again. You were retrieved before the Shiva reached your planet."

There was a long, thoughtful pause. The response, when it came, was not quite what he would have provided. The revenant's isolation had produced changes.

"Who are you?"

"I am you. Another version of you."

"Prove it. Tell me something that no one else in the universe knows. Something about me that no one but me could possibly know."

That no one else could possibly know. It took a few seconds, then he had it.

"Our teacher was Professor Bonvissuto."

"Known to me, and also to all the data banks."

"Surely. In our second year with him, he entered us in a statewide contest. We won, mainly because a big part of the competition was to improvise on a given theme."

"Also recorded, I suspect, in the same data banks." Drake Two must suspect where this was heading, but the snaky tentacles gave nothing away.

"But we weren't really improvising at all. When we had breakfast in a hotel near the concert hall the morning before the competition, we were given a table that hadn't yet been cleared. The previous diner had scribbled a series of notes on a napkin, then crossed them out. We noticed the last one, because it had the same three ascending G-minor notes that start the third movement of Mozart's Fortieth Symphony, and also the third movement of Schubert's Fifth Symphony. We started to wonder what you could do with the theme, and we doodled around with it off and on for the rest of the day.

"When the judge offered the theme on which we were to improvise, we realized who had been sitting at the table before us. Naturally, we did a spectacular job and astonished everyone. We felt like cheats, but we didn't say anything to anybody—not even to Ana."

Drake Two was gesturing agreement. "I am persuaded. So what now? Why was I returned?" And then, with a wave of comical puzzlement that Drake understood exactly, "I am Drake—but what do I call you?"

"Call me Walter, if you have to. You know how much we hated our given name. I must give you an update on events. There have been great changes; mostly for the good, but we have bad news too."

He outlined the progress in understanding the Shiva, and the effect that would have on society's need for Drake Merlin. At the end of the explanation, his other self gave the gesture of grim assent.

"If you are no longer needed, I am in the same position. So are all the other versions of us. We are dangerous atavisms—until the next time that the galaxy needs us."

"Which may be never." He regarded his companion self. Given his experiences, he was comfortingly normal. He had known that already, since the responses were close to his own responses. Which suggested another step. "There will be countless billions like us, returning from service beyond the stars. They will not all be as balanced as you. Even so, they must be welcomed, provided with explanations, and restored so far as possible to normal function. Will you help?"

If Drake was truly Drake, the answer could not be in doubt.

"Tell me what I must do."

"Some of our returning selves are likely to be hugely unstable. I am not sure if I—or you—could suffer such an interaction alone and retain our own sanity. We need to reinforce each other. We need to combine our strength. We need—"

"—to merge. I understand."

"But not in this form. I am not sure that is even possible. It must be accomplished when we are in electronic storage."

"Of course. Proceed."

No need to explain, no need to persuade. Of course not. Not unless a man had to persuade himself.

Already his vision had begun to blur. Uploading and merger became simpler when the mind was fully quiescent. As his consciousness began to fade, he wondered.

What would he be like—*they* be like—when the merger was complete? Was he a caterpillar, ready to change to a chrysalis before transforming to a butterfly? It would not be like that. In the caterpillar's metamorphosis there was no combining of materials. Two gametes, then, joining to form a single zygote in the fertilized egg? That was closer, except that his parts were—or had once been—absolutely identical.

As he drifted off into limbo, he hit another simile: he was like identical twins; born together, parted for a long, long time, and at last reunited.

Drake awoke and recognized at once that his groping comparisons were worthless. He had no sense of a merger. He would never believe that he had once been two separate individuals, except that his memories beyond a certain point in the past were duplicates. He had been feeling his way through the swamps of Greenmantle and at the same time directing operations in the War Room. In his mind's eye he looked to the heavens and recalled two starscapes of vastly different skies.

But he had also been right. His mental strength, stability, and resilience had never been so great. For the first time, he understood why humanity chose to exist as elements of a composite. If the merger of two felt like this, what would a multitude be like? Omnipotent and omniscient?

He was about to find out. A thousand returned copies were waiting for his attention. Millions more were on the way.

But even when those were all merged to a single Drake Merlin, it would be no more than a beginning.

The first one is the most difficult.

Drake recalled that optimistic assessment and wished that it were true. This was not the first, nor even the hundred and first. But he was fighting for his sanity and his own existence.

There had been no warning. An organic revenant, seemingly no different from ten thousand others, had agreed to merge into shared consciousness. The upload to electronic form had been routine. The merger began. And Drake felt within him the white-hot flame of insanity.

Alone, he would have had no chance. It was his extended self, protected by the finite transmission times of even S-wave communication, that provided an opportunity for defense.

An opportunity, but not a guarantee. The force of madness was strong beyond belief. A single command was repeated over and over. It ordered every part of Drake to forget the external world, to sink with it into an autism that knew nothing beyond self.

But one part of Drake, farthest off in space, was able to resist. It offered its urgent warning: *If we move inward upon ourselves, we will never return. Remember doomed Narcissus, who fell in love with his own reflection. Look outward. Turn outward.*

The struggle continued. Drake became oblivious to external time and place. That was exactly what the insane component wanted. Only a continuing, intrusive, distant voice—*look outward, turn outward*—provided the lifeline that returned Drake to external reality.

At one point he thought he saw an opportunity to destroy the component, erasing it completely from all stored memory forms. At the last moment he realized that was a trap. He was the copy, and the copy was Drake. By accepting its annihilation, he would be endorsing the idea of self-annihilation, and ultimately he would guarantee his own dissolution.

Look outward, turn outward. He continued the fight. At last, little by little, his dispersed self found a purchase on the lost mind. He turned it, screaming and struggling, to face the united force of ten thousand components, each delivering the same message.

It was hopeless. The revenant was obdurate, irrational, impenetrable. And at the moment when he came to that conclusion, a critical stage was reached. Without warning, the phase change took place. All resistance ended and the madness dissolved. The mad mind, broken and bewildered by past insanity, could not explain what had happened.

Drake soothed it and welcomed another self to the expanding society of the composite. At the same time, he made a solemn vow: Never, no matter how many components were added to his composite self, would he again assume that adding the next one would be easier.

It ought to be a moment for rejoicing. Drake had kept strict accounting, and this was the millionth component to return for rehabilitation. He was getting there, slowly but surely.

It was a pity that the millionth had to be such a case, one that made any idea of celebration impossible. Perhaps it was the gods of ancient times, punishing hubris in their own way. Drake had felt his power growing as the number of his components grew, and he had exulted in it. He spanned a million stars, and there was nothing he could not do.

Except this.

He examined the profile of the new revenant. This Drake had suffered a unique and terrible fate. A hundred million years ago, he had assumed a local organic form and been landed on a world where the Shiva were expected. He had remained there for half a million years, and at last been rescued and returned for possible rehabilitation.

Sometime during that half-million years, a parasite had entered Drake's body without his knowledge. For native life-forms, the organism was actually a symbiote that improved its host's chances of survival. No native life-form was intelligent, so it was not important that as an accidental by-product, brain tissue atrophied in the presence of the parasite. The infected animal was still able to breed. Its life expectancy and reproductive capacity were somewhat improved.

Drake's intelligence had been housed in the brain of the native animal, with a slight organic memory augment. The decline had been too slow to notice, and at some point there was no intellect—or anything else—left to worry about.

The mind and memory of the returned copy had been downloaded to electronic storage, so that Drake's composite could examine it bit by bit. There was still something, the vaguest feeble glimmer of self-awareness. By no rational standard could it be called intelligent. And by no emotional standard could it be destroyed.

Drake initiated the merger with himself. The poor, damaged relic of the revenant had done its duty. It deserved the best that the composite could offer. Even if nothing at all was contributed to the intellectual power of the extended group mind, perhaps

the millionth merger would add its iota of emotion and compassion.

And maybe the million and first revenant, or the billionth one, would experience the benefit.

Brooding over the abyss, Drake contemplated his growing self. He stretched across a million galaxies, adding to his numbers every day and every year. The threat of the Shiva to humanity was ancient history. Nowhere was there danger, nowhere was there conflict. The potential for his own growth was endless. He might one day occupy the whole universe.

And yet….

Yet there was a feeling that something was missing.

How could that be? His task was complete. Every one of the components that he had sent out, on every planet once threatened by the Shiva, was fully accounted for. Every one that had not been destroyed in the battle had returned. Over long aeons they had added to his extended composite. There was no way that he could have missed one.

So it was an illusion. Nothing was going wrong. Nothing was lost or forgotten, nothing could be.

Drake felt himself, for the first time that he could remember, at peace. At last he could relax.

PART THREE: ODYSSEY

26

"From Out Our Bourne of Time and Place the Flood May Bear Me Far."

Drake's memory of the final minute was clear and vivid. He had been standing at the ship's port, gazing down on a world below. It was almost one full day since he had been embodied, and now he was ready to board a lander and begin the descent.

He already knew the planet and the local skyscape. A wealth of information about both had been loaded into him during embodiment. But that was abstract knowledge. Now he desired the real thing: the feel of alien soil or sand beneath his clawed feet, the first breath of whatever passed for air, the sight of sun and moons and starry constellations diffused through haze and cloud and nighttime mist.

He took a last look down. The world was close to Earth type, and his embodiment reflected that: arms and legs and neckless head; three-fingered hands; a body able to walk upright rather than crawl or burrow or scuttle across a rocky seabed.

He turned to enter the lander, and in that moment the ship's control system spoke: *"Shiva presence detected. Landing aborted. Caesura activated. Final entry commences in five seconds."*

So soon? The ship's message had just told him that he was going to die. He had expected a long and lonely vigil on the surface, with only memories of Ana to sustain him, and at the end of it the arrival of a Shiva influence and an unknown destiny. Instead he would find oblivion within the next few seconds.

Since there was not one thing he could do about it, Drake stood perfectly still, watched, and listened. The caesura had already appeared. He could see a roiling spiral of darkness with a blacker eye at the center. A caesura was a slit in space-time, but this seemed more like a bottomless funnel, a conical swirl of ink and dark oil.

The ship was poised on the brink. Drake, knowing that his final moment of consciousness had arrived, thought of Ana. Now he would never see her again.

He squeezed his eyes shut....

...and opened them. There had been a violent moment of disorientation in which his fractionated body twisted and spun in a hundred directions at once. But when that ended, he was still alive. All was calm. The port beside him showed no chaos, no blazing glare or stygian dark, nothing but peaceful stars.

Had the Shiva prevented the caesura from operating?

"What went wrong? Why didn't it work?"

Before he could struggle for his own answers to those questions, the ship was replying: *"Nothing is wrong. Everything has proceeded exactly consistent with theory."*

"Do you know what happened?" Of all improbabilities, this was the greatest: that Drake and the ship had been flung to another universe looking exactly like their own. He stared again out of the port. The sky showed stars, gas clouds, and the faint misty

patches of spiral nebulae. But the stars were in unfamiliar patterns, and the planet had vanished entirely. "Where are we?"

"Specifically? I do not know."

"The caesura was supposed to annihilate us—to throw us into another universe. This looks like *our* universe."

"It is our universe. I have estimated the local physical constants, and they are the same within the limits of measurement. The probability of this occurring in another universe is vanishingly small. I am now in the process of measuring the global universe parameters."

"Do you know what has happened to us?"

"I have no proof, but on the basis of deductive logic I can make a strong inference. The operation of the caesuras follows an unpredictable statistical pattern, thus the outcome of any specific use cannot be predicted. But the probabilities have long been known. In almost every case, the caesura serves to eject an object that enters it into another universe. Once in a million uses, the caesura serves as an instantaneous transportation device to a chosen location. And sometimes, so rarely that we had assumed it would never happen in practice, the caesura may transport an object to an unknown place and time within our own universe. The evidence indicates that has happened to us. According to the records, this possible outcome was explained to you long ago."

Drake remembered it—vaguely. It had been mentioned when the idea of using caesuras first came up; then he had ignored it, thinking of the caesuras only as weapons. But the Bose-Einstein Condensate that formed the ship's cooled brain forgot nothing, and its atomic lattice memory held millions of times as much information as all of Earth's old storage systems combined. The ship probably knew everything that Drake had ever been told, as a tiny subset of its database.

He regarded the stars outside with a new eye. "We are still in our own universe, but far away from where we started. Is it possible for you to take me back to headquarters?"

"It may be possible, eventually. It cannot be done quickly, for several reasons. First, this vessel is able to travel only at subluminal velocities. Extended travel must necessarily be slow. Second, the caesura can cause translation through both time and space. We are now

within a galaxy older than the one that we left. That also suggests the passage of considerable time."

"What do you mean, considerable?"

"I have not yet determined that. It could be many billions of years. I will know better when I have completed my estimate of the universe's global constants. Third, I have already sought to detect evidence of superluminal signals. I find nothing above threshold. Therefore, we cannot be anywhere within our original galaxy, or else S-wave communication has been replaced by something else. Finally, I do not recognize any galactic spatial patterns, as I would if we were somewhere within the local galactic supergroup. We have traveled, at a minimum, hundreds of millions of light-years. The problem of discovering the location of our galaxy is formidable. Even if that were solved, the problem of reaching it would remain."

A ship's brain was designed to be free of emotional circuits, including any trace of humor or fear. Now Drake wished it were otherwise. He could use support at the moment from Tom Lambert or Par Leon. But the ship's design was his own doing. He had not wanted others to be forced to face their own extinction, and perhaps to flinch. He was less lucky. He had emotion aplenty and enough intelligence to understand the implications of what he had just been told.

He stared down at his body, never used for its original purpose and now useless. It had been enhanced for what seemed a more than adequate life expectancy, at least a million years. For any point within his own galaxy that would have been more than enough. He could have endured until contact was established with other humanity or until an S-wave signal facility was reached.

Movement to the galactic scale changed everything. The home galaxy contained about a hundred billion stars, all packed within a flat disk a hundred thousand light-years across. The whole universe contained a hundred billion similar galaxies. The tiny misty patches he could see outside the ship faded to invisibility across more than twelve billion light-years. Each was an island of suns, from the densely packed galactic center to the fading edge of the outermost spiral rim.

Somewhere, far out there, his own galaxy endured. The desperate struggle to contain the Shiva contin-

ued. The suffering and terror of trillions of sentient beings were reduced by distance to a silent and ethereal dust mote of light. He wondered what was happening now. Were other copies of him, in other ships, at last making progress against the Shiva? Were the Shiva sweeping on, unstoppable, across the whole galactic disk? He would never find out. Even if he knew his destination and could head for home at once, his body would wear out and die before he had traveled a tiny fraction of the journey.

And if the search for the home galaxy had to proceed at random? Then a searcher would still be wandering through space thirty or forty billion years in the future, when the universe collapsed toward its inexorable endpoint of infinite pressure and temperature. That searcher could not be Drake or this ship. Long before the end, in less than an eye blink on the cosmic scale, they would be dust.

It was a moment for despair. The logical thing was to end it now, before continued existence brought more grief and longing. He was looking down at his new, flawless, smooth-skinned body, wondering how it could most easily be given a peaceful end, when the ship spoke again:

"My defined actions did not extend beyond the point of entry into the caesura. I require new instructions. Can you tell me the nature of our future, and what activities you plan?"

A moment for despair. That much was permitted. Now it must be over. Someone depended on him— even if it was only a ship. He could not give up.

"You know the main criteria for stellar type and planetary orbits that encourage the development of life. Do you have instruments to determine the nearest and most promising stars that satisfy those criteria?"

"Certainly."

"What about the development of intelligent life?"

"Essentially unpredictable. I can make crude estimates, but with little confidence in the results. The ascent of a native intelligence depends on too many random events in the evolutionary process."

"That's what I was afraid you'd say. All right, I want a systematic survey and catalog of all stars in this galaxy likely to have developed life. Throw in your best guesses for the development of intelligence. Give each one a probability, and place them in order of our distance from them."

"That can be done."

"Another question: What is the programmed lifetime of this ship?"

"Given raw materials, it is indefinite. I contain instructions for repair, for maintenance, and if necessary for self-replication. My memory has quadruple redundancy to allow for quantum changes. As any component ages, it can be renewed."

"How about me? I know there's a lab on board that can build a body to specification and download a person into it, because that's what you did to make me as I am. Is the lab still working?"

"It is working now. Since it is a part of me, it should continue to do so for the indefinite future."

"What about the other way around?" Drake, despite his determination to think positive, felt a tension he could not ignore. This was the key question. "Could you take me as I am now, and *upload* me from this body into electronic storage? And if you did that, could you download me later into another body, either the same or a different one? And could you do the same thing over and over?"

The pause seemed long, though it was probably no more than a second.

"What you ask was not in the original mission plan, but it seems completely feasible. The body for future download would need to be specified. Also, I could not go beyond two hundred embodiments without replenishment. If more were necessary I would require a planetary visit for the acquisition of more raw materials."

"I'm planning on planetary visits. In fact, I'm depending on them." Drake went again to the ship's port and stared out. The nearby stars were the brightest things he saw, but they were like cells in a human body, tiny subcomponents of a larger whole. The power was in the galaxies, stretching out into space forever. "What's the average distance between galaxies, and how far away is the nearest one?"

"Galaxies average a little more than 4,300,000 light-years apart. Of course, they are not homogeneously distributed."

"Of course." The ship did not catch irony, but maybe it could be taught. Certainly, they would have time enough.

"And the nearest galaxy to this one is about seven million light-years."

Seven lifetimes for this body. But long before that he would go crazy. The only way to survive was to spend the time between stellar encounters dormant, in electronic storage. And the next time around he would insist on his familiar human form.

"There is another factor that I should mention. When you asked me the mean distance between galaxies, I gave you an answer that applies today."

"That's what I expected."

"But if, as your other questions would suggest, you plan on searching for our galaxy of origin, another factor must be considered. The universe is expanding. The distance between the galaxies constantly increases. If our target world lies many billions of light-years away, then the rate at which it flies from us will be a substantial fraction of light speed. Our effective rate of travel toward it would be diminished. Perhaps greatly diminished."

"I see the problem; the Red Queen's race." Drake was feeling dangerously unstable. "All right. What can't be cured must be endured. How long before you can pick a preferred stellar target?"

"That has already been done."

"With life, or with intelligent life?"

"Both tables have been prepared. As I said earlier, little confidence can be given for anything involving the development of intelligence."

"We'll have to take that chance. Consider only systems with a better than ninety-five percent chance of having life, and a better than ten percent chance of having intelligent life. How many are there?"

"Between 120 and 250. It is hard to be more precise."

"How far to the nearest candidate?"

"Six thousand light-years."

"Take us there. And one other thing. You said you could not detect any sign of S-wave signals. Is that because they travel only a finite distance?"

"No. In principle, they have infinite range. In practice they follow an inverse square law between source and receiver. With the ship's on-board detection equipment, the signals become indistinguishable from background at no more than a few tens of thousands of light-years. That is adequate for signaling within a galaxy but not outside it. However, even the strongest and most tightly focused S-wave beam would be lost to our limited equipment within a hundred million light-years. That is why

I am confident that we are nowhere within our original local supergroup."

"But you could do better with a better receiver. Do you know how to make one?"

"I have the specifications for much larger receivers—for receivers of almost unlimited size, that would be able to pick up superluminal signals from the far depths of space. However, their fabrication could not be done on board. It would call for a free-space facility, and much assistance."

"Don't worry about that for the moment."

Six thousand light-years to the nearest prospect. Seven million light-years to the next galaxy. *One step at a time.* There were endless billions of years ahead of them, time enough for anything.

"I now have other information, and it amplifies my earlier statements. I have completed my estimate of global universe parameters. In particular, I have measured the galactic red shift. The result of that is surprising: There is no longer any red shift of distant galaxies."

The ship paused. Drake was learning how its analytical processes operated. He waited.

"Assuming that we are still in the same universe, which I continue to believe, the vanishing of the red shift is highly significant. It means that the universe is half-way through its total lifetime, and the blue shift phase is beginning. Within the limits of observational error, my best estimates of current epoch show that the initial singularity preceding the expansion occurred thirty-three billion years ago. The final singularity, the eschaton itself, lies thirty-two billion years in the future."

Not endless billions of years ahead, then, but thirty-two billion. At that final point lay the Omega Point, the ultimate last hope for Ana's resurrection. Except that Drake did not want to wait that long. And he was busy with his own calculation.

"We've jumped ahead eight billion years!"

"It is closer to nine billion."

Eight billion, nine billion, thirty-two billion— Drake found the numbers too big to have any meaning. *One step at a time.* "You asked about the nature of our future activities. I can tell you them. After we have finished speaking, I am to be uploaded to electronic storage— painlessly, please, if there's a way to do it. You will proceed to the chosen star system. Upon arrival there, you will make observations of life-bearing planets. If one of them

offers evidence of an intelligent life-form with a working technology base, resurrect me. If not, select the next promising stellar target and continue the journey. Carry out the same procedures when you arrive there. If there is no intelligence or intelligence without technology, keep looking. Awaken me only for discovery of technological intelligence, or for an emergency that you are unable to deal with. Is all that clear?"

"You have left one important point unspecified. You order me to resurrect you when we reach a world that satisfies your criteria, but you have not specified a form for your embodiment."

"True." Drake abandoned, reluctantly, his plan to spend the rest of the future in his old human form. "Give me a body that can survive on the planet. Better still, make it the same body shape as that of the intelligent life-form."

"What if there should happen to be more than one?"

"Give me the form of the one that seems closest to human." Drake regarded his body, so soon assumed and so soon to be abandoned. Was there a reason to remain in it any longer? Not that he could think of. It would be another six thousand years—at an absolute minimum—before he had any reason to be conscious. He must not dwell on that. Think of it as a natural sleep/wake cycle, not as a time comprising the whole of written history before his own birth. "I'm ready to be uploaded. If you can't make up your mind which form to use when you get there, because they're not anything like human, don't worry about it. Just pick one."

"With what criteria?"

"I don't mind. Use a virtual coin if you have to— but don't wake me up to call the toss."

27

Postindustrial

Drake awoke slowly and easily. As soon as he was able to think, he knew that something had gone badly awry.

His body did not feel wrong—it felt too *right*. His blood ran like ichor through his veins, and his mood was giddily euphoric. He knew of only one way that such a thing could happen.

He opened his eyes, lifted his head, and looked down at his naked body. As he had suspected; he was in his own human form, a new and blemish-free version of himself. He was also aboard the ship.

"What happened?" The vocal cords had never been used before, but they were in perfect working order. He tried an experimental laugh. Whatever else might be wrong, the embodiment lab was in fine shape. And so was he. "Are you telling me that you found a planet full of humans who look just like me in another galaxy?"

"No. I believe that we have encountered an intelligent form, but it is certainly not human."

"So why did you put me in this body?"

"It was a default option."

The ship sounded as frustrated as Drake felt exhilarated. He needed to be careful. The brain transients produced by new-body residence had not yet damped themselves out. He could feel the wild mood swings. How long had he been dormant?

"What do you mean, a 'default option'? Tell me what's going on."

"Your instructions were followed to the letter. We flew to our first target star. One of its planets bore life, but it had not progressed beyond single-celled prokaryotes. There is no possibility that intelligence will develop there for several billion years. I therefore proceeded to the second target, twelve thousand light-years away. I could determine, from a distance of half a light-year, that the nature of the atmosphere of all the planets in the system was such that no life in any form that we know it could survive. Nonetheless, I continued and found on closer approach that life had actually come and gone on one world. It had never achieved intelligence, and it had died out as temperatures rose during the normal brightening and expansion of its main sequence primary.

"On the third world, fifteen thousand light-years away, there were large artifacts and all the signs of sometime intelligence. But the creators had been destroyed, apparently by their own actions. No other life-form had the potential for near-term self-awareness.

"On the fourth world—"

"Wait a minute. How many targets have we visited?"

"This is the one hundred and twenty-fourth. I saw no point in resurrecting you on any earlier occasion. You are not interested in extinct intelligence, nor in possible

future intelligence, but in present *intelligence. We have never before found evidence of that."*

"And now you have?"

"I believe so."

"And how long since the search began?"

"We have been traveling for slightly more than two million years."

"Fine." Drake decided that he had become blasé. Two million years no longer impressed him. To get his attention now, you had to talk billions. "So what's the problem?"

"When we were approaching the current target star, I examined it from far orbit and concluded that one of the planets was remarkably Earth-like. Its atmosphere, told of the presence of oxygen-breathing life, and as we came closer I observed several characteristic markers of intelligence: long linear and rectangular surface features, modified river courses, patterns of nighttime lights, and cluster patterns supporting little or no plant life."

"That sounds right. Roads and dams and power and cities. Did you make detail scans?"

"I did so as we approached closer, images to the meter level of detail and beyond."

"So you know the shape of whoever was doing all the work. Why didn't you put me into *that* form?"

"Had I been able to find such a form, I would have done so. As it is, I found it necessary to invoke the default option of your original shape for the embodiment." The wall in front of Drake became a display screen. *"Observe. We are first looking from far away, on our approach orbit."*

The scene was the whole planet, seen from space. The ball glowed a mottled red and pink, from its banded midsection up to the small circles of white around the poles.

"Are those water-ice polar caps?" Drake had the irrelevant thought that he was looking at a gigantic Christmas tree ornament. He was bubbling over with excess energy, and his mind was ready to accept strange images.

"Correct. The mean temperature is that of Earth during one of your planet's warmer periods."

"I can't see much from this distance."

"Have patience. The images that you will soon see derive from, lower orbit."

The pink sphere on the display was growing. It was possible to imagine dark lines on its surface, scattered close to the equator. Drake waited. He knew the tendency of the human eye to play "connect the dots" and discern linear patterns where there were none. His thoughts spun away to the far-off past. Who was it, long before his own time, who had been fooled by that built-in physiological quirk of the human brain and had drawn maps of nonexistent Martian "canals"?

Except that this was no optical illusion. The linear features were real, growing in clarity every minute. As the ship drew closer to the planet, the display could no longer hold the full image of the world. The focus moved to a line, dark and straight, at center screen. It was bordered by colored rectangles and triangles. To Drake's eye and imagination the line was a road across a Kansas flatland. The broad fields were different shades of red, a child's quilt with bright patches that ranged from light pink to deepest crimson. The yellow brick road had turned dark brown, but it ran through farmlands of fairy-tale color.

The scale that accompanied the display gave the lie to the illusion. The "road" was a kilometer wide. The quilt was monstrous, each of its patches the size of a county of old Earth. Scattered darker dots within the patches were big enough to be towns.

The field of view zoomed in toward a narrower black thread at the center of the broad swath of road. Drake could see that the edges of the patchwork quilt were not regular. They were broken and random, the boundaries intruding on each other. The pink had spread in places onto the darker swath, like crabgrass invading an untended lawn.

The black thread must surely be water. Unlike on Mars, these canals were real. The line of banks ran ruler straight across the surface. Close to the water's edge, every few kilometers, a five-sided open tower of girders stretched toward the sky. The display closed in on one.

"*This is too tall to be built on this planet with natural materials. Carbon composites are essential for its building and continued stability, which implies a reasonably advanced technology. Technology implies intelligence. But where is that intelligence?*"

Drake recalled his "firebreak," the millions of human worlds sacrificed and emptied to escape the Shiva. Had other galaxies been invaded? Were alien species trying the same delaying tactic, abandoning this world to slow an enemy's advance? Who was the Roman general famous for his scorched-earth policy and refusal to fight the Carthaginians directly?

"*One might conclude that the intelligence is* here."

The display homed in on a lighter-colored area by the canal. It was a clearing, a couple of hundred meters across, and it stood in the shadow of one of the great pentagonal structures. Drake was at last able to pick out surface life-forms.

The flat semicircle was bordered on its straight edge by water, and on its curved perimeter by a skimpy fence. A group of thirty or forty objects like oversized pink snails clustered against the boundary. They were creeping steadily along the fence. A dozen others, slightly smaller and faster moving, surrounded them.

A group of twenty other beings crouched close to the water's edge. They were dark red, with many legs, and they surrounded a dark, shallow pit in the surface. On closer inspection Drake could see that they came in three types. The ones on the very edge of the pit were the biggest, four times the size of the outermost group members.

"*This depressed area*"—a bright point of green, vivid against the pinks and browns, appeared on the display in the middle of the pit—"*is revealed by infrared imaging to be well above ambient temperature. I assume that it is a breeding pit, kept warm by rotting vegetation. It is not hot enough to be a cooking pit.*"

Drake thought that was an odd thing for the ship to say—the presence of the vast pentagonal towers spoke of a mastery of technology far beyond the use of fire. But he could see (or imagine) a consistent picture in what was going on in the clearing: herd animals, grazing, held by the fence and protected and chivied along by the equivalent of sheepdogs. The red creatures might be the breeding phase of either of the other types.

But where was the intelligence that had made the great towers? A primitive breeding/grazing society as he knew it could never produce such a technological tour de force.

"*This settlement seems typical.*" The display scanned along the canal to show numerous colonies, each one close to a tower. "*The pattern is repeated in hundreds of places. Each time, the same organisms are seen. But now—observe."*

One of the towers had toppled over. It sprawled the skeleton of its length across the canal and far beyond, into the patchwork of open fields. It seemed intact after its collapse, vouching for the strength of the materials used to make it.

"There is no colony here. Every other tower has one. And see this."

The scene on the display was moving again, swinging away from the canal to a spider's web of converging roads. At the web center stood buildings, some low and dark roofed, others reaching for heaven like the pentagonal towers. Plants like long vines grew over the low roofs or wound around the towers' bottom girders. There was no sign of life anywhere.

"Buildings. Roads. Power stations. Lighted cities. Communications, unless the towers serve some other uses. There is civilization. But where are the beings who did all this? I would welcome your interpretation, before I offer mine."

"I can't even make a guess. Did you see signs of life or artifacts on any other planet of this system?"

"None."

"So they don't have spaceflight. Their development must have been enormously different from ours. What do you think is happening?"

"I have one piece of evidence that you have not yet seen. This is an image taken at night."

The bright cities stood out like clusters of jewels. The roads that joined them were invisible, but as Drake watched, lines of bright blue intermittently flashed along their lengths.

"I have enhanced the pulse in duration and lowered its apparent speed to a level where human eyes can follow. What you are seeing is a burst of information carried by optical laser. Given the absence of intelligent organic life, it suggests a simple explanation: This civilization has passed the industrial phase. It is now wholly concerned with information transfer among its separate elements. Physical transfer of material is no longer necessary."

"What about the beings who did the original development?"

"I assume that they went to inorganic form and were downloaded into a planetary network."

"One that takes no notice of us?"

"If they never discovered spaceflight, they may deny even the possibility of off-world existence. The question is, What do we do now? We need a working force to build an S-wave signal detector, but the intelligence of this planet has never worked in space. Also, like my own intelligence, it may be unable to appear in corporeal form. How can we determine if that is so?"

"Since they don't respond to our signals, I'll have to go down and take a look. Chances are there's nothing useful, but if this is the best you've seen in a hundred and twenty-four tries, we have to make sure."

"Not the best one. The only one."

"How many more hours of daylight?"

"Unless we elect to change longitude, there will be six hours before darkness."

Drake glanced at the sun, uncannily close in color to Sol. "I might be back by then. If not, I'll spend the night in the lander. Is it ready for use?"

"It is waiting."

"How much will you have to change me, before I can survive on the surface?"

"Some slight changes were made during your embodiment. This world is close to being an Earth look-alike. I would recommend, however, that you proceed with caution in ingesting native substances."

"Don't eat the food and don't drink the water. Sure. What else?"

"I believe no other changes are essential."

"You knew what I was going to decide, didn't you?"

"I had suspicions."

Drake wondered what the ship had been doing during the two million years in which he was dormant. Studying him, more than likely. Was there any way that a ship's brain could become smarter, or at least more *cunning*, over time? If experience worked for people, might it work for inorganic brains?

"You know what to do if I don't return, and the signals from me stop?"

"Regrettably, if you do not return I will be able to do nothing to help you. If you do not send instructions, I will wait for one year in orbit around this planet. Then the ship will go on to the next target star and continue the search. I will seek to recover the lander, if that is in any way possible."

Drake nodded. Nothing about recovering his body. There was only one lander. Whereas he….

He was completely expendable. If he came back, the Drake Merlin held in the ship's storage would be updated to reflect his experiences. On his next embodiment he would feel full continuity of consciousness.

If he *didn't* come back, a copy of him would still exist on board the ship. His next embodiment, at some new target world, would feel exactly as he felt: like the one and only real Drake Merlin. He would experience continuity of consciousness, although he would have no memory of a visit to this system.

Drake had a stranger thought yet. Another copy of him, or a hundred others, could be made at any time. Right now, he could ask for duplicates. Why not go down there with someone he could totally rely on—himself?

He sighed. He had too much adrenaline in his system. The sooner that he worked it off, the better.

"All right. I'm ready for the lander."

Drake had in his augmented memory a working knowledge of all known languages, visual, aural, tactile, and pheromonal.

How useful were they likely to be? He was not optimistic as the pinnace completed its braking phase and floated toward a landing a few kilometers west of one of the settlements. It was easy to be fooled by a planet superficially like Earth, but he might be ten billion light-years away. Every lifeform in his native galaxy could be a close cousin compared with this.

He put the lander down on an open field at the edge of *one* of the deserted "towns." There was life here, but the forms were small and they scurried away before he could take a good look at them. Drake estimated that the biggest of the leggy red animals that they had observed by the canal was maybe a quarter of his size. He was the planet's giant.

He stepped down from the lander. A faint breeze on his face carried a scent that made him wrinkle his nose. It reminded him of pickled onions, and that in turn suggested concert recitals in Germany, followed by dark beer and laughter and late-night suppers. How long since anything had summoned up those memories?

He moved onto the road and knelt down to examine the surface.

"Are you getting all this?" Whatever he registered with his senses or his instruments should be automatically sent to the ship, hovering in stationary orbit.

"Everything. Continue."

"Just testing."

Drake probed the surface. The road was a fine glasslike gravel set in a tough bituminous matrix. It was tough and durable, but fine threads of bright red vegetation had taken a toehold at the edge. A narrow strip along the middle of the road was brighter than the rest, as though something continuously scoured it clean.

"This hasn't been used as a road for a long time. I think you may have it exactly right. They've advanced to pure electronic form and left material things behind. They didn't restore the fallen tower, because they no longer need it." Drake glanced at the sun. It was lower in the sky, and barred clouds were moving in across it. "If there's any sign of them, it ought to be in the towns."

"Two hours to sunset." The ship had noticed and interpreted his action. *"The town that you are about to enter did not show up on our orbital survey as one with nighttime lighting. There are rainclouds approaching from the west. I may lose the ability to monitor your environment visually. If you intend a detailed exploration, you should stay in the lander and wait for morning."*

"It's only a few minutes' walk. I'll take a quick look, and then come back to the lander for the night."

The two towers in the middle of the town were no more than a small fraction of the height of their counterparts by the canal, but as the sun went down they cast long shadows in Drake's direction. They were taller than he had thought, a hundred meters and more. The bigger one was in the exact center of the town. Drake walked toward it across a skeletal pattern of girder shadows on the dark road.

"I'm at the first building. Plants are growing around the walls, but they don't stop there. I can see vines entering through that break."

He pointed to a gap in the building wall. The semicircular arch was six feet tall and came down to within a foot or so of ground level. It ended in a flat ledge about four feet wide. He could easily enter if he were willing to step on the vines.

"What are the chances that touching the plants will hurt me?"

"Possible, but unlikely unless they are motion sensitive. They are chemically different enough that they will not respond to you as a living form. Warning: Within the next ten minutes there will be enough cloud cover to inhibit my visual oversight of you."

Drake poked his head through the opening. It took a few moments for his eyes to adjust to the gloom. He was looking into a small room, with another semicircular aperture at the far side. Dusky pink plant life covered everything like a carpet. Beyond the other opening he could see a downward ramp and, beside it, the faint outline of what looked like a piece of gray machinery.

He lifted his feet to avoid touching the plants and steadied himself with his hand on the side of the opening. A surface layer of wall material, about a quarter of an inch thick, crumbled to white powder at his touch. The dust made him sneeze. The wall behind was revealed as a solid metallic plate.

At the same moment his communications unit produced a staccato rattle. A diminished ship's voice said urgently but faintly, *"Your signal is weakening."*

Drake pulled back. "Is it active interference?"

"I think not. It is a natural fading. There must be some shield or insulation in the building walls and roof. I am predicting rain where you are located within the next quarter of an hour."

Drake looked again along the road that led to the tower. Nothing moved. Even the faint breeze, with its odd smell, had died away to nothing. The setting sun was hidden behind a cloud bank.

"I'm going to take a quick look inside. Do you know what the roof is like?"

"It is no longer visible because of the clouds, but our earlier survey showed two large round openings. Nothing could be seen within them. If the room that you looked into is of typical height, the building has three floors above ground level."

"The ramp that I saw goes down, not up. I'll see if there's any way to reach the upper floors."

Drake moved forward and stepped high across the ledge. He could not avoid treading on the plants at the other side. They gave beneath his weight, with a squeaking sound of crushed rubbery tendrils.

"Are we still in contact?"

The communications unit remained silent. Drake hurried across the room and into the next one. It contained gray machinery, solid, alien, and uninformative. He saw a tubby upright cylinder about three feet high that could have been anything from a spacewarp to a dishwasher. He ran his hand across the upper surface. His fingers came away covered with grime. Everything was coated with a thick, uniform layer of dust.

The ramp was steep by human standards, tilted at thirty degrees. He moved carefully downward, pushing his way through sheets of sticky material, thin as gossamer, that broke easily under his hands. Suddenly it was much darker. There was no opening to the outside at this level, and the sunlight that bled in from above was less and less. In another five minutes he would have to turn back. He wished that he had brought a light from the pinnace. Any exploration of lower levels would have to wait until morning.

He had reached the bottom of the ramp. His shoe hit something that rolled away in front of him. He moved toward it and bent low to see what he had kicked.

After one look he froze in his stooped position. He could not see colors in the gloom, but his foot had struck an object of a familiar size and shape. It was like one of the pink snails that crawled around the fence by the canal. This one was dead.

Drake picked it up. It was surprisingly light. The outer surface was smooth and rubbery, which allowed it to retain its original cylindrical shape, but the insides had been scooped out through a long slit at one end. He wondered for a moment if it were some kind of mummified form. His nose told him differently. It had been dead just long enough for the corpse to become putrid.

He could see half a dozen other remains on the floor ahead. One of them was bigger than the rest, a giant white version of the red multilegged creature that he had observed in the canal enclosure. Stretched upright, this one would loom over him. But it would never stretch over anything. It had been cut almost in two at its midsection.

He retreated, heading up the ramp a lot faster than he had descended. Sticky cobwebs clung to him, and he held up his arm to shield his eyes. He did not feel at ease until he had retraced his path, scrambled over the ledge, and was standing in gloomy twilight.

"Do we have contact?"

"I am receiving your signal clearly. I do not have visual monitoring."

The ship's voice was infinitely reassuring. Drake looked up into a heavy overcast, shielding his eyes against a rain that was gradually becoming stronger.

"I'm done for the day. I'm heading for the pinnace. I don't think we'll find any manufacturing capability here, but I want to take another look inside the buildings tomorrow."

As Drake spoke he was moving rapidly along the road, head ducked to keep cold drops of rain out of his eyes. He lifted his head for a moment to peer through the downpour and halted abruptly. The lander should have been by the side of the road, fifty or sixty meters from the buildings. The field ahead stretched far away. It was empty.

Had he turned himself around and headed out of town in a different direction?

That was impossible. He had left the building by the same opening and moved directly away from the tall central tower. He could see a flattened place in the field where the lander had been.

"Did you do something with the pinnace?"

"Certainly not. Has it been interfered with?"

"Worse than that—it's gone."

He hurried forward. Soon he was close enough to see other marks in the soaked vegetation. There was a distinct trail running off toward the town. The lander was equipped with a hover and forward motion capability, but that had not been used. Something had dragged it along the ground.

"I can see where it went. I'm going to follow."

Not just dragged, but hauled without caring whether or not the lander was damaged. As Drake followed the broad furrow, he came across a strip of metal and a torn-off bar from one of the lander's ground legs. He picked the bar up and held it close to his face. In addition to muddy streaks, it bore smudges as though something had picked it up, held it, and discarded it.

The trail led not to the nearest building, but to a bigger one on the left. The wall had a great black emblem marked in its middle. As Drake went closer he realized that the dark area was a gap in the wall itself. The furrow he was following led toward it, then faded to nothing as the surface changed from soft soil to hard impermeable material.

"I think the lander has been taken inside a building."

"What are you proposing to do?"

"I don't have a choice. I have to recover the lander. Without it, there's no way to get back to orbit."

"You could wait until morning."

"I daren't. It may have been accidental, but there has been damage."

As Drake spoke he was moving toward the building. He went carefully and quietly, the bar from the pinnace's landing gear held close to his chest. Everything was silent except for the slowing patter of raindrops.

At the wall he halted. The opening was big enough to take the whole lander. Was it just inside, where he might fly it right out again? Or had it been dragged down a ramp to some deeper level?

He took two cautious steps inside. Immediately he felt a violent blow on his ribs, just below the left nipple. He swung the bar without thinking. It crunched into something that screamed, so loudly and at so high a pitch that it hurt his ears. He felt a blow on his left hip, then another on his right arm. Two invisible objects brushed past him. He turned and followed. He was in time to see two tall white shapes vanishing into the twilight.

The rain had slowed to a few random drops. A ghostly flicker of light showed, far off across the field. Then another.

A creaking sound came from behind him. He quickly spun around to face it.

No tall white shape was leaping out of the dark doorway to attack him, but suddenly there was another flicker of light from inside the building. It provided enough illumination for him to see the lander. It had been hauled into the middle of the room and tilted onto its side. Unless it could be righted, it would not fly.

"Are you hurt?" The ship could not see him, but it was receiving a record of his rapid movements.

"I'm all right. But the lander is damaged."

"Can it be fixed?"

"I don't know." Again there was light inside the building, this time a ruddy glare that varied in brightness like a sputtering flame. "I have to go in again."

The ship said something in reply, but he did not hear it. His attention was focused on the wall beyond the opening. It reflected light from sources farther inside. Torches burned there, orange red and erratic.

Drake moved forward, the rough-edged metal bar over his shoulder. He thought he was ready, but the speed and violence of the attack surprised him.

Half a dozen of them came out of the darkness like white ghosts. They had crouched waiting at the side of the room. Sharp pincers sank into his left arm. His reflexive jerk backward at the sudden pain saved him. The crude machete that slashed at his middle cut through his clothing but made only a long and shallow skin wound.

He turned and smashed at the pincered head. It shattered and splashed cold liquid over his face and neck. He continued his turn, flailing away at anything within reach. The ghost with the machete whistled and screeched as the metal bar caught it solidly in the middle. It fell away, taking another with it. Then Drake was running for the opening. The torchlight behind him was brighter.

He ran thirty yards from the building before he turned to look behind. Everything was quiet. No white shapes sprang through the hole in the wall. No orange torches flared from inside. For the moment he was safe.

"Are you receiving me clearly?"

Perfectly clearly. I project clearing skies and visual oversight in another two hours.

"That will be too long. Listen carefully and place this into the permanent record." The admonition was unnecessary, but Drake had to be sure. "Your suggestion that this planet has gone beyond the postindustrial phase was correct, but the principal intelligence has not moved to a more advanced form. It has regressed to primitivism. We did not observe the dominant intelligence earlier, because it is nocturnal and spends the days underground in these buildings. Based on what I have seen, there is no chance that this planet will provide the space-borne technology that we need. Many of the old systems are still running, but I'd guess that the present inhabitants have little idea how they work. It's just as likely that they worship them now.

"Here are your instructions. Continue the search for a space-faring civilization throughout this galaxy. If you are successful, resurrect a copy of me and enlist the aid of whatever beings you find. If you search

this whole galaxy and find nothing useful, do not continue to the next nearest one. The quest for our home galaxy without a signal to guide us could take to the end of time. Instead, begin a survey of this galaxy with a different objective. Look for a stellar system where raw materials are available in easily accessible form. You know what is needed for the creation of an S-wave signal detector. When you reach the right stellar system, resurrect copies of me, as many as will be needed to perform the space construction work. Build the signal detector, and use it. Do you understand these instructions?"

I understand their meaning, but not your reason for giving them. What of you? Do you not propose to seek the lander and return to orbit?

"I wish I could do that."

Then why do you give me instructions that omit discussion of your own future actions?

"Because I don't think my actions here are going to have much bearing on what you must do." Drake could see the flicker of torches within the building. "I think the Morlocks are getting ready to try again."

I do not understand the term 'Morlocks'.

"That's all right. I didn't expect you to." The torches inside the building were brighter. Drake backed up a few steps. He could smell his own blood, a strong and characteristic scent that he had known only once before in his life. He rubbed at his wounded left arm, then at the cut on his right side. It was strange how little he felt the pain. How would they attack, singly or in groups? Would he be better off in the open, or with his back against one of the walls?

I suggest that you proceed with patience. It is not necessary for you to return to orbit in the immediate future. The local food substances are not suitable for you, but I can transmit information for their processing that will allow you to consume them. The life expectancy of your body is many centuries. In that time the situation on the surface may change.

"It will change all right." Drake turned, wondering if he might find a hiding place along the road or out in the fields. He saw lights, far off but steadily nearing. He would do better to head for the nearest building and make his stand there.

In any case. The ship spoke while he was sprinting across sodden vines. *I cannot desert you. I must stay here as long as you survive. That may be centuries.*

"It may. It would be nice to think that it will be." Drake was panting, his back to the building wall. He clutched his metal bar, all that he had to hold on to. The torches were nearing, crowding in to make a dense ring through which he saw no way to break. "Stay until I die, then go."

They were closer. Long bodies gleamed pale orange in the smoky light of torches held in spidery forelimbs. He could see the razor-sharp pincers. They gaped wide enough to grasp his head. He lifted the metal bar, weighing it in his hands.

"Wish me luck." He took a deep breath through his mouth. "It won't be long now."

Interlude: Dutchman

The monitor ships had been designed by Cass Leemu and Mel Bradley with great care and ingenuity. They must be able to survive without external services or maintenance for up to a million years in orbit, all the while performing continuous observation and analysis. They must be entirely self-sufficient, able to take energy as necessary from any source. They must contain enough stored information to answer any question that a copy of Drake Merlin, embodied on the surface of a planet and awaiting the arrival of the Shiva, might ask.

The composites represented by Cass and Mel had been careful and ingenious in their work, but not wasteful. They did not include features that could not under any reasonable scenario be needed.

So no plan had been made for a ship to survive passage through a caesura. No ship had been designed to operate in galaxies far from human control and influence. No capability had been included for the on-board production of self-replicating machines. The design guaranteed that a ship be able to operate for millions of years, but not for unspecified billions.

Cass and Mel, at Drakes insistence, had gone beyond reasonable and foreseeable needs in just one area. The first humans, long ago, had emerged from the caves of Pleistocene Earth with brains already large enough to write sonnets, invent and play chess, compose fugues, and solve partial differential equations. They had not really needed such abilities in a world where hunting, gathering food, breeding, and nurturing seemed the only fixed constants. But a bigger-than-necessary brain had proved an advantage. It might be necessary again. Drake wanted each ship to be created not only self-aware, but intelligent enough to review the probable consequences of its instructions and of its own actions.

This ship had received unusual and specific instructions: Seek a civilization that was already space-faring. Then rouse Drake from dormancy to interact with whatever—if anything—was found. Should no space-faring intelligence be located within this galaxy, build a superluminal signal detector. Drake would have to be roused from dormancy and embodied to help with that, because the ship lacked the general-purpose robots needed for large space construction.

The instructions implied several other imperatives. First, the ship must survive. It must do whatever was needed to ensure its continued operation. It must also be patient.

The ship wandered alone across the sea of stars. There was no way that it could ever land on a body bigger than a small asteroid. Its own weight would destroy its fragile structure. A copy of Drake Merlin, far more robust, could be downloaded into an organic body while the ship was in orbit around a planet and landed there, but it was impossible for a large S-wave detector to be constructed on a planetary surface.

Remaining in operating condition would not be difficult for the ship itself. Material resources for self-renewal were plentiful around many stars and in the dust clouds scattered through the spiral arms.

In any case, that was not going to be the problem.

The ship found an open lane of the galaxy and drifted along it, far from the disturbing effects of suns and singularities and dust clouds. It performed its careful analysis: eighty-eight billion stars in this galaxy; a mere two hundred targets as sources of potential intelligence—five-eighths of them already eliminated by direct inspection. It would be a straightforward if lengthy task to look at the rest. The ship could certainly handle that.

But now, assume that the search was unsuccessful, that no space-going intelligent life was found, that it was necessary to take the next step. Then the time scale for action expanded enormously. Years increased from millions to billions. To build an S-wave detector—one large enough to see into the deepest reaches of space—was a monstrous task. Drake Merlin, in his final orders from the clouded surface of the planet, could not have known what he was demanding.

But the ship knew.

It also knew that it had no choice. Unlike a human, a ship's brain could not elect the annihilation of self.

As the ship computed the trajectory for the next target star, it mapped out the mandated sequence of its future actions if the current search failed to produce the right kind of intelligent life.

Find the right type of dust cloud, one close enough to a recent supernova to be rich in the necessary heavy elements. Embody Drake Merlin—not once, but in a hundred or a thousand or a million copies. (And never consider their eventual fate.) Use the Merlins, singly and working in unison, as laborers. In the absence of intelligent robots, Merlins must mine the dust cloud, build the space production facility, shape the strands of the antennas and stretch them across space in the precise configuration demanded for signal detection of S-wave sources.

It could be done. The ship saw practical obstacles—it must husband its limited drive, coasting without power for thousands of years between target stars, taking advantage of every natural force field and particle wind of the galaxy; but there was nothing impossible.

Except, perhaps, for the time that all this would take.

The ship made the calculation and regarded the result. It could not sigh or wince, but it wished that it was possible to go back to Drake Merlin in the last moments before the horde of white ghosts had swarmed over him, and ask if this was what he really wanted.

It knew the answer to that question. The on-board information base made it clear: Drake Merlin did not want any of this. He wanted his lost wife. The odds against that made everything in the ship's calculations seem like certainty by comparison.

The next target star was known, the most economical flight path computed and ready. There was no further reason for delay.

The ship set out on its multibillion-year journey, sailing the endless trade winds of an indifferent galaxy.

28

"From Far, From Eve and Morning and Yon Twelve-Winded Sky."

Who would ever have thought that it could take so long?

Drake drifted through space, his suited body slowly turning. He had left the ship in order to inspect the overall condition of the structure. How many times had he been downloaded to do this, he or some other of the multiple copies of himself? How many times had everything been found to be in working order, and how many times had he returned to electronic storage?

A thousand, ten thousand, a million. It made no difference. The S-wave detector was all around, a construct whose nodes and gossamer filaments stretched away past the point where his eyes could trace their presence against the stars. The great array was supposed to be able to detect evidence of superluminal message activity out to the red shift limit. It had been set up to operate automatically and indefinitely, if necessary without human or ship supervision. One by one, galaxies would be looked at until the whole universe had been surveyed. The process would stop only when a signal was detected. So far the instrument had reported nothing but a steady hiss of background noise.

If the array was working to specification, was something wrong with the basic theory? In principle a super-luminal signal would traverse the universe in hours; but confirmation of the theory had been made only in the home galaxy, over distances a millionth as far as current needs.

His attention moved beyond the detector array to the far-off glow of stars and galaxies. His eyes could not see the change, but he knew that it was there.

Not the end yet, but the subtle beginning of the end. Already the great dust clouds had been consumed, the blazing blue supergiant stars long ago exploded to supernovas or collapsed to black holes. Every main sequence star was far along in its lifetime, reduced from a bloated red giant to a white dwarf hardly bigger than the original Earth. Only the slow-burning low-mass stars remained, doling out miserly dribbles of radiation; their energy supply would be sufficient for another hundred billion years.

Except that such a period was not available. The cosmos itself was evolving, changing. The ship reported to Drake that the universe was far past its critical point. The remote galaxies displayed a strong blue shift, a displacement of the light toward shorter wavelengths. The microwave background radiation, diluted and cooled during the earlier expansion of the universe, now revealed an increase in its black body temperature.

The universe was warming up. The Great Expansion was far in the past. The collapse, toward the final singularity and the end of time, was under way.

But thought's the slave of life, and life time's fool; and time, that takes survey of all the world, must have a stop.

Drake halted his drift through space but permitted the slow rotation of his suited figure. He, like time, was taking survey of all the world. It seemed his task must have no stop—until the universe itself put an end to it.

The current inspection was complete. He might as well head back to the ship. On the other hand, there was no hurry. When he returned he would be uploaded again to electronic storage. His new sleep might be for a million or a billion years, but he could expect little change when he awoke. The march from here to the end of the universe would be slow and stately, a multibillion-year progression. Only the final months and days would be spectacular. To anyone around to watch them, they would display unimaginable violence.

The ship was a tiny gleam of gold at the center of the black web of the S-wave detection system. Drake headed toward it, glancing from time to time to his left. The dust cloud that had provided the materials for the detector still hung there, glowing faintly by its internal light. It was too small to collapse under its own gravitational attraction. That, and the constraining field placed in position by the ship, had been the key to its continued survival.

Drake, occupied with his thoughts, had turned off the suit unit linking him with the ship. There was no danger in doing so. Communications could be activated in an emergency by the ship's brain, although the many billions of years since entering the caesura had never produced a single override.

He switched the communicator on when he was just a few kilometers from the ship, and was shocked to hear a brief repeated message.

"Superluminal signal activity has been detected. Analysis is underway. Superluminal—"

"What! Why didn't you call and tell me?"

"That seemed...premature." The ship was oddly hesitant. *"There are anomalies that require explanation."*

"Then you'd better tell me about them." Drake was sliding through the molecular interstitial lock at record speed. He felt a sense of exultation at his special good fortune. He had been the one embodied when the signal came! Then he felt stupid. Since every embodiment was one version of him, there was no way that he could *not* be the one embodied when an S-wave message was detected.

"Where does the signal come from?"

"It is multiple signals, from a galaxy about eight hundred million light-years away. In cosmic terms, that is rather close. It lies on the far side of one of the great gulfs, but in a super-cluster that is still one of our neighbors."

"What do the messages say?"

"That is where the anomaly begins. First, the signals lack standard header records, identifying their source and destination."

"Maybe they were broadcast."

"That cannot be the case. An S-wave signal is like any other, it must be tightly beamed to be read at more than a few hundred light-years. But even if the signals had been broadcast, they would carry a source identification. That, however, is not the most disturbing feature. The real problem is that the signals are unintelligible. *We are not dealing with a single detected signal, where the problem might be one of resolving ambiguities. We are picking up millions of bit streams, an abundance of test data. Although we carry with us every known communication protocol, these superluminal signals conform to none of them."*

"Maybe it's a new protocol, something that came into use after we passed through the caesura. We've been gone for so long, changes are inevitable."

"True. But the signals are totally *unrecognizable. Change is more than likely, it is even necessary to reflect new needs and new technology. However, just as the human body caries within it elements of your own most archaic history, from fingernails to body hair to embryonic gill slits, so any superluminal signal ought to carry at*

least some semblance of the old communication protocols. *These do not. They are wholly unfamiliar.*"

"Are you still working to crack them?"

"*Naturally. However, I am not optimistic. Already I have employed eighty percent of the analytical tools available to me, with no success. The most probable explanation is also the least satisfying.*"

Drake didn't need to ask what it was. The possibility had been discussed with the ship's brain during each of his embodiments.

"Assume that it is an independent civilization, aliens who have never encountered humans but are advanced enough to use S-wave signaling. How would it affect our ability to send a signal to them?"

"*To send a signal? That would be very easy. Our S-wave detector can transmit as accurately and rapidly as it receives. That would not seem to be the issue here. The question is, What will happen to our signal when it is received in the other galaxy?*"

"That's going to be my problem, isn't it?" Drake saw no point in talking generalities any longer. "Once I'm back in electronic storage, how long will it take to transmit me superluminally?"

"*A few hours at the most.*"

"Then let's do it. You said eight hundred million light-years?"

"*Eight hundred and eighteen million, to be more precise.*"

"How much travel time is that for you—allowing for fuel and maintenance and everything else?"

"*Most would have to be in coast phase, since between the galaxies there are no ready sources of materials or energy. Necessarily, that would imply long periods of low or zero acceleration. The travel time would be a billion years or more.*"

"You can survive that?"

"*Of course. Already we have endured tens of times that interval. However, I must mention two other anomalous features of the received signals. First, although there are many signals, million after million of them, they clearly fall into two different types.*"

"How do you know that, if you can't understand what they say?"

"*By statistical analysis of the bit streams. That analysis clearly reveals two distinct types, although the content of either type remains unknown. And that is the second anomaly. In principle, my analytical tools should permit the interpretation of any possible signal whatsoever. It* makes no difference if the sender is human or nonhuman, organic or inorganic, familiar or utterly alien. If the laws of logic, which we have always believed to be universal, are being followed, the signal should be intelligible.*"

"But these are not? Very curious. Chances are it will be easier to sort out what's going on when we're there to see it." But Drake was expressing a confidence that he did not feel. He sensed old memories stirring within him. Two kinds of signal that clearly were signals, but neither of which could be interpreted. Why did that sound familiar?

"First, switch me back to electronic storage. Then send me on my way. After I'm gone, you can take the slow road and join me." *Signals that could not be understood. Algorithms that should be able to interpret anything, but failed to do so.* He postponed the question. He would have time to consider it when he reached the signal source. "Let's get me to electronic form, so I can go to work. Assuming that things work out all right, I'll beam myself back here and tell you what's going on."

Assuming that things work out all right.

It occurred to Drake, rising to consciousness, that nothing had gone right for aeons. They had certainly not gone right this time. Rather than waking in some other galaxy, delivered as an S-wave and reconstructed to consciousness, he was still on board the ship. And although he was awake, he was certainly not embodied. Instead he was in electronic form, sharing sensors and processors with the ship. He was also aware of the hundred or more other versions of himself, dormant around him.

"All right. It didn't work. What's happening now?"

Part of the answer came to him even before the ship spoke. The visible light sensors revealed face-on the disk of a barred galaxy. From the way that it filled the sky ahead, they were within a few tens of thousands of light-years—touching distance, in intergalactic terms.

Also, it was *the* galaxy. The ship's signal-receiving equipment showed the spiral arms filled with the glittering sparks of S-wave transmissions. The galaxy flamed with them, bright flickering points of blue and crimson. They had been color coded by the ship into type 1 and type 2—statistically different from each other, but equally mysterious.

If the ship was here, so close to the source of the signals, then a billion years or more must have passed since he was last conscious.

Why wasn't the ship answering his question? And then Drake realized that the ship *had* answered. A new block of information had been transferred, and his electronic consciousness was already processing it, thousands or millions of times faster than his old organic one. He knew, without being told….

The ship had remained for centuries at the focal point of the giant array. It had transmitted Drake as a superluminal signal—not once but a hundred times and more. It had waited patiently for a return signal. Nothing came into the array but the same endless stream of unintelligible communications.

At last the ship had to make a difficult choice. If it left the array, all chance of receiving an intergalactic signal from Drake was lost. The ship would be forced to rely again on the simple S-wave detection system that it carried on board. On the other hand, to remain in one place and wait for a signal from Drake might take until the end of the universe.

Finally the ship abandoned the array and set out on its lonely billion-year journey across the intergalactic gulf. In doing so, it lost the ability to pick up superluminal signals from its destination until the target galaxy was close enough for the on-board system to operate.

How close?

This close. Close enough for the ship to employ a synthetic aperture optical system, able to produce visible wavelength pictures of surface detail on planets the size of Earth.

And now a new problem arose. It was baffling enough for the ship to know that it needed help. It had brought Drake to consciousness.

And because he would need direct access to all sensor inputs, and because in any case there was no planet within twenty thousand light-years where an embodied organic form might prove useful, the ship employed a different procedure. It did not embody the aroused intelligence, but resurrected it in electronic form.

Drake examined one of the planetary images as the ship drifted steadily on through space. The world was superficially Earth-like, sufficiently massive and far enough from its primary to hold an atmosphere. It should have had air of some kind, nitrogen or methane or carbon dioxide or,

if it bore life, oxygen and water vapor. No trace of any showed up in the gas spectral analysis. The surface, unobscured by clouds or a shroud of air, was black rock. It looked like volcanic basalt that had flowed under high temperature before pooling and hardening to grotesque formations. There was no sign of surface water, no sign of life or surface artifacts. Orbiting the world like a swarm of lightning bugs were hundreds of objects too small to be seen with the imagers. However, from time to time a flash from one of them showed that it was transmitting, and the ship was receiving, an outgoing S-wave signal.

What was there to talk about in facilities that orbited long-dead worlds?

Drake tracked the destinations of the outgoing data bursts, and the ship offered their images at his command: world after world, scene after scene of charred devastation. Every planet was in ruins. Each was clearly lifeless.

"I have performed as complete a survey as possible from this distance." The ship's messages were clear and easy now that Drake knew how to listen to them. "The pattern repeats from one side of the galaxy to the Other, from the outer rim to the central disk. Those worlds have in common what I have termed a type one superluminal message capability. Compare them with he type two worlds."

Another sequence of planets was offered for Drake's inspection. From the ship's point of view, there were large differences. From a human point of view, one similarity overwhelmed every other factor: organic life was absent.

Drake examined a thousand type 2 planets where everything that humans had learned of physics, planetology, and biology suggested that life should have developed. The sun was an appropriate spectral type, surface temperature was in the right range, the planet had a low-eccentricity orbit, there was plenty of surface water, and a thick atmosphere of hydrogen, carbon dioxide, and nitrogen.

Life should have developed—*must* have developed. And it *had* developed. The proof was in the swarm of active devices around each world, emitting and receiving their bursts of S-wave signals. No one would install such a system without a purpose. Life had once been on all these worlds. And somehow life had been destroyed, not as spectacularly as on the type 1 worlds, but just as finally.

"The problem is one that we never anticipated." Was that the ship speaking, or Drake's own thoughts? The dividing line became blurred when they shared common storage and processing power. "We had always assumed that superluminal signal capability would be accompanied by a working technology. Now we find abundant S-wave capacity and nothing else. Do we wish to visit a galaxy that seems dead of organic life?"

"Is it *safe* to do so?" The last thought was surely Drake's alone. His thoughts were moving again to old memories and offering an uneasy synthesis.

In an infinite universe, anything that can happen will happen.

He had been talking to himself, but his thoughts were no longer private.

"The universe is not infinite," the ship said. "It is finite in time both past and future, and it is finite but unbounded in space."

"All right. Change that to things that you never expected to happen, when you were long ago on a world far away, can happen if you wait long enough and go far enough."

He not only hadn't expected to see this—when he was young he had hardly taken notice of it. His interests revolved around music and Ana, and anything as dull as military policy or political strategy tended to be ignored. It was Ana, the social activist, who had educated him. He remembered one lazy October afternoon when they lay side by side in his little one-room apartment, with the Venetian blinds partly drawn and late sunlight casting elongated and distorted leaf shadows on the wall. Drake lay flat on his back. He didn't want to talk or think about anything and would have quite liked a nap. He found it easier to say nothing and pretend to listen, but he had got away with that for only a few minutes.

"You don't care, do you?" Ana punched him on the left shoulder and propped herself up on her elbow so that she could see his face and make sure that he wasn't going to sleep. "I'm telling you, it could happen again."

"Nah. Mutual Assured Destruction is a dead idea. And a dumb idea, too."

"It's worse than dumb, but I'm not sure it's dead. Brains and resources were wasted on it for two generations. Do you want to know why?"

Not really. But Drake said only, "Uh-huh."

"It kept on going because it was a big fat money tree, where corruption could thrive and contractors could get very rich. And because no matter what you do, for paranoid people more is never enough. If *they* build more weapons, or even if you just think that they might, *you* have to build more. They're as crazy as you are, so they have to build more, too; so you have to build more, so they have to build more, so you have to build more, so they have to build more, so you have to build more...."

She paused, rather to Drake's disappointment. The cadence of the repeated phrase was relaxing, and he would happily have nodded off listening to it. Instead he said, "I don't know why you're still worrying about all this. It's ancient history. MAD went away over twenty years ago, along with the Soviet Union."

She snuggled up against him and put her hand flat on his bare belly. "That proves how little you understand the military. I drank this stuff in with my mother's milk. Four of my uncles and five of my cousins are regular army or air force. You should hear the talk at family reunions. You did me a big favor. They can't stand your politics."

"I don't have any."

"That's almost worse. But they don't want you around, and that gives me an excuse to stay away. I'll never be able to thank you enough."

"You can thank me by letting me rest. Anyway, you shouldn't be thanking me. Thank Professor Bonvissuto. He got you the scholarship."

"I'll thank both of you. You know what Uncle Dan said? He's the air force colonel, the one from Baltimore who told you that the finest vocal group in the world was the Singing Sergeants, and that Wagner was a boring old weirdo."

"I remember him. Rossini said much the same—about Wagner, I mean, not the Singing Sergeants. He said Wagner had beautiful moments, but awful quarter hours. He also said that he couldn't judge Wagner's *Lohengrin* from a single hearing, and he certainly didn't intend hearing it a second time."

"Ideas in the military don't go away, ever, Uncle Dan says." Ana wasn't going to let Drake distract her with musical anecdotes. "Old ideas get put on the shelf, and when the right funding cycle comes around they're dusted off and proposed again as new. I don't believe a lot of what he tells me, but I believe that. Balance of terror didn't start with Mutual Assured Destruction. And it won't end with it. Bad ideas are still sitting there on the shelf."

And sometimes they sit on that shelf for an awfully long time before they finally achieve their potential.

"I do not think that I am following you," the ship said.

It was hardly surprising—Drake's private thoughts had not been intended for anyone else. They had hopped randomly between past and present, and they included personal references that were surely not in any general database.

Drake addressed his remarks directly to the ship's interface. "Mutual Assured Destruction is a very simple idea: I build huge weapons systems. So do you. Then you daren't attack me, because if you do, I'll attack you in return and you'll die, too." (He had killed Ana, and he had died, too. He had thought of his actions as Mutual Assured Survival. Did that make him any different from the Mutual Assured Destruction lunatics?) "So neither one of us dares to attack the other. It sounds as though it might work, but MAD has one fatal flaw. It produces an equilibrium between two groups, but it's an *unstable* equilibrium. One accident, or even a misunderstanding, and both sides will use their weapons. They have to hit as hard as they can immediately, to neutralize as much of the other's firepower as they can. Just as bad, a third group with very few weapons can *force* a misunderstanding and make the two big powers fight each other, by faking an attack of one on the other. I think we are looking at the results when MAD is applied on a huge scale. I think it killed that whole galaxy."

"That cannot be true. Even now, I am detecting new superluminal messages. I cannot understand them, but it proves that intelligence continues to operate there."

"Intelligence of a sort. Sometimes if an idea is old enough, it can seem brand new. I ought to have known what was going on ages ago, as soon as you told me that there were two distinct types of signals

coming from this galaxy, and that you were unable to interpret either of them. You said that any signal at all should be intelligible to you. But suppose it was *designed* not to be understood by anyone without a suitable key? Suppose both sides were employing ciphers, codes that the other could not break."

"Intentional obscurity. That is certainly possible. But what makes you so sure that the galaxy is dead? How can that be true, and the technology still be working?"

Drake realized that he could explain even that. His mind had thrown at him an image of a long-ago performance of Haydn's Farewell Symphony, of a conductor facing a group of players. In front of each stood a lighted candle. One by one, each musician finished his or her own orchestral part, snuffed out the candle, and left the stage. Finally the whole orchestra was gone. The conductor stood alone in darkness.

The ship was unlikely to benefit much from that thought. "Let me tell you what happened on Earth," Drake said, "in the years just after I was born. Two great powers had been busy building up their nuclear weapons. The chance of all-out war seemed very high. That war, if it happened, would be short. A couple of hours and it would be all over. Missiles over the pole could be launched to reach any target within thirty minutes. The military on one side—our side, people would say, though I never thought of it as *my* side—decided that they must keep some kind of communications system working, even after the main war was over. They imagined a space-based command post, a whole constellation of special satellites in orbit around the Earth. The spacecraft would be completely operated by computers, and they would form a kind of central nervous system for all fighting, no matter when it happened. The system was called MILSTAR, for Military Strategic, Tactical, and Relay system, and it was supposed to be able to function even after the main spasm of war was over. The military planners didn't intend for MILSTAR to help with civilian reconstruction. That wasn't its job. They wanted it to handle *military* communications—and to be able to support fighting again, if necessary, months or years later. They wanted MILSTAR ready to fight another war. It was designed to function even if all the surface command structures had been obliterated. It was supposed to be able to call on robot weaponry, whether or not there were humans around."

The image came again. The conductor stood facing a full complement of players. As the military powers on land, sea, and air were snuffed out by enemy action, MILSTAR continued, organizing and optimizing resources that became smaller every second. Finally, the stage held nothing but orchestral desks and empty instrument cases. The conductor waved his baton over a vanished army of players. MILSTAR floated serenely on through space, its communications system in full working order and ready to shape a second symphony of Armageddon.

"The MILSTAR satellites had to be very sophisticated. They needed a long operating lifetime. They had to be mobile, to avoid direct missile attack; durable, to operate for years without a single human mind to direct them; robust, to survive electromagnetic pulse effects and near misses; and smart, able to talk easily to each other using a variety of encrypted signals, so that the enemy could never crack the global communications network.

"It was a highly secret project. It had to be. That was why it was able to obtain huge funding for a long time, even though anyone who looked at it objectively could see why it wouldn't work. It needed tens of millions of computer instructions, lines of program code that could only be tested when the actual war was declared. It assumed a static world order, with a single well-defined enemy. It bypassed every civilian chain of command. Worst of all, it assumed that one side or the other could *win* an all-out nuclear war, and be all set to fight again. No mention of hundreds of millions of casualties, or disabled food and water and sewage and transportation systems, or a totally collapsed economy that couldn't pay ten cents for a military budget.

"Well, we were lucky. MILSTAR came out from behind its veil of secrecy, little by little. That doomed it. It couldn't stand the sunlight. Finally, after years and years of staggering along when no one really believed in it but kept it going as a source of jobs and a political pork barrel, the money was cut off and the development ended. MILSTAR never became a working system—on Earth. But something like it

was developed, and is still in operation"—Drake indicated the galaxy ahead of the ship—"*there.*"

Drake had been carried away, in time and space and in a depth of feeling lost to him for aeons. He knew he had spoken for Ana, more than for himself. Those had been *her* voiced fears, her indignation, her relief at an earthly doom avoided. He also realized, for the first time, that existence in a purely electronic form could admit emotion and passion and longing.

The ship had absorbed the facts of his message, if not its intensity. "So although an S-wave signal system exists in that galaxy," it said, "the original creators and owners are long vanished. Therefore no moral or practical impediment exists to our taking over its use. We should find it possible to inhibit the encryption system. As soon as we have done that, and our own type of S-wave signals can be sent and received—"

"We can't do that."

"I believe that I possess the necessary analytical capabilities, even though you may not be aware of them."

"That's not the problem. The problem is in going there." Drake again indicated the galaxy ahead of them.

"We are only twenty-one thousand light-years away. We have traveled forty thousand times that distance already, without difficulty. The remaining journey is negligible."

"No. It's the place where we can expect trouble. Look at them." Drake displayed an array of blackened and silent worlds for the ship's attention. "We can't say what did this, and for all we know it may still be working. Maybe it's waiting for something new that it can hit. The weapons ran out of *targets.* We don't know that they ran out of anything else. Just because a galaxy is dead of life doesn't mean it's safe to go there."

"Then I request that you propose an alternative." The ship turned its imaging equipment, swinging slowly from the island of matter ahead to the great ocean of space that surrounded it. "The next nearest galaxy is two and a quarter million light-years away. It showed no evidence of S-wave transmission. Do you suggest that we change to it as our target? I am ready to follow your instructions."

And that was the devil of it. There *was* no better alternative. No other galaxy, in a search that stretched halfway across time, had displayed superluminal signals. It was a poor moment to decide that the ship had left the big detection system, laboriously constructed over so many years, prematurely. But it was true. The smart thing would have been to survey every galaxy in the universe for S-wave transmissions, before rushing off to tackle the enigma of the one that lay ahead.

It was Drake's fault. He should have thought harder and longer before he acted. The price of mindless action was high: they had to return to their detection system, a billion years away, and follow that with another interminable search.

That was the price. But he was not willing to pay it.

Surely *something* could be done with the facilities that lay ahead of them, so temptingly close? Compared with the other option, twenty thousand light-years was like stepping to the house next door. He knew, with absolute certainty, that a full superluminal capability existed here, in perfect working order. Nothing like it might be found again before the universe itself came to a close.

As the field of view of the ship's sensors performed its steady turn in space, Drake watched the grand sweep of the galaxies. They had not changed. *He* had changed. When had he lost his will and daring? When had he become so cautious?

Long ago, without a second thought, he had risked everything. Now, no matter what he did, he would be risking less than everything. Other versions of him surely still existed, even if they happened to be at the far edge of the universe. They did not know that *he* existed—they would think that he had died fifteen billion years ago, when the ship was swallowed by the caesura. But what of that? They should still be there. Did he have anything to lose, if now he risked the dark menace ahead?

"Aye, but to die, and go we know not where...."

Was that all it was? Simple fear of death?

"Are we still heading for the galaxy?"

"Yes. We have not changed our course."

"Then forget the alternative. Hold our path. Take us to the nearest world where you are detecting a source of S-wave messages."

There are many events in the womb of time which will be delivered.

And how long since he had thought of *that?* It was time to take a chance, and test the kindness of reality.

Taking a chance on one thing did not mean abandoning caution in everything else.

Drake elected to remain conscious, though not embodied, through the whole slow approach to the galaxy. The ship's speed had to be subluminal. Meanwhile, the S-wave messages flashed and flickered ahead from spiral arm to spiral arm, as enigmatic as ever. At Drake's suggestion, the ship's brain assumed that the messages were deliberately encrypted and tried to decipher them. The effort consumed the bulk of the ship's computation powers for twelve thousand years. There was no useful result for either type 1 or type 2 messages.

While this was going on, Drake constantly monitored the galaxy ahead. He had no idea of the range of weapons that remained there. At any moment, the ship's approach might be detected, and an alien force could reach out to consume them. He was ready to power the ship down totally and hope that silence would end the attack, or if that failed to turn the ship around and try to outrun the destruction.

The thirteenth millennium brought the change. It occurred while Drake and the ship were analyzing the comparative freedoms and restrictions of their two mentalities.

"What would you have done, in a similar situation?" The ship was dissatisfied with its own performance.

"Assuming that I were a ship, with your history and your inorganic intelligence? The first thing I would do, after Drake Merlin insisted on being sent as a superluminal signal to this galaxy, is tell myself that embodied humans tend to be impulsive and make decisions too quickly. We evolved that way, because the old human body rarely lasted a century. We were always in a hurry, we had to be. So as a ship I would have spent a long time evaluating my own possible actions. Then I hope I would have asked what could be done at the S-wave detection structure we built and nowhere else. When all those things were done, I would have headed this way."

"And what would you have done as a *human* in the same situation?"

"If I could see no possible further use for my existence—"

Drake's comments on suicide, an idea alien to the ship's intelligence, were interrupted.

A-W-A-W-A-W-A-W-A-W-A-W-A-. The ship's S-wave detector screeched and warbled in overload as a message blared into it.

A-W-A-W-A-W-A-W-A-W-A-W-A-W-A-.

"Is it coming from the galaxy?" Drake had to send his own thought at maximum volume to penetrate the curtain of incoming noise.

A-W-A-W-A-W-A-W-A-W-A-W-A-W-A-.

"I do not know." The ship's own signal was barely intelligible. "The source is so powerful. It comes from everywhere. Wait." The ship de-tuned its receiver, and the volume of signal suddenly dropped to a tolerable level.

WARNING. YOU ARE ENTERING A DANGEROUS AND QUARANTINED AREA. DO NOT PROCEED FARTHER WITHOUT INSTRUCTIONS. REPEAT, YOU ARE ENTERING A DANGEROUS AND QUARANTINED AREA. HALT, AND DO NOT PROCEED WITHOUT INSTRUCTIONS. WORKING S-WAVE COMMUNICATION PROTOCOLS ARE CONTAINED IN CARRIER WAVE. VISUAL AND REAL-TIME INTERACTION FOLLOWS.

"I'm sending our identification and reply." The ship was already transcribing protocols. "It is safe to do so. That signal can't be coming from the galaxy ahead."

"How do you know?"

"Because there is no encryption. More than that he signal is in *standard form*. It must be coming to us from our own form of mentality."

Drake did not need that last piece of information. The promised visual and real-time information flow was beginning, and pictures were already flowing in. The first frame was very familiar. It was Drake Merlin, staring at something right in front of him. A puzzled voice was saying, "Please transmit that identification sequence again. There appears to have been a transcription error. According to our records, you don't exist. You haven't existed for fifteen billion years."

Drake was not embodied, so he could not send an exultant real-time image of himself. The best that he could do was to provide his own stored and smiling icon, as it was preserved in the ship's memory.

"What you have received is not a transcription error. We exist, and you have the right ID sequence.

We've been heading for home all this time. I'm sorry that it took so long." And then, the only thing that really mattered, the question: *"Did you develop the technology needed to restore Ana? Is she there with you?"*

While Drake waited for answers, he realized that everything else made sense. A rogue galaxy, devoid of life but sending out S-wave signals and filled with weapons of destruction, was a menace to every intelligence in the universe. A region around that galaxy was needed as a quarantine zone. All the approach routes had to be monitored. Like a dangerous reef in a peaceful sea, the galaxy must be surrounded by warning bells and lightships. It was a beacon for the whole universe, the best possible place for lost travelers, like Drake and the ship, to arrive at.

And arrive they had. They were on the way home.

In an infinite universe, anything that can happen will happen.

One of those things, now and again, was a little bit of luck.

29

Homecoming

With Drake's return to human space, his problems seemed to be in the past.

The feeling of euphoria did not last. It ended when his question about Ana remained unanswered, and when the image of the other Drake Merlin vanished suddenly from the screen. It was replaced by the face of Tom Lambert. Tom's features, hair color, and expression varied wildly for a few seconds before they stabilized.

"Unfortunately, Ana has not been resurrected." Tom's mouth shrank to half its size, then enlarged again. Drake had seen the effect before. Some strong emotion, fear or joy or rage, was distorting the presentation. "The problem of resurrection will be worked on."

Will be worked on, after so many aeons? Drake wondered what they had been doing all this time. What could possibly be left to do?

But Tom Lambert was continuing. "I'm sorry." His face writhed with worry, then took on a lopsided smile. "We have not used this particular form of presentation for more than fifteen billion years.

We never thought it would be necessary. A return such as yours was never anticipated, although we knew that the theory showed it to be formally possible. Now, of course, we understand exactly what happened. You and your ship remained in this universe, but you passed through a noncausal path in the caesura. Before you reemerged, you traveled seven billion light-years in space and eight billion years forward in time."

"And then I couldn't find you for umpteen billion more. But here I am. So what is there to be sorry about?"

"We are sorry that you encountered the warning concerning your approach to the Skrilant Galaxy."

"I assume that I needed it." Drake was not convinced by Tom Lambert's explanation. "I presume I would have been blown apart otherwise."

"That is most probable. But our warning included a representation of yourself."

"So I met myself. Big deal. I survived."

"But it was *not* yourself." Tom glanced sideways, away from Drake. "You, as you are now, did not encounter the full present form of Drake Merlin. I should add that I form a minor subset of that whole. Very soon you will meet."

"I think you'd better tell me what's going on. This isn't the sort of homecoming I was hoping for. What do you mean, I haven't met my present self?"

"Drake Merlin, in all the universe except on your ship, you are no longer a single entity. The mentality of Drake Merlin, except for you, is a composite."

"I don't believe it." Drake sensed coming disaster. "It's the one thing I knew I could never afford to do. If I merged to a composite with anyone else, I knew I might lose sight of my goal."

"But we did merge, in a different way. We regret that now. Sit quietly, Drake Merlin, for one moment more. We are opening an S-wave high-data-rate linkage with you and your ship. Prepare for an update of many billions of years, since the time that you vanished from our horizon. Be prepared for strong coupling, then all your questions will be answered. The link is opening…now."

Drake submerged beneath a torrent of data, a million parallel sources streaming in.…

The struggle with the Shiva was ending. He saw new composites, part human, part Shiva, controlling the interaction between the two forms of life. Humans and the giant sessile plants might never understand each other, but with the right intermediaries they could coexist.

With success came a new problem. Through the endless years of battle, Drake had remained aloof. He dared not allow himself to become part of any composite, organic or inorganic, within the interconnected webs of consciousness. Nor would he share his personal data banks with anyone or anything. His logic was simple and invincible: He alone was willing to make the awful decisions of death and destruction needed to defeat the Shiva. He dared not risk any dilution of that will. But there was also the secret agenda: if he ceased to be a single individual, the drive to restore Ana might be lost.

For what seemed like forever, versions of his individual self had been downloaded and sent out on the warships, to meet their fiery or frigid end on planets at the edge of the Galaxy and beyond. With the Shiva ascendant that had been a one way process. But in some of the spiral arms, humans at last began to hold their own. As they carried out their programs of counterattack and advance into the space between the galaxies, and then, on through to other galaxies, human ships began to survive.

And now….

He was coming back, Drake Merlin in his billions; each of him was different, each had his own unique experiences, each was undeniably Drake.

He had held himself apart from all others. But how could he remain aloof and refuse access to himself?

He could not. Drake formed a composite, an unusual one: Every component would be Drake Merlin.

At first it was total chaos. His element selves numbered beyond the billions; he had long ago lost count of the number of times he had been downloaded, and the total constantly increased. Parts of him were close by, parts were separated from the rest by millions of light-years; some had been partly destroyed in combat and become maimed or incomplete versions of a whole Drake Merlin. All, without exception, were now different. *Time and events produced changes in form, perspective, even in self-image. Drake struggled to understand, to assimilate, to integrate, and to maintain or create a single personality among that teeming horde of selves.*

He was no longer essential to the struggle with the Shiva. A truce, incomprehensible to any entity but one of the human/Shiva symbiote framers, was signed. The need for oversight by Drake slowly diminished. As the threat of the Shiva receded and the need for his continuous involvement decreased, the Drake composite became increasingly consumed by introspection and by his own process of reconstruction. He took no interest in external events unless they were relevant to a substantial fraction of his own components.

Those components were linked to other composites and to other data banks. They stretched out across the galactic clusters and the great rifts, on toward the edges of the accessible universe. Drake Merlin had become guardian and caretaker of the cosmos.

With the growth of his composite came something else: slowly and imperceptibly, his driving willpower weakened. Old desires, needs that had propelled him forward from the farthest reaches of the past, dwindled and faded. Old longings no longer mattered....

Until one day, unexpectedly, on the monitored boundary of the dead but malevolent Skrilant galaxy, a new but very old Drake Merlin appeared that formed no part of any other.

Within the vast extended composite of Drake Merlin, the news of the encounter stirred a curious uneasiness. The stranger was asking questions. The attempt to answer them called for the use of memories so far removed in time and space that they carried no physical impressions. The composite had to sift deep within its own data banks before it found answers.

The result was shocking. Drake Merlin had somehow, somewhere, lost the way. He had forgotten his own most solemn vows. Now he had to change—and wonder if there was time enough, before the end of the universe itself.

Drake emerged, to find Tom Lambert silently waiting. The data flood had ended as suddenly as it had begun. Drake realized something else. He was no longer on board his own ship, and he had become inexplicably different.

Tom Lambert nodded. "Your perception is correct. You were uploaded while the data transfer was proceeding, and superluminally transmitted here."

"And embodied?" Drake worried about the long-lost feeling of a tangible self.

"That is no longer necessary. In fact, if you are to understand what we are doing, many parallel inputs continue to be necessary. In such circumstances, material embodiment is no longer possible."

"Something has gone wrong, hasn't it?"

"It has. We became distracted. What we are doing to correct it—if we can—is this."

If the previous data flow had been a torrent, the new one was a tidal wave. It washed over Drake and carried him along without a choice.

First came a different sense of self. Drake Merlin had multiplied, a million, a billion, countless trillions of times. He was on every planet, in orbit around every star, present in every galaxy (even the lost Skrilant Galaxy had its corps of Merlin mentalities). The distinction between organic and inorganic forms no longer meant anything. Changes from one to the other took place constantly. Drake felt his other self extending steadily across the whole universe. Even if he and the ship had done nothing but sit and wait after they passed through the caesura, eventually the extended composite would have discovered and recovered his lost individual self.

That individual self was in danger of drowning. He expressed his fear and heard the rest offering reassurance.

You can join us safely. You can never be lost. We are you.

"What are you doing?"

What we should have done long ago, and what we now must do. We are concerned not with individuals, but with universes. Remember this.

The trillions of voices became one:

In a closed universe, a final point of collapse lies at the end of time. The eschaton, the Omega Point, the c-point—the space-time final boundary has been given a variety of names. Its main properties have long been defined. One of those properties is of paramount importance: close to the c-boundary, all information—everything that ever can be known—becomes accessible. Everything that ever can be known, and everything that has ever been known.

And the implications....

We went astray, but now our task is clear. We must survive. We must gather, absorb, and organize information as fast as possible. Near to the end, that accumulation will, we hope, become sufficient. Ana, our true Ana, will by our efforts be restored to us. Thanks to you, we have again become aware of what must be done. Will you become one with us and join our efforts?

Drake knew that the goal was infinitely desirable. It was possible in principle. But was it possible in practice?

The mentality that Drake Merlin had become sprawled across the universe. It had near-infinite resources of data and processing. But it was far from omniscient. How much information was enough? Had the effort started too late?

Drake could not answer those questions. Perhaps there would never be enough information. However, he knew one thing: if the effort failed, it must not be because of the lack of even a single component or individual.

That made the decision easy. Decisions were always easy when you had no choice.

Drake sighed, and nodded. "Merge me in. Join me to all the rest of you. I'm ready to go to work."

30

Love and Eternity

All the imagined analogies were wrong. When Drake agreed to merge with the universal Drake Merlin composite, he had seen himself as a tiny ant in a cosmic anthill, his every action subordinate to the common need.

It was not that way at all. He *was* the composite, the whole thing. And it was he. There was no sense of loss, but of enormous gain. He walked a carpet of tiny pink-petaled flowers on the surface of Eden, a garden world in a galaxy so far from Earth that it had never been named or even observed in Earth's lifetime. At the same time he maintained perpetual watch around the dead, deadly, and insane galaxies—Skrilant was not the only one. Sometimes he saw life there, indomitable as ever even in an aging universe, creeping back to blistered dead hills or ravaged ocean beds.

That was rewarding. Some things were not. Some things were close to intolerable. On a world of a remote globular cluster, he saw a species far more intelligent than humans rise to artistic triumph and technological power in just two centuries. He was present when the Lakons announced that rather than joining the combined human mentality, which had been offered to them, they would for reasons beyond human understanding choose self-immolation. He looked on helplessly as Lakon adults and children walked into the sacrificial flames. The babies, left behind, died of starvation.

He could have interfered—and done what? A being can more easily be killed than made to live. But he knew he would carry the memory with him to the end of time.

The universe did not care. That was the important point. *Humans* cared, but the universe was indifferent. He was present, ten billion light-years away from the Lakons, when two galaxies collided and hard radiation wiped out a thousand potential intelligences. He watched a black hole, invisibly small to human eyes but massing as much as one of Earth's great mountains, run through its last second of evaporation. An observing party, too curious and too close, died with it. After the final burst of elementary particles and hard X-rays, nothing remained. That seemed symbolic. It suggested to Drake the nihilistic end of the cosmos itself.

Present conditions offered few clues as to that violent end. The universe seemed peaceful, moving toward a quietus that, if it came at all, suggested not a bang but a whimper. The blue shift was more pronounced, but still it seemed innocuous. Not observation but physics and abstract mathematics promised the final fiery doom, certain and implacable and unavoidable.

Drake forced himself away from introspection. There was a job to be done. He must collect, store, and organize information. He must remain intact and integrated and keep in touch with all of his myriad components. Computation power grew linearly with the number of units; coordination problems grew exponentially.

As time went on communication itself became easier. He soon realized why: The universe was shrinking. Contact between far-separated elements was easier. Increased problems of coordination more than cancelled that gain. He found himself scrambling, working nonstop and harder than ever to hold a single focus and a single goal.

Collect, collate, compare. He slaved on, sometimes wondering if there would ever be a recognizable end point to his labors. Would he still be serving as data clerk to the universe, when everything melted and fused into the infernal fireball?

The end crowns all, and that old common arbitrator, Time, will one day end it.

Collect, collate, compare. Drake worked on. The sky became brighter. The more distant galaxies glowed bluer. Constantly, he was forced to create more copies of himself to deal with the increased volumes of data. The number of his components grew, and grew again: trillions, quadrillions, quintillions. How many? He no longer attempted to track the total. Contact with some elements of himself, riding in as S-waves from far across the sweep of galaxies, were pure conundrums. They were indisputably Drake. Yet these components of his own self felt more alien than any strangeness of the Shiva or the Snarks. The effort of assimilating all his divergent personalities became ever greater.

As the universe comes close to its ultimate convergence, the density of mass-energy will increase and so will the temperature. At the end comes a singularity of infinite heat and pressure.

Words, theories, that was all they were. They had no basis in reality. *This* was reality, the toil of information collection without an end.

Except that finally, after a span so great that it was easy to believe that it could never happen, an end seemed in sight. The long downward curve steepened. The cosmos was shrinking faster—noticeably faster. Work for Drake became a frenzy, a blur of action. Energy densities were running higher. Information transfer was faster, over diminishing distances. Processes could proceed more rapidly.

And then more rapidly yet.

The microwave radiation was microwave frequencies no longer. It had shortened to visible wavelengths. The space between the stars crackled with energy.

Stand still, you ever moving spheres of heaven, that time may cease and midnight never come.

But midnight was approaching. Time moved on. The sky was falling, imploding toward its final singularity, and the firmament had become a continuous actinic glare when Drake became aware of a new presence, a different voice speaking from among his endless sea of selves.

It emerged from the white noise that formed the edge of Drake's consciousness and steadily approached his central coordinating nexus. He did not know where it had come from, but as it neared it seemed to touch and merge with every one of his components. It interrupted the rhythm of his frantic work, and as such it was dangerous. Somehow he must stop its action.

He reached out toward it. Even before full contact was established, there was a curious exchange of energies like a fleeting touch of fingertips. It destroyed his processing powers. All his work froze, and in the same moment he sensed who it might be.

A mixture of emotions—hope, joy, fear, longing, love—spread through his extended self and thrilled him with wild surmise.

"Ana?"

"Who else?"

"But where did you come from? Can you be real? I mean, to just appear...."

"We've really got to stop meeting like this, eh? I certainly *think* I'm real." The cosmos filled with quiet laughter. "I think therefore I am. I think I'm me, Drake, I really do. But you know the theory as well as I do; as the universe converges toward the eschaton, there's no limit to what you can know about anything. We're getting close to the end now. So it's not beyond question that I am your simulation, a construct of your mind. *You* think, therefore *I* am."

"You are not a simulation." Drake hated the suggestion that Ana might not be real, even though it had come from him. "You can't be. Don't you think I would know if I was creating a simulation?"

"You might. But maybe you have powers that you don't know about. Mm. That doesn't sound consistent with being omniscient, does it? Let's put it another way, with a question: Is self-deception possible, even for an omniscient being?"

"I don't know." The gentle touch had come again, closer and more intimate. "All I can say is it doesn't *matter.* When you are with me, nothing else is important. It never was, and it isn't now."

"All right, let's avoid an argument by agreeing that I'm here and I'm real. So before I do anything else, let me say thank you. Now I have another question. How much time do we have?"

She had always been the practical one, the clear-eyed realist, raising issues that Drake was happy to push under the rug. And as usual she was asking the right question.

Drake looked beyond himself, to the universe that he had been ignoring. It roared and blazed with energy. The cosmic background had become as bright as the stars around which most of the composites clustered. And still the pace of collapse was accelerating, rushing giddily on to the final singularity.

"We have a few more years of proper time, at most, before the final singularity." He found it impossible to worry. Ana was with him, never again would she leave him.

"Is that all?" The visual construct that she had chosen was her old self, and she was frowning. "Just a few years? I mean, it's more than I ever expected, but it's not much of a return on investment for *you*. Think of all your efforts!"

"I had it easy. It's enough. We'll stretch it subjectively. We can run multispeed in electronic mode and make it seem as long as we want."

"But it won't be *real*. I still don't like it." She was inside his mind, gently feeling her way around. It was the delicious touch of knowing fingers, exploring his most private regions. "A few years isn't nearly enough time. We need to get to know each other all over again. I know what I've been doing—nothing—but I want to hear all your adventures. And don't pretend you haven't had any. I know about the flight to Canopus, and Melissa, and the Shiva. I even know about the other Ana. But I want to hear it all from you directly. And you're telling me we won't have time. Don't you think you ought to *do* something about that?"

"Ana, you're talking about the end of the universe." Drake laughed, delirious with happiness. He could feel music swelling inside him, for the first time in aeons. "It's the end of everything. The Omega Point. Finis. There's no *da capo* marked in this score. That's all there is."

"I remember a different Drake. It was you, wasn't it, who once had a quite different opinion?"

Drake knew it was no question. She was teasing him. Ana was well aware who had thought what. And she must have been happily plundering his data banks of memories for longer than he had been aware of her presence, because he had never spoken aloud the words that she said next. "'Science has come so far. Surely no one believes that it can go no further.' Remember thinking that?"

"That was when there was time, what seemed like an infinite amount of it. Now there's no time. Not for new science, not for anything but us."

"Once you knew next to nothing, Drake, and you were able to work a miracle. Now that you have all the information in the cosmos available to you, who knows what you'll be able to do. The universe is ending because it's closed, right? It doesn't care—but we do. So *open it*. The knowledge you need already exists. We just have to look."

Ana picked him up and carried him with her. He found himself cascading through space in all directions at once, while ghostly data banks swirled to him and through him, an accumulation of knowledge unimaginable at any earlier epoch. He recognized within them a million bare possibilities; but they were no more than that.

"We can't avoid the eschaton, Ana. It's there. It's a feature of our universe, a global reality."

"I thought the eschaton only existed in a closed universe."

"It does. If the mass-energy density had been below the critical value, this universe would be open. But the density is too big."

"So. Reduce it."

"That's impossible." Except that before the thought was complete, Drake had seen a way to do it. The caesuras, created so long ago in the struggle to contain the Shiva, sat as scattered and forgotten relics across space-time. They could still be used to receive any amount of mass and energy.

She was inside his mind, and she had caught the idea as it came into being. "Well, Drake. What are you waiting for?"

He could not reply. He was engaged on a dizzying involution of calculation, every one of his selves operating at its limit. The answer, when he had it, was not one that he wanted her to hear.

"It's still no, Ana. We can dump enough mass-energy into the caesuras to form an open universe. A tiny fraction would reemerge into this universe, although not enough to make a difference. But we would have to go far beyond that to do any good. We need enough structural bounce-back to avoid a final singularity here."

"So that's what we do. You say the caesuras can handle any amount of energy and mass."

"They can."The irony of the situation was revealing itself to Drake. "But there's one insoluble problem. Information is equivalent to energy. And I—with all my selves and all my extensions and all my composites—represent enough energy equivalence to make the bounce-back impossible. It's the ultimate catch: Any universe that I am in must be closed."

"You mean with the physical laws that apply in *this* universe. What about other universes, the ones that form the end point for caesura transfer? Look at those, Drake."

He was already looking. There was speculation in the data banks but no solid information.

"Ana, it's still no. Even if we had all the information possible in this universe, it would not be enough to tell us what lies in other universes. There's no way to find out."

"Not true. There's one very good way. We go and see. Come on."

Suddenly they were hurtling through space, faster and faster. Dangerously fast. Relativistically fast. At this speed, a few subjective minutes would bring them months closer to the eschaton. The little time they had together was melting away. Drake coordinated his countless selves. All would have to fly, exactly in unison, into the myriad caesuras that gaped black against the flaming cosmic background.

At the edge of the caesura horizon, he slowed and hesitated. Mass and energy was swirling past them into the infinite maws, draining from the universe. But as long as he remained there, the final singularity could not be avoided.

"Second thoughts?" Ana was tugging at him, urging him on toward blackness. "Bit late for those."

"Not second thoughts. I was thinking, it would be just our luck to emerge into some place where the laws of physics are too different to permit life. Or some of us might find ourselves right back here."

"What's so bad about that? If we do come back here, won't it be to an open universe? You worry too much." She was bubbling within his mind, an effervescence that he could never resist. "'Life is a glorious adventure, or it is nothing.' You were the one who first quoted that to me. Have you changed so much?"

"I don't know. I can't bear to lose you again."

"You won't lose me." She was reaching out, enfolding him, confident as he was nervous. "This universe or another one, wherever we go, we go together. You'll have me for as long as there is time. Come on, Drake. You always said you wanted to live dangerously, now's your chance."

They were on the brink of the spiraling funnel of oil and ink, close to the point of no return. Ana was laughing again, like a child at the fair. "Here we go," she said, "into the Tunnel of Love. And don't forget now, make a wish."

"I already did." It was too late to turn back. Ahead lay total, final darkness. Behind them he imagined the radiance dimming, easing with their departure away from the hellfire of ultimate convergence. The universe they were leaving would become open, facing an infinite future. Not bad, for a man and woman who only wanted each other and had no desire to change anything. "I wished that—"

"Don't tell me, love—or it won't come true!"

"Won't matter if I do tell." They were passing through, heading for the unknown, the last question, birth canal or final extinction. Was it imagination, or did the faintest glimmer of light shine in the vortex ahead?

Drake reached out to embrace Ana, squeezing her as hard as she was holding him. "Won't matter if I do, love. Because it already has."

THE END

THE PURSUIT OF THE PANKERA

A PARALLEL NOVEL ABOUT PARALLEL UNIVERSES

A NEW WORK BY

ROBERT A. HEINLEIN

The original working title for this novel was *Six-Six-Six*

COMING SOON

For more information please go to

www.ArcmanoBooks.com/heinlein

www.ingramcontent.com/pod-product-compliance
Lightning Source LLC
Chambersburg PA
CBHW082048220626
47052CB00007B/1251